The Lost Fisherman

JEWEL E. ANN

THE LOST FISHERMAN

BOOK TWO

JEWEL E. ANN

Copyright © 2021 by Jewel E. Ann

ISBN 978-1-955520-05-8

Print Edition

Cover Designer: Estella Vukovic

Formatting: Jenn Beach

CHAPTER ONE

Six months in Thailand turned into twelve months in Thailand with Brendon. Rory was right. Friendships had a way of turning into more.

Playful nudges.

Teasing.

Flirty glances.

Hand-holding.

Stolen kisses.

All the little things checked off the boxes. If the boxes were checked, it had to be love. Right?

A stop in Tokyo and another in Los Angeles was all that stood between me and my mom—between me and the naked fisherman.

Brendon spent the month prior to our trip home hinting about marriage.

Did I see myself having a destination wedding or a church wedding?

How many kids did I want?

Would I choose to live in the city or in the mountains?

A dog and two cats? Or no cats and two dogs?

Brendon still had his job waiting for him at the law firm in Denver. He would make good money with room for advancement, maybe even make partner one day.

I had the chance to do ... nothing. Well, not true. There would be kids to raise, dogs to walk, and cakes to bake.

Fisher made good money. If I was destined for the life of a wife and stay-at-home mom, why did I leave him? I thought about Fisher more in the days leading up to our departure than I had done for the previous twelve months.

Brendon convinced me to prolong our trip by a few days so we could spend a few nights in Tokyo.

"Reese, slow down," he mumbled over my mouth— my anxious mouth—as we took the elevator to the hotel room.

I had this clawing feeling that Brendon's reason for the extra days in Tokyo had everything to do with a marriage proposal.

Proposal.

Wedding.

Sex.

That was his plan.

I had other plans. For some reason, I didn't want to

lose my virginity, or what was left of it, on my wedding night. What if I married Brendon and the sex wasn't good? What if I spent every second comparing him to Fisher?

I had to know.

"Whoa ... seriously, what's up with you?" Brendon pulled my hand away from his crotch just as the elevator doors opened.

"I don't want to wait. I know ... I know it's wrong, but I don't want to wait."

He narrowed his eyes. "Reese, I think you're just experiencing some mixed feelings over going home after being away for a year. Go take a shower, drink some water, and sleep on it. Okay?" He stopped at the door to my room.

His answer to sex was shower, hydrate, and sleep on it? Would every man I met reject me? Would I ever have sex?

"Okay." I nodded. "You're right. Night."

That night, I showered, thought about Fisher, and I touched myself.

The next morning, we were first in line to go to the observation tower of the Tokyo Skytree. With Mt. Fuji visible in the distance on the clear day, Brendon got on one knee and proposed to me with his grandmother's diamond ring.

Onlookers smiled and gasped, all eyes on us. No ... all eyes on *me*.

"You're the woman of my dreams, Therese

Capshaw, and I think I knew it from the day we met. Do me the honor of being my wife."

My brain was paralyzed. But in the moment, all I could do to make everyone stop staring at me, including Brendon, was nod.

"Yes!" He slipped the ring on my finger and stood, pulling me in for a big hug and a kiss on the cheek.

I was engaged, and I got a kiss on the cheek.

On the way back to our hotel, I pulled on his arm, tugging him into a drugstore.

"What are you doing?" He laughed.

I led him up one aisle and down the next, stopping at the condoms.

He narrowed his eyes. "Reese ..."

"It doesn't mean we have to; it just means ... we're prepared."

"Prepared to sin?"

"Prepared to not have to explain why we need to rush our wedding if we do happen to sin."

Brendon shook his head, and I knew he wasn't comfortable with it, but I wasn't comfortable marrying him and not having sex with him first. And that should have been the only sign I needed.

But I was still that teenaged adult with *so* much to learn, and my favorite teacher happened to be half a world away and retired from teaching me any more than tough love and the oh-so-important "sink or swim."

With a miserable grimace and his teeth digging into his lip, Brendon nodded.

That nod led to anticipation.

Anticipation led to the allure of the forbidden.

He might not have initiated it on his own, but when we found ourselves in his hotel room after dinner that night, things quickly moved in the direction of that box of condoms.

"I love you so much," Brendon chanted over and over between kisses and amid discarding our clothes. Maybe he thought God wouldn't be so critical of our decision if he kept reminding me (and God) how much he loved me. It wasn't merely a physical need—and hopefully not an immoral act; we were in love and committed to each other.

And by "we" I meant Brendon more than me.

I just wanted to know what it felt like to have sex with him. And I loved him; it just didn't feel like it did with Fisher. Maybe it wasn't supposed to feel like it did with Fisher.

"I'm so nervous my hands won't stop shaking," Brendon said as he fumbled the condom.

After he rolled it on, I closed my eyes—another sign things weren't great with Brendon. He touched me, and I imagined it was Fisher.

He started to push into me, and I replayed moments with Fisher. But Brendon didn't touch me like Fisher had touched me. He didn't really touch me at all, just his cock suited up between my legs and his lips nervously hovering over my lips.

Did he not notice my breasts? Maybe he wasn't a breast man.

Did he not want to kiss me between my legs? Locate my clit? Run his tongue along the length of my neck before biting my earlobe?

It was all so different.

I winced when he pushed all the way into me. It didn't feel great, maybe because he wasn't doing anything to make it feel at least a little less than awful and painful.

For the next five minutes, maybe not even, he jabbed me with an erratic rhythm. He missed my clit every time while his heavy breaths washed over my face—grunting and occasionally pressing a limp, sloppy kiss to my mouth.

"Oh my ..." Brendon squeezed his eyes shut and stilled for a few seconds before a full-body shiver shook him. He opened his eyes and grinned. "That was..." he blew out a breath "...amazing. I love you *so* very much."

When he rolled off me, I slowly sat up with my back to him and tears in my eyes. I gave him my virginity, and I didn't regret it, not on my part. Brendon deserved it because it meant something to him. I think it meant more to him than it meant to me.

The tears?

Guilt?

Not because I'd sinned.

Because I tempted him. He sinned for me. He did it because he loved me. He did it because it seemed a little less wrong since I agreed to marry him.

Tears ... I couldn't stop the tears because I knew I couldn't marry him.

And I couldn't go home to Rory ... to Fisher.

It was time to do something for myself. It was time to fall in love with endless possibilities. Time to walk alone. Time to grow up.

Time to *"fucking think for yourself."*

CHAPTER TWO

Four years later ...

"Oh my BABY GIRL!" Rory threw her hands in the air and charged me like she did at the airport in Denver after getting out of prison.

I was a teenaged adult then. Deer in the headlights. And no clue where my journey even began, let alone where it might take me.

It took me to Fisher, then it took me to Thailand, then it took me to Ann Arbor, Michigan. In Thailand, I volunteered to help a woman named Alesha. She was fifty-three. A midwife. Much like working for Fisher, I was grunt labor. No experience needed. And much like Fisher, Alesha taught me a lot. I watched (sometimes helped) her deliver thirty-three babies during my year in Thailand. But I knew after the very first delivery, that she had the best job in the world.

After breaking Brendon's heart that night in Tokyo, I changed my travel plans. Instead of going back to Colorado, I returned to Houston. My grandparents helped me make financial arrangements for college.

Nursing school at the University of Michigan.

A new place where I didn't know a soul. The perfect place to follow *my* dream.

"Your dad would be so proud." Rory hugged me the day I received my bachelor's degree.

I loved her for acknowledging Dad. He really would have been proud of me.

My mom's parents were overjoyed for me too. My dad's parents plastered on their fake smiles, watching Rory and Rose congratulate me. They were not okay with my mom and her lesbian partner. I loved my mom, and I loved Rose too. During my four years in Ann Arbor, they averaged three visits a year. I never made it to Denver, but they didn't mind coming to me.

The sour looks on my dad's parents' faces didn't bother me. They were old. Set in their ways. And their opinions no longer shaped mine.

I thought for myself. I found a way to love God without fear or guilt—the most liberating feeling ever.

Sex? Yes ... I'd had a handful of boyfriends during my four years in Michigan. And they were *all* better lovers than Brendon. To be fair ... it was his first time too.

Alcohol? I wasn't a binge drinker, but I enjoyed a fun night out with friends.

Friends ... I had so many friends from nursing school. They felt more like sisters and brothers to me.

I even got a tattoo ... but no one, aside from my lovers, had seen it. Fisher wasn't the only one who deserved a harem.

"Lunch?" Rory asked.

"Sounds perfect!" I hugged my grandparents just before we headed toward the parking lot. Mom and Rose rode with me while my grandparents drove their rental cars.

"So when do you start your new job?" Rose asked.

I laughed. "First I have to pass my NCLEX exam. Then I'll find a job."

"Then you'll be able to start your master's degree next fall, correct?"

I nodded. "That's the plan."

"We're moving out of the basement. Getting our own place. There will be plenty of room for you if you decide to come back to Denver," Mom said.

"Moving out of Fisher's basement?" I shot her a quick side-glance. It felt weird saying his name. I'd thought about him a lot, but I hadn't actually said his name.

"Did you ever get to meet Angie?" Rory asked.

I swallowed hard and nodded. "Um, I think so. His childhood sweetheart?"

"Yes. Well, she moved back to Denver last year for good because her mom wasn't doing well. In fact, she recently passed. She and Fisher just got engaged."

It didn't matter. I said this to myself over and over

again. My brain got it, but the translation got messed up somewhere between my brain and my heart, causing unnecessary pain.

Five years ... it had been five years since I'd seen or talked to Fisher. I thought I made a nice clean break. So why did the edges of that hole in my heart feel so jagged, like they hadn't healed? Like they would never heal.

"So it's time to move out. Angie is nice, but I think they want the house to themselves to start a family," Rory said.

I nodded slowly. "Yeah," I whispered past the lump in my throat.

At the restaurant, Rose grabbed my hand after I got out of the car. She gave it a quick squeeze and offered me a soft smile, an "are you okay" smile.

All those years ... and she never told my mom about Fisher and me. It was another reason I loved Rose. Another reason why I knew my mom fell in love with her.

Channeling the happiness from the morning's events, from my special day, I squeezed her hand in return and smiled.

Rose winked and released my hand, leaving Rory none the wiser.

Fisher and I ended in the best possible way. I felt his love, and I always believed he felt mine. It just wasn't our time.

Life took over.

I didn't wait for him.

He didn't wait for me.

And that was okay. That was life.

With the news of his engagement, it solidified what I had always feared. There would *never* be a time for us.

"Oh ..." Rory turned around just before we entered the restaurant. "Speaking of Fisher, he sent a card." She dug through her bag and pulled out an envelope.

"Thanks." I took it and slipped it into my bag. I couldn't read it until I was alone. Even if it was nothing more than a generic graduation card with his signature, I needed privacy to deal with anything Fisher Mann.

IT TOOK me three days to open his card. My family went home. And my two roommates (fellow nursing school graduates) were gone for the day.

As I slowly unsealed it by wedging my finger into the corner, I took a deep breath. It was, in fact, a generic card, but there was more than just his signature. He'd left me a long note taking up the entire left side of the card.

Reese,

Can I say how proud of you I am without it sounding condescending? Without you thinking it's an age reference? I am. More than that, I'm happy for you. Rory said you plan to be a midwife and deliver babies. I knew you'd change the world, touch lives ... like you touched mine.

I'm sure Rory's told you that I'm getting married. It feels like the smart choice at this point in my life. My family is thrilled, and I'm good, in case you do care, which you might not. Go be the amazing woman I knew you would be. Find your place, your people, the life you deserve.

Congratulations,
The Naked Fisherman

I laughed through my tears. So many tears. He signed it The Naked Fisherman. It made me happy and incredibly heartbroken at the same time. Was he waiting for me? Did he, one day, decide to stop waiting and please his family by proposing to Angie? Good ... he was good.

CHAPTER THREE

I passed my NCLEX.

I got my own apartment.

And I had an interview scheduled with a pediatric office.

Life continued to give me sunny days despite the Fisher Mann engagement news.

The morning of my interview, Rory called me.

"I haven't had the interview yet," I said as I made my way to my car. "I'm on my way there now."

"Reese," her voice hit my ear with a chilling gravity.

It stopped me in my tracks. "What is it?"

"Fisher was in an accident on his motorcycle. He's in surgery now. We don't know the extent of his injuries yet. I just thought I'd let you know in case you wanted to say a prayer for him."

"W-what?" I covered my mouth with my hand as tears instantly filled my eyes.

"I'll let you know when he's out of surgery ... if he comes out of surgery."

If ...

"Okay?" she asked.

I nodded and pushed a tiny "okay" past the boulder in my throat.

After Rory ended the call, my phone and keys fell to the ground, cracking my screen. Sobs racked my body, one wave after another.

All I could see was his face. Those eyes. That wink. The smile he gave me just before he said something that made me blush.

"Are you going to kiss me?"

"I'm thinking about it."

"A-are you m-mine?"

"You know the answer to that."

"I'm trying so hard to not fall in love with you."

"I know."

I was okay ... maybe not good ... but I was okay not having Fisher in my life, but I wasn't okay with him no longer being *in* this life. If that happened, I would never be good again.

Picking up my phone, I managed to bring up the number to the office where I had the interview. Canceled it and booked a flight to Denver.

When I arrived, I called Rory.

"No news yet. He's still in surgery. Did your interview go okay?"

"I'm here in Denver, at the airport."

"What?"

"What hospital is he at?"

"Reese, there's nothing you can do. I was planning on calling you as soon as he got out of surgery and we knew more."

"Mom!" It was a rare time of me calling her Mom instead of Rory. "What. Hospital?"

"I'll come get you," she said in a calmer tone before ending the call.

Forty-five minutes later, Rose climbed out of the passenger's seat when they pulled up to the curb. "We're all praying for him," she whispered when she hugged me.

I blinked back the emotions burning my eyes and nodded in lieu of actual words.

When we arrived at the hospital, Fisher's family and other familiar faces from work crowded the waiting room.

His parents and siblings.

Hailey.

Angie.

We shared a few sober "hellos" before I tucked myself in the far corner of the room with Rory and Rose. And then we waited. When the doctor came out, his parents and Angie gathered in a circle around him. A collective sigh of relief could be felt. It was good news. He made it through surgery.

When we determined only family would be allowed to see him later that night, I went home with Rose and Rory to their new house.

"You didn't move that far." I found a small grin

when they pulled into the driveway of the home that was maybe three blocks from Fisher's house.

"This was a foreclosure. We basically stole it. Works great. We find ourselves taking a walk several nights a week and still ending up at Fisher's house, drinking beer and wine on his front porch or the back screened-in porch." Rory shrugged, shutting off the car. "What can I say, he's family. Only ..." She frowned. "Not enough to get to see him tonight."

Rose squeezed my mom's leg. "We'll see him tomorrow."

Rory nodded.

We ordered dinner, but none of us were that hungry. Instead, we shared funny Fisher stories as if he was dead and we were reminiscing about his life.

"Oh..." Rory drained the rest of her wine "...how'd your interview go?"

I shook my head while pouring another glass of wine for myself. Finally, I was able to join the real adults in the room. "I canceled it. Told them it was a family emergency."

"I was a little surprised when you called from the airport," Rory said. "I know you two worked together for a while, and I joked about you acting like siblings, but when was the last time the two of you even spoke?"

Rose gave me a nervous glance. I considered just telling Rory about Fisher and me. I was nearly twenty-four—what would she have been able to say or do at that point? I'd moved on. He'd moved on.

For whatever reason, with him in the hospital and

engaged, I opted to wait. Maybe until a better time. Maybe never. Did it matter any longer?

"I don't know ... it was weird. I mean ... it's been years since we've spoken, but when you told me, it hit me hard. I'm not sure why. And I didn't even think; I just canceled my interview and got the first flight to Denver. Maybe it's because I know how close *you* are to him."

"I'm sure he'll be thrilled to see you, even if the circumstances are crappy."

I nodded slowly. Would he be *thrilled* to see me?

THE NEXT MORNING, we made our way to the hospital after Rory talked to Arnie. He said Fisher was a little fuzzy in the head, but otherwise okay. The accident was just that, an accident in the rain. A large truck couldn't stop and ran into Fisher.

When we reached the waiting room, Angie was in tears as Fisher's sisters consoled her.

Did he take a sudden turn?

It wasn't impossible. I'd seen my fair share of patients come out of surgery, seem stable and fine, only to flatline hours later.

Arnie broke away from the pack of women. "Long time no see. How have you been?" He gave me a hug.

"Good." I lied. "Are you famous yet?"

He released me and chuckled. "Almost."

"What's going on?" I nodded to Angie and his sisters.

Arnie frowned. "Oh, my brother's acting a little drunk that's all. I'm sure it's the pain meds. The doctors aren't too concerned yet."

"What do you mean he's acting a little drunk?" I asked.

"Memory issues. He doesn't seem to know everyone. Well, he knows me. Our sisters. Our parents. But nobody from work thus far. In fact, he doesn't remember building homes. And..." he scrunched his nose and whispered "...he doesn't recognize Angie at the moment."

"Oh no." Rory's eyes widened as her jaw fell open.

"Come on, might as well see if he remembers his favorite drinking buddies." Arnie smirked at Rory and Rose.

I followed the three of them to Fisher's room.

"More visitors. Pretend like you recognize them." Arnie teased Fisher as we filed into his room.

I stood behind Rory and Rose as they paused at the foot of his bed. I could only see bits and pieces of him.

His bandaged face.

His casted arm.

"Rory and Rose," he said in a rather weak voice.

It didn't matter how weak his voice was; it still did things to my crazy heart.

"Ding. Ding. Ding." Arnie gave Fisher a slow clap. "Two for two, Bro."

"No more motorcycle for you," Rose said as she

moved to one side of his bed while Rory inched closer on the other side of the bed, leaving me in clear sight.

He knew them, so he would know me. I was quite certain of it. I gave him a small smile.

He smiled back. "Hi."

"Hi."

"Please tell me we haven't met. I fear I've already made too many people feel insignificant today," Fisher said.

Rory and Rose exchanged a look.

"How has your brain misfired so badly that the hottest women in your life are just ... poof ... gone?" Arnie shook his head at Fisher.

Fisher narrowed his gaze, as if doing so increased his chance of recognizing me, as if it were his eyes' fault and not his brain's fault.

"This is Reese, my daughter," Rory said. "But you haven't seen her in years, so don't stress. She lived with me in your basement for a few months. And she worked with you for less than ... what?" She glanced at me. "A few months?"

I nodded. It was all I could do. Of course Angie was crying. When the man you love (loved) didn't recognize you, it wasn't a great feeling.

"She just graduated from nursing school in Michigan. She's going to get her master's starting next year. Midwifery. She's going to deliver babies."

Fisher returned a slight nod. "Congratulations."

I cleared the thick emotion from my throat. I think only Rose sensed my true level of emotions. "Thanks,"

I managed to say. "I'm really happy to see that you're okay."

"Yeah. That's what they tell me. I don't remember the accident either."

"The doctors think his memory loss is probably temporary," Arnie said.

I knew it could be temporary. Or it could last a long time. Or it could be permanent. The brain was hard to predict.

"I hope so." Fisher stared out the window for a few seconds. "That um ... woman was really upset. My fiancée?"

Oh my gosh ...

That woman. He reduced Angie to "that woman." I was never an Angie fan, but I also wasn't a monster. I felt her pain. He didn't ask me to marry him, but I felt total devastation at his lack of recognition. I could only imagine how Angie must have felt.

"Well..." I returned a nervous laugh, feeling Rose's gaze on me "...I'm sure it must be heartbreaking to be a stranger to the one you love most."

Fisher's brow tightened into lines of wrinkles. "I'm sure you're right."

"We'll let you get some rest." Rory leaned down and kissed the side of his head. I wanted to be that close to him.

Feel the warmth of his skin, the brush of his lips, the intensity of his eyes as he looked at me with wonder and anticipation.

The irony? Had I "given" him my virginity, he

wouldn't have remembered. I don't regret it being Brendon, even if I hurt him. Had it been Fisher, I wouldn't have been able to walk away. I would have treated losing my virginity like donating a kidney.

More Fisher Mann lessons ...

It wasn't about firsts. *Every* moment mattered. Every touch. Every word. It was selfish to think of our lives as nothing more than an endless series of giving and taking. It implied we were, more or less, just moving from one moment to the next with no meaning. I knew ... deep down I *knew* it was never about my virginity. Not with Fisher. It was always about my heart.

Looking at Fisher in that bed and being unrecognizable to him was a clear reminder that I, nor anyone else, shouldn't rely on another human to be a measure of self-worth and success.

"Ready?" Rory asked me.

I nodded slowly.

CHAPTER FOUR

"I've missed this ... you know ... time with you two,"
I said on a long sigh as the three of us took a hike in the
mountains several days after seeing Fisher in the
hospital.

"We never took our trip up here," Rory said,
reaching for her water bottle in the side pocket of her
backpack as we stopped at a clearing. "I promised to
bring you here. Remember when you were adamant
about coming up here by yourself?"

I nodded. "Can I be honest now?" I smirked.

She rolled her eyes. "You drove up here anyway?"

Shaking my head, I chuckled. "No. Fisher brought
me ... on his motorcycle."

"Oh, Reese." Rory shook her head. "I didn't need
to know that, especially since his accident."

"I said you wouldn't be happy about it, but he said
we didn't have to tell you. He really was a terrible
influence. I can't believe you left me with him."

Rose rubbed her lips together, enjoying the way I was telling Rory so much, yet nothing at all.

"Well, as soon as he gets out of the hospital, I'll have a word with him."

Rose laughed. "You're going to talk to him about taking your daughter on his motorcycle when he doesn't remember her? Good plan. Make sure I'm with you when this conversation takes place. I want to listen."

I laughed too. It wasn't funny, but it was.

"What do you think will happen if he doesn't regain all his memory?" Rory slipped her water bottle back into her backpack. "Do you think he will fall back in love with Angie?"

Rose shrugged. "If it happens, it will be incredibly romantic. What is there? Over seven billion people in the world? And he falls in love with the same person twice? Sadly, I fear it won't happen like that. I mean, I can see him being the nice guy who marries her anyway because everyone adores her, and he'll trust the people he does remember."

"He's known her forever," Rory said. "I think he'll remember her. She owns too much of his heart."

"Unless ..." My big mouth opened without me realizing it. Then it was too late.

"Unless what?" Rory asked.

Abort!

"Unless it's not about time. I mean, you said you knew there was a connection between you and Rose from the day you met. Sure, Fisher's known Angie for years, but why did it take him so long to decide to marry her? It wasn't like you and Rose. Nobody was standing in their way. Just the opposite. Everyone wanted it. Except Fisher. I'm just saying ... the length of their history isn't necessarily an indicator for the likelihood that he'll fall back in love with her. What if he wasn't truly in love with her? What if she was just the obvious choice for lack of a better one?"

Rory blinked slowly. "Okay, everyone make a note that Reese is never allowed to talk to Angie."

"I'm not saying she isn't nice." We started walking again. "Or a good catch. But there must be more. That's all I'm saying."

Rose nudged my arm. "We know ... you're *just saying*."

I smirked. Yes, despite my life experiences and emotional revelations—a lot prompted by Fisher—I still liked the idea that he fell in love with me in a matter of weeks, despite it making no sense to anyone else. And since he couldn't dispute it, because he had no recollection of me or us, I felt perfectly fine with letting that version of our story live in my head forever.

"I LOVE HAVING YOU HERE. Are you thinking of moving back to Denver? There are jobs here. You can get your master's here," Rory questioned me as we drove back to Denver.

"Let her be," Rose scolded my mom.

"I'm not pressuring you. I'm simply asking the question and stating a few facts."

"She's not staying." Rose rolled her eyes at Rory.

"It's not a terrible idea," I murmured from the back seat.

"What?" Rose twisted her body to give me a wide-eyed expression.

"See? I know my girl. She's always been *my* girl."

I didn't break Rory's heart by disputing that. I *was* her girl, and maybe part of me always would be, but my intentions for considering a move back to Denver had little to do with her.

And from the look on Rose's face, she knew it. And she wasn't happy about it.

I didn't care.

I wasn't the eighteen-year-old girl she found on the floor with Fisher. A lot had happened. And while I had no expectations of him ever remembering me, I just ... I wanted to be near him. I needed to know that he would be okay, even if that meant standing by while he fell in love with Angie again, while he married her, while he started a family with her.

My faith hadn't completely died. I did have faith that things would work out, whatever that meant.

CHAPTER FIVE

"Hey, girl!" Hailey pushed her desk chair back as I opened the office door.

"Hey, yourself." I hugged her.

"Congratulations, Nurse Capshaw."

I laughed, releasing her. "Thank you. I'm not done. But I'm excited to spend the next year working instead of being in school. Then I'll finish up my master's."

"We didn't get a chance to talk at the hospital. But ... a midwife, right?" She sat on the edge of her desk.

"Yes. I worked with a midwife in Thailand. I didn't make an instant decision that I wanted to be a midwife, but I looked forward to every day with her. I got butterflies whenever she announced that someone was in labor. And I couldn't sleep for hours after a birth. The adrenaline. The sheer amazement. And it never got old. I witnessed nearly thirty births, and they were all a little different. They were all special in their own way.

So ..." I didn't have to grin. I realized I'd been grinning since the second she said the word midwife.

"That is awesome. I'm thrilled for you. Maybe you should move back here and deliver my babies when I have them. Hopefully sooner versus later." She held out her hand.

"Oh my gosh! You're engaged?"

"Married." She shook her head. "Hawaii wedding. Less than ten people were there. His name is Seth and he's a mechanical engineer. Met him online. We're actually coming up on our one-year anniversary."

"No way! I can't believe my mom didn't tell me. Congratulations."

"Thanks. So ... did you make it in the room to see Fisher? I hear he might go home in a few days. What's it been? Three weeks now?"

I nodded. "Yeah. I heard he's going home soon. And I did see him once."

Her nose wrinkled. "Did he recognize you?"

My head inched side to side. "But at least I'm not his fiancée."

"Oh my god! Right? I feel so bad for Angie. Like ... what if he never gets back those lost memories? And will he be able to work? He doesn't remember anyone from work except his dad and uncle. Does he remember his skills?"

I shrugged. "Hard to say. He might not. Or he might get all his memories back tomorrow. But what does Angie do? Wait for them to come back? Or settle into the possibility that he won't remember her, and she needs to see if they can fall in love again?"

"Not Fisher." Hailey shook her head. "I'm not saying the accident hasn't possibly changed other things about him, but I can see him just doing it. Like ... his family telling him how much he loved Angie. How they had gone through so much over the years to finally be together. And how he was all in, ready for that life. I see him nodding and just ... marrying her. Figuring the rest out later."

"That would be..." I wrinkled my nose "...interesting. It would feel like an arranged marriage on his part. The whole 'Trust us, you're perfect for each other.' I couldn't do it. I was engaged to the wrong guy for a day, and I couldn't go through with it."

"Wait, you were ..."

I put my finger to my lips. "And Rory doesn't know. Nobody knows. I don't know if he told anyone. Since I broke it off, I highly doubt he told anyone."

"A day?" She laughed. "What happened?"

He wasn't Fisher Mann.

"It was impulsive. On his part and mine. And I still hadn't made a clear decision on the direction of my future, so I couldn't say yes to marriage and a family. Not yet."

"Smart girl."

"How are things here? Who's in charge now that Fisher's recovering?"

"Me of course." She winked. "His dad and uncle have been covering things. He has great guys working for him. There's not a lot to worry about. Houses are still getting built."

"That's good."

"So when do you go home? You've been here for weeks, right?"

"I don't have a job at the moment, so there's been no rush to get back home. It's been nice spending time with my mom and Rose. But I'll probably head back to Michigan soon."

After Fisher goes home.

"Sure you don't want to stick around here?" She tilted her head and gave me a goofy smile.

"Actually, I'm not ruling it out, if I can find a good job. And I'd need to look into the master's program. But ..." I shrugged.

"Do it!" She giggled. "I'm a little biased, but DO IT!"

I laughed. "I'll see what happens in the next month with job prospects. Rory and Rose are already on top of looking for things around here. When I get back to Michigan, I'll see where things stand with a few openings that were available before I came here."

Before I skipped out on an interview because my heart was more mature but still just as foolish as ever when it came to the naked fisherman.

"Well, don't be a stranger. Five years is too long." She winked.

"Agreed." I hugged her again. "Good to see you."

UNDER THE GUISE of job searching, I stayed just long enough for Fisher to get released from the hospital. Rory didn't complain at all. Rose didn't either, but I knew she was on to me.

"I called Angie and told her we'd drop dinner off but not stay long. I don't want her to worry about food or have the burden be on his family." Rory packed containers of food into bags. It was more than one meal's worth.

"Good idea," Rose said from the kitchen table, working on lesson plans.

"Peanut butter cookies." Rory shook a container filled with cookies. "Fisher loves peanut butter. I bet that makes your stomach turn, huh, sweetie?"

Fisher didn't make my stomach turn. He still made it do things, but only good things. But peanut butter was not back on my food list yet.

"I've tried it several times during school, but nope ... still can't do it." I glanced up from my phone. "Ready?"

She nodded.

"Don't hate me, but I'm staying here. I'll stop by this weekend to see him. I'm just behind with my lesson plans." Rose frowned.

"He'll understand." Rory kissed Rose's head. "Love you. See you in a bit."

"Love you too," she muttered.

All the terrible things I was told about homosexuality. All the terrible, *judgmental* things that went through my head. And there I was watching my mom and Rose so in love. How could so many awful things be said and done in the name of God? It wasn't His fault. It was a flaw with humanity's need for control.

"Maybe being home will spark something with his memory," Rory said as we drove to his house.

"Maybe. Is Angie living with him?"

"Yes, she has been since her mom passed. I bet tonight will be weird for them. Getting in bed with a stranger."

I nodded slowly, preferring not to think about Angie and Fisher in bed. The last time I recalled her being in his bed, he was in the basement with me, and we were on the pool table doing very naughty things. Maybe the pool table was what they needed to show him.

Don't be that person ...

My conscience berated me and rightfully so.

When we pulled into the driveway next to Fisher's work truck, I grabbed one of the bags from Rory, just to have something to do with my hands to hide my shakiness, my nerves.

"He got a new work truck?"

"Yeah, I think it was about two years ago," Rory said, ringing the doorbell.

"Hi. Come in. This is so generous of you." Angie took the bags from us as soon as we stepped inside.

Fisher was in a leather recliner, TV on, blanket over his legs.

"Hey, handsome. Welcome home." Rory took the liberty of being one of the people he knew, and she kissed him on the head and patted his good hand. His other arm was still in a cast.

Fisher lit up like a child at daycare when a parent picked them up. Familiarity. "Hi. It's good to be home." He eyed me.

I smiled. "I saw Hailey the other day. She assured me things were fine. You need to just recover."

"Hailey?"

"Hailey runs your office. Reese worked for you briefly. Remember? I told you that in the hospital. Reese stopped by to see Hailey."

"Sorry." He rubbed his forehead. "A lot happened in the hospital."

"It's fine. How are you feeling?" I asked.

"Pretty good. Can't sleep well yet, but I'm tired a lot. I don't like how the pain meds make me feel, but everyone seems to think I should still take them. I think they just want me to shut up and sleep while they pray my memory fully returns."

Just as he said that, Angie appeared from the kitchen, and just as quickly, she returned to the kitchen. Rory gave me a look. "I'm going to see if Angie has any questions about the food we brought."

I nodded.

"You can have a seat." Fisher lifted his chin, signaling to the sofa.

"Thanks." I eased my butt onto the edge, gripping my knees to keep my hands steady. Everything was so weird, so awkward.

"What do you do?" He caught nothing Rory said to him at the hospital.

"I just graduated from nursing school."

His lips twisted. "Did Rory tell me that? Is that something I should have known?"

"I think she mentioned it, but it's fine. You sent me a graduation card." With a goofy, tight smile, I shrugged. "So ... thanks."

He chuckled. That was the Fisher I remembered. That soft chuckle accompanied by a slight head shake. "You're welcome. Did I put money in the card?"

"No money."

"Hmm ..." He frowned. "Kinda cheap of me. Sorry about that."

Okay, maybe he wasn't the same Fisher. It was really hard to tell at that point.

It was my turn to laugh. "It's fine. I don't think college graduations are like high school graduations."

"Maybe. Did I write something nice in the card?"

I found his genuine interest entertaining. As heartbreaking as his accident was, as his memory loss was, I couldn't deny the new Fisher brought a smile to my face. "Yes, I believe you wrote something nice in the card."

"Was it lame like, 'The future is yours,' or 'Much success?'"

On another laugh, I shook my head. "No. If I recall correctly, you were way more original than that."

"It's funny. I'm trying to remember if I ever recall Rory talking about having a daughter."

"Well, if you don't remember me, then it's unlikely you'd remember her talking about me."

He stared at the television, but I sensed he wasn't focused on the show. "Did you like working for me?"

Biting my lips together, I gave that careful thought. That wasn't an easy question.

"You're hesitating. Is that a no?"

"You were focused and driven. I was young and, honestly, a little clueless in my life at the time. You hired me as a favor to my mom, but I'm certain you had some days that you questioned why you made that offer."

"Oh? Why do you say that?"

Before I could answer, Rory and Angie returned. Angie's eyes were red. She'd clearly been crying.

"Everything okay?" Fisher asked, concern etched into his face. "Did I mess up again?"

Oh, Fisher ...

It was hard to fully put myself in his shoes, but I tried. I tried to imagine a complete stranger coming up to me and telling me they were my fiancé. We were in love. And I simply didn't remember. How does one navigate that? Would I have been able to play the part? Pretend to be in love?

It wasn't that I didn't see it from her side—clearly, he didn't remember me either—but I kind of saw it from his side a little more. Probably because I wanted to see it more from his side.

"You didn't do anything, babe. It's just been an emotional few weeks. You're home now. Life will start to feel normal again, and I'll get past my silly emotions." Angie kneeled on the floor next to Fisher's chair and held his good hand, giving it a kiss and pressing it to her cheek.

Fisher visibly stiffened, and when Angie glanced up at him, he forced a smile. The smile one would have given to a stranger.

She had no choice but to put her heart out in the open on a platter for him to cut into tiny pieces with his unintentionally insensitive comments. However, I kept my heart a little more guarded.

We ended.

I moved on.

He moved on.

End of story.

That was my brain's version of the story. Another reason I kept my heart guarded was to keep it from fighting with my brain. It didn't feel like I had moved on. It didn't like to think of Fisher moving on. And it definitely didn't like to think our story had ended.

"We'll give you two some privacy. I'm so glad you're home," Rory said.

Before she could take a single step toward the door, Fisher spoke up. "You should stay for dinner. I know you sent way too much food for two people."

"Oh ..." Rory shook her head, giving Angie a questioning expression on a quick glance. "No. Rose is home. And I made the food for you two. You don't have to eat it all in one night. We'll drop by another night. Maybe we'll bring pizza and beer."

"Yeah, babe. You need to rest anyway." Angie continued to pet his hand and arm. He didn't want to be alone with her.

"What's so funny?" Rory asked.

"What?" I narrowed my eyes.

"You're smiling. What's so funny?"

"Nothing. Sorry. I didn't mean to smile. I'll rein that in."

Fisher snorted a laugh. "Yep. She's your daughter, Rory."

With no success, Rory attempted to hide her grin from me. "Let's go, *Daughter*. Don't you have a job to find or crosswords to construct?"

"Crossword puzzles?" Fisher did that head tilt that I'd always adored. My little puppy dog. More like a wolf back then.

"Yes." I smiled, wondering if that would jog his memory. "A cruciverbalist. Ever heard of that?"

I knew Rory missed it, and Angie did too, but I didn't. I saw that tiny twitch at the corner of his mouth just before he shook his head once. "I ... I'm not sure."

"Fisher's not a crossword puzzle guy. But he did win a spelling bee. Right, babe? I think your mom told me that once." Angie tried to demonstrate her expertise.

It *thrilled* me to know that he shared that secret with me and not her. And his memory might have cherry-picked things from his brain, but not the crossword puzzles because I saw it, the twitch, even his eyes

37

changed a tiny bit into something along the lines of curiosity or satisfaction.

"A cruciverbalist is a person who enjoys crossword puzzles or constructs them," I said.

Fisher ...

That look. Was it the look he gave me the very first time I told him about my pastime? Was *that* the look I missed? Was that the moment he knew I was more than just an eighteen-year-old girl with freakishly long arms and unlikely to wear socks with my tennis shoes?

I wasn't trying to take him away from Angie. I was only trying to find *my* naked fisherman.

My naked fisherman *did* enjoy crossword puzzles.

My naked fisherman wouldn't marry someone just because his family thought it was the right thing to do.

My naked fisherman ... well, I didn't know if he still existed.

But I sure wanted to find out.

"No offense, but it sounds like a nerdy hobby."

"Fisher, that's not nice." Angie, bless her ignorant heart, came to my rescue.

"Reese's dad used to construct puzzles." Rory played the middle ground. Very matter-of-fact. She wasn't trying to make anyone feel bad.

Fisher nodded several times. "Your ex-husband died. Right?"

Wow.

Fisher remembered that, but not me.

"Yes. Shortly before Reese turned fifteen."

"Well, I'm on a roll today. Another asshole remark

from me. Maybe I should just take my meds and go to sleep."

"It's fine," I said. "I'm sure someday I'll find my nerdy, cruciverbalist soul mate. And he will find my affinity for clues and words to be endearing. Maybe even sexy." I winked.

A wink.

For my naked fisherman.

Then it happened again. The corner of his mouth twitched.

Yes, Fisher. You're my cruciverbalist soul mate, you stubborn ass with a broken brain.

"I'm sure he's out there. Good luck." Fisher kept his gaze on me.

"He's probably in hiding. Not all cruciverbalists are brave enough to admit their passion to the world."

"Mmm ..." he hummed while giving me an easy nod.

I had his attention.

Not his memory.

Not his engagement ring.

Not his bed.

Shaky ground at best, but I took it.

"Well, goodnight, you two," Rory said as I followed her to the door.

"Thanks again," Angie replied.

"Yes. Thanks," Fisher added.

CHAPTER SIX

Dear Lost Fisherman,

I just got home after spending weeks in Denver making sure you'd be okay. You don't remember me. That's fine. Maybe it's best if you don't.

After five years, the world's shortest engagement, college, a tattoo, and some serious sinning, I thought I was over you. I found my passion and followed it. I gave my virginity to a worthy man who might have cherished it more than I did. And I found my fucking voice.

Then I saw you. And it was …

Nine across: Eleven letters. Hint: A calamity.

Catastrophe.

I found it therapeutic to write down my thoughts

and feelings. It was the easiest way to let go of them. It had been years, not since my father died, that I felt the need to journal my thoughts. But losing Fisher brought out *everything*.

Anxiety.

Unsettled emotions.

Destructive hope.

Loss of direction.

I gave myself some time. Some time to sort out my feelings before taking a job anywhere. I let my resurrected naked fisherman emotions sort themselves out.

Rory kept me updated on Fisher during my break for perspective. It didn't help my perspective.

Rory: Fisher's doing better. A little stir crazy.

Rory: Fisher can't sleep. Terrible anxiety.

Rory: Fisher tried to go back to work today. Angie is not happy.

Rory: Feeling so bad for Angie. It's going to be a long road for her and Fisher.

Most of my replies were short like, "Sorry to hear that," or "That's too bad."

Two weeks later, Rory called me.

"Hi."

"I found you a job," she said.

I laughed. "What makes you think I'm still looking for a job?"

"Because it's two in the afternoon on a Thursday

and you answered your phone on the first ring. And if you had a job, you would have told me by now."

"Speaking of jobs, don't you still have one?"

"My next client canceled at the last minute. Anyway, speaking of clients and jobs ... this morning I had a new client. Know what she does?"

"As a matter of fact, I don't," I said.

"She's a midwife. She works in a clinic with three other midwives. They practice midwifery and all kinds of women's healthcare. I'm actually going to start seeing her. She tests for hormone imbalances and stuff like that. I could use a good balancing. I told her about you, and she said she'd love to talk to you about possibly working with her, assisting in the clinic and during labors because she just lost her nurse whose husband got transferred to another state for his job. I told her I'd call you right away. I also gave her your contact information, so expect a call. She's really excited that you assisted a midwife in Thailand for nearly a year."

"She's in Denver?"

"Well ... yes. Of course."

"How do you know I'm for sure still thinking about moving back to Denver?"

My relationship with Fisher was much better when there was a good twelve hundred miles between us. Going back to Denver would magnify everything again.

"Because you love Rose and me and you miss us. And did you hear me say *midwife?*"

It was a great opportunity.

"I'll talk with her. No promises. How's ... Rose?"

"She's fine. I guess a few of her students are driving her crazier than normal. She's thinking it might be time to look for a new position, something in high school."

"That's probably smart. How's ..." I worked my way to my real question. Not that I didn't care about Rose. "Fisher?"

"Oh, Fisher ... I don't know. I mean. He's upset that he's still in a cast. Upset that he can't sleep. Upset that he can't remember the people who work for him or anything else about his job. But if I'm reading between the lines correctly, he's upset that he can't remember the woman living with him. And I feel *so* incredibly bad for Angie. She's considering taking a new job in pharmaceutical sales because it involves traveling, and she thinks it might be good for her and Fisher to have some separation. She's hoping absence makes the heart grow fonder, but I gotta be honest with you, I'm not sure he'll miss her. And it's not *her*. It's him. He's hating life at the moment. Drinking more. Smiling less. Rose and I feel like enablers more than friends when we stop by to see him. It's like he's dying for an excuse to drink. And he knows Angie won't drink with us because she's too busy researching memory loss and a million ways to bring it back. It's all very awkward."

"Is he seeing a therapist?"

"No." Rory laughed. "Angie is, but Fisher won't. Not yet. He doesn't feel comfortable talking to a stranger about a bunch of other strangers. His words."

"Sounds about right. Well, everyone needs to let him find his own way through this. If he doesn't want help, you can't force it on him. And maybe Angie's right. Giving him space might help. Stress doesn't help the healing process, and his brain needs to heal."

"Yeah, Rose and I told her to take the job, but Fisher's family isn't so sure. They think her job should be getting Fisher to fall in love with her again. But unrequited love is very hard on the heart."

I nodded to myself. "Yes. It is."

"Call me after you talk to Holly. That's the midwife. Holly Dillon."

"I will. And thanks. It does sound like the perfect opportunity, even if I'm not looking forward to moving again."

"I know. Talk soon, sweetie."

THE PHONE INTERVIEW with Holly went well. Perfect, in fact. Breaking my year lease wasn't the ideal way to manage my money, but I took the loss, rented a small U-Haul trailer to pull behind my car, and drove to Denver over the course of three days and two nights.

What I didn't expect to find was Rory, Rose, *and* Fisher sitting on Rory's and Rose's front porch when I arrived around dinnertime. My nerves did stupid things along with my heart and the butterflies in my tummy. He didn't remember me. Why did I act like a naked student on the first day of school?

"She's home!" Rory set her wine aside and ran toward me.

"Hi." I hugged her when she did her attempted tackle move on me.

"How was the drive?"

I sighed, blowing my hair out of my face. "Long."

"Hungry?"

"Starving," I said.

"Let's eat first then we'll unload your stuff. I made chili and cornbread muffins."

"Sounds amazing." I followed her toward the porch.

"Hey, girlie girl." Rose stood and hugged me. "So good to see you."

"You too."

"I'm just going to pop the muffins back in the oven for a bit to warm up." Rory opened the front door.

"I'll get the table set." Rose followed her.

The door shut, then it was just us.

"Hi." I smiled. It was difficult to approximate the proper size of a smile to give Fisher. Nothing too exuberant. Nothing too pitiful like I felt bad that he was in a cast and suffering from anxiety ... maybe even on the verge of alcoholism as his favorite coping mechanism.

"Welcome home. And congratulations on your new job."

"Thanks. I hear you're recovering well."

He grunted a laugh before taking a pull of his beer. "Who told you that?"

"Rory."

"I'm recovering. Well? Not so sure about that."

"Where's Angie?"

"My fiancée?"

On a nervous laugh, I nodded. "Um ... yeah."

He shrugged. "Not sure. I said something to piss her off *again*. So she left. She'll return. She always does."

"Well..." I leaned against the corner pillar of the porch "...you sound like a bundle of joy. I can't imagine why she'd leave your cheeriness."

That brought a tiny grin to his face, and he slowly shook his head before scratching the back of his neck. "She's fine. Really. A beautiful *stranger*. I was clearly a lucky man."

"Was? You survived a pretty intense accident on your motorcycle. I'd say you're still lucky. And you still have a fiancée. What's the problem? Are you having erectile dysfunction issues? It's not uncommon after accidents."

He choked on his beer and wiped his mouth with the back of his hand. "What the fuck? No. Why would you ask me that?"

I took his beer and helped myself to a long swig. A little mixing of saliva.

He raised a single eyebrow.

Yeah, Fisher ... I'm not the deer-in-the-headlights girl you don't remember. I swap saliva. Drink beer. And have sex. Sometimes I even touch myself because it feels "good."

"I'm a nurse. It's strictly a medical question. It can be hard on relationships when accidents impair sexual function. And sometimes it's not a physical disability as much as it's an emotional issue."

"My dick works just fine."

"Maybe you should do something that takes your mind off your situation."

"What's my situation?" He grabbed the beer bottle back from me and frowned when he noticed it was empty.

"Your arm is still in a cast. I'm sure your family is still coddling you. And you're living with a stranger who wants you to get fitted for a tux so she can take your name and have your babies."

His lips twisted. After a few seconds, he nodded several times. "That's not entirely inaccurate. So what distraction do you suggest?"

"I could give you some of my crossword puzzles to work on."

There it was again. That look. The one I missed as a nervous eighteen-year-old girl with an insane crush on the naked fisherman. The one I *didn't* miss when we took dinner to his house after he came home from the hospital and I told him about my hobby.

"Why do you keep mentioning puzzles? I'm not sure I even like crossword puzzles."

"No?" I did his signature head cock. "Huh ... I thought I felt a vibe. Must not have."

"A crossword puzzle vibe?"

"Something like that." My lips pressed together to conceal my grin.

"Dinner's ready," Rory said as she opened the door.

Fisher's gaze stayed glued to me, just where I liked it. Where it belonged.

"Need help standing?" I pushed off the pillar and held out my hand.

Shaking his head, he leaned forward and stood on his own while mumbling, "I don't need help getting anything up."

"Believing you can is half the battle," I murmured back to him as I headed into the house.

It was just a whisper, but I felt pretty certain he said, "Smart ass," as he followed me into the house.

"LET'S GET YOUR STUFF UNLOADED," Rose suggested right after dinner.

"I don't have a lot. I sold the big pieces because I knew you wouldn't have room for them, and I didn't want to store them." I headed out to the driveway.

"Fisher, do you want a ride home?" Rory asked as she set the dinner dishes by the sink.

"It's three blocks. I think I can manage. Besides, I should help unload Reese's things from the trailer."

"No." I turned just as I stepped outside. "Your arm is in a cast."

"So?"

"So we've got it."

"I have one good arm." He stepped outside, forcing me to take a step backward.

"Save it. We've got this. You know my arms are freakishly long." I said it, and I couldn't unsay it. For a second, I let myself forget that Fisher didn't remember me or anything about me.

"They are?"

I nodded slowly before turning and making quick strides to the trailer. "That's what some jerk told me once." Opening the trailer, I grabbed one box while Rose took another box.

Fisher grabbed a box too and wedged it between his arm and chest, following us into the house, into my bedroom.

Rose set her box down and headed back outside. I set my box on the bed and started to brush past Fisher as he set his box next to mine.

"Was I the *some jerk*?"

I stopped in the doorway with my back to him. After a few seconds to figure out an honest answer, I glanced over my shoulder. "You were my favorite jerk." I shot him an exaggerated smile, using fake humor to hide the depths of my emotions. "But yes ... you made fun of my long arms." Without waiting for his response, I strode outside again.

Rory joined us, and the four of us had everything unloaded in less than ten minutes.

"Thank you, Fisher." Rory thanked him before I got the chance to do it. "You sure you don't want a ride?"

"No ride. Thanks for dinner."

"Night, Fish," Rose called from the kitchen as she started washing dishes.

"I'm going to lock the trailer and my car," I said to Rory as I followed Fisher out the door.

"Okay."

We said nothing while strolling down the driveway. I veered off to the left to lock the trailer.

Fisher stopped, sliding his good hand into his back jeans pocket. "I don't really think I'm going to care for them, but if you want to drop off some puzzles ... just..." he shrugged "...whenever. I'll give them a try. No rush. It's really ... no big deal."

I locked the trailer and leaned my back against it, crossing my arms over my chest. "Okay. I'll drop some off tomorrow."

"There's no rush." He tried so hard to be nonchalant with me.

"Okay." I nodded several times. "So ... I'll drop them off tomorrow."

He fought his grin, but it won.

I won.

"I guess tomorrow is fine."

I didn't know who Angie got when they were together. I didn't know the anxiety ridden Fisher my mom had told me about.

My Fisher was still in his skin. Too cool for his own good.

A streak of crudeness.

And a little *extra*.

"I was uh..." he tipped his chin to his chest "... looking through pictures on my phone. And I came across some of you and one of us. We were in the mountains. Your hair was longer. But other than that, you looked the same. Do you remember that?" Fisher forced his gaze up to meet mine. Confusion ate into his face along his brow and at the corners of his eyes.

I smiled. "Yes. My memory is fine."

"And ... what were we doing? Was Rory there too? She wasn't in any of the pictures."

"No. It was just us. Rory was in California for work. I had never been in the mountains, and I really wanted to go. But both you and Rory had a little fit over me driving there by myself. So you took me. On your motorcycle. We stopped at that lookout point and snapped a few pictures. Then we ate pizza at Beau Jo's pizza on our way home. It ..."

My grin swelled. "It was a good day. A great day, really. My first time in the Rockies. My first time on the back of a motorcycle. My first time dipping thick wheat pizza crust in honey."

He nodded slowly. "So we did stuff outside of work?"

"Sometimes. We went on a double ... well ... triple date once. Arnie invited me to one of his concerts. You and Angie were there, and my friend and her boyfriend joined us as well. I was underage; therefore, I was the DD that night."

"Huh ..." He inched his head side to side. "It's so weird. Like Angie showing me a million photos and videos from our time together, and nothing is familiar. I don't remember the trip to the mountains or the concert."

On an easy smile, I stood straight and uncrossed my arms. "Well, I remember for the both of us."

"You don't appear bothered that I don't remember. Angie seems on the edge of going nuclear after we've spent hours trying to jog my memory with the photos and videos."

I nodded slowly. "I think love—the good kind—holds an equal mix of wonder and familiarity. That feeling like you know someone, yet you also know parts of them are still a mystery that you can't wait to slowly discover. If there's no wonder, I think the love *can* die. If there's no familiarity, I think the love already feels dead. If I were the one marrying you, I would be bothered more than I am. But you chose her."

Oh ... my ... sweet ... lord ...

That was not the right choice of words. And as much as I hoped and prayed Fisher would let my word choice slip by without a second thought, it didn't happen.

"I chose her?"

FUCK!

Yes, I adopted that word into my vocabulary, like a favorite tool in a toolbox that I used only on a need-to basis.

"Gosh..." I twisted my lips and rolled my eyes dramatically "...that sounded really weird, didn't it?" For good measure, I threw in an awkward laugh. "I'm so freaking tired from long days of driving. I meant *proposed*." I shook my head. "Yeah, that's what I meant. You *proposed* to her. Just her. Not like you had a choice between her and someone else. At least ... not that I know of. And definitely not me, of course, because until your accident, I hadn't seen you in five years. Gah ..." I covered my face with my hands. "Please just tell me to shut up."

He smirked just like the Fisher I knew five years earlier. Like the Fisher who *didn't* choose me. The Fisher who was finally willing to take my virginity with the understanding that *my husband* (not him) would thank him someday.

"I find your rambling too entertaining to tell you to shut up."

"Go home and find your fiancée entertaining."

Something between a grunt and laugh left this chest. "I'll do my best."

"Night, Fisher. Thanks for your help."

He turned and headed down the sidewalk. "Anytime."

CHAPTER SEVEN

I PLAYED it cool the next day for a full three hours after waking before I walked the crossword puzzles over to Fisher's house. Rory and Rose were at work, and I didn't start my job until the following week, so no one was keeping tabs on me.

I knocked on the door several times.

No answer.

I rang the doorbell.

No answer.

As I gave up and started to retreat down the sidewalk, Fisher opened the door.

Just my luck ...

He was wet and holding a towel around his waist. The past replayed itself. I liked the idea of a redo with Fisher.

"I'm running late, babe!" Angie appeared in the doorway in a pantsuit and her handbag dangling from one arm. She lifted onto her toes and kissed him on the lips. He kissed her back.

It wasn't a long kiss, but it wasn't one sided either.

"Morning, Reese. Can't stay and chat. Byeee!" She waved to me with her left hand, big diamond, and manicured nails, just before hopping into her car.

I mumbled a barely audible "hi" and turned my attention to the resurrected naked fisherman. As I made my way to the front porch, he watched Angie back out of the driveway before shifting his attention to me.

"Good morning."

My gaze struggled to stay on his face.

"Not pretty, huh?" he said.

I shook my head as if I hadn't been staring at his road rash that was healing fairly well. "You're alive. I think the prettiness of your skin should be an afterthought."

He retreated into the house, leaving the door open —which I took as an invitation to go inside.

"Angie seemed in a good mood. You must have done something right for once."

He continued down the hallway toward his (their) bedroom. "Apparently she just needed to get laid. Had I known, I could have obliged her sooner." He shut the door behind him.

That was a pretty hard hit. It took a good pep talk to get my emotions in check before he reemerged from the bedroom.

He proposed to her.

She said yes.

Even if he didn't remember her, it didn't mean they couldn't have sex. Sex didn't have to involve emotions. Men paid for sex with prostitutes—not that Angie was a prostitute or Fisher was the kind of guy who would pay for sex. I needed a way to wrap my brain around it before the disappointment sent me spiraling out of control.

I took a seat at the island in the kitchen. A few minutes later, he came into the room in jeans and a white tee. Hair still wet. "My dick works, Nurse Capshaw. In case you're still concerned." He poured himself a cup of coffee and dropped two slices of bread into the toaster.

My breakfast was a mini vomit in my mouth that I swallowed back down. "Still so crude."

"Crude?" He turned and leaned his butt against the counter, sipping his coffee. "Was I crude to you?"

Did he want the truth?

"Had my mom not been living in your basement, I'm pretty sure I could have won a sexual harassment lawsuit against you and your crudeness." I might have been feeling a bit feral and defensive after confirmation that he screwed Angie the previous night.

How dare he have sex with his fiancée. (Internal eye roll at myself).

"Are you..." he squinted at me "...serious? I was inappropriate with you?"

Wow! It seemed to really bother him.

I gave my answer some thought. Of course, my

knee-jerk response would have been, "You zip-tied me to a stool and *ate me out*." That response gave away too much information. I wasn't actively trying to break up his engagement. Not consciously, anyway.

"You had a gift for making me blush. That's all."

He kept his mouth hidden behind his coffee mug. Was he grinning?

"Do tell. What kinds of things did I do to make you blush?"

"I ..." I laughed. "I'm not going to tell you. I'm sure most of it was because I was young. I'd spent the previous three years in a Christian academy, and Rory was gone, so I think you were bored. Embarrassing me became your favorite pastime."

After another sip of his coffee, he set his mug on the counter. "Well, I'm sorry." He seemed serious.

The long moment of silence conveyed a level of genuineness. Then a case of untimely giggles hit me. I just ... started laughing, and I couldn't stop.

Even with my hand cupped at my mouth, my laughter continued. "I'm ... I'm sorry. I just don't believe you."

"What don't you believe?"

"That ..." I took a deep breath to control my laughter. "That you're sorry. You told me your dick still works."

"Only because yesterday you asked me if it worked."

"As a nurse. I asked you in a professional way."

"But you're not *my* nurse, so it made you look like

57

my friend's daughter simply asking about my dick." He retrieved the butter from the fridge.

"No peanut butter? You can't possibly be out of peanut butter."

He shrugged. "Yeah, I don't know what's up with that. Everyone tells me I love peanut butter. Rory made peanut butter cookies. I mean, it's all right, but I don't feel a big love for it."

"I hate it."

"Really? That's interesting. I don't know what I hate. Or I don't remember what I hate. It's weird how some things are clear and other things just don't exist. Not like I don't remember them well, it's that they are not there at all."

I nodded. "The brain is a mysterious place. For everything we do know about it, there seems to be so much we still don't know and may never fully understand. Don't stress over it."

"I'm not, but I feel the stress from everyone around me."

I didn't know what to say. So I said nothing more about it for a minute or so before changing the subject. "I brought you some crossword puzzles." I set the folder on the counter.

"Oh ..." He glanced over his shoulder. "Are we done talking about my memory and my dick?" That smirk ...

Different guy, yet same guy. Just missing a few memories.

"I hope so. Do you need help spreading that on your toast?"

"Do I look like I do?" He had butter on his cast and his toast kept slipping off his plate onto the counter as he tried to spread it.

"No. You don't. You look like you have everything under control."

He hugged the tub of butter to his chest with his casted arm and used his good hand to press the lid back onto it. After he returned it to the fridge, I noticed a glob of smeared butter on his shirt. Rolling my lips between my teeth, I kept silent.

"You not working today?" He looked down, frowning at his shirt.

"I start my new job on Monday. Are you not working today? Because you clearly could do about anything. That cast isn't holding you back one bit." I snorted.

Fisher glanced up, eyes narrowed. "Are you picking on a disabled person? How Christian of you."

"Sorry. What can I do for you today? Rake the leaves in your yard? Shave your scruffy face?"

"My face?" He paused his chewing. "Angie said I needed to shave or at least trim my beard. She offered to do it, but I said I could do it myself."

"Of course you did." I smirked. "If you were left-handed, you'd be fine. But you're not left-handed."

"You know my handedness?"

"Yes, but if there was any question, that butter fiasco I just witnessed confirmed it."

"Smart ass." He ate his toast.

I watched him eat it. And we shared familiar glances. Well, familiar to me.

"I'll let you trim my beard. But you can't tell anyone."

"Okay. Why is that?"

"Because I want Angie to think I did it on my own."

"You do realize ... this is the woman you asked to marry you. The whole 'in sickness and in health' thing. Right?"

He shook his head. "I didn't propose. She did."

"Uh ... you remember that?"

"She told me. She's told me everything. I officially have all the memories of our life thus far; they just aren't mine. They're hers, which makes it about as real to me as someone reading me a fictional book."

"And she proposed?"

"Yes."

"How do you feel about that?"

He shrugged. "I don't know. I asked her if she knew why I hadn't proposed."

"What did she say?"

"She said I needed a nudge."

"Interesting." That shocked me. Rory didn't tell me Angie was the one who proposed. "Well ... are you done? If I'm going to secretly trim your beard, I should do it now. I have some errands to run."

"Okay. We can do it now." He set his plate in the sink and nodded toward the hallway.

I followed him to the master bathroom where he shrugged off his shirt with his good arm and tossed the shirt on the floor.

"Have you trimmed a beard before?" he asked, pulling the trimmer from its base and turning it on like he was testing the battery.

"Yes. I've trimmed lots of things." I plucked the trimmer from his hand. "Sit." I nodded to the vanity bench that wasn't there when Fisher lived alone.

He sat down, draping a towel over his lap to catch the hair. I focused on his face. Not his scars. And definitely not his abs or happy trail. Nope. I was a total professional. Except for my thoughts. They played in my head like a day at an amusement park.

I've been in that tub naked.

I know what your penis looks like because I gave you a blowjob in that doorway to your closet.

"What's so funny?" he asked.

"What?" I turned on the trimmer.

"You were grinning."

I really needed to practice a straight face while fantasizing about the naked fisherman.

"Sorry. I won't smile again." I started near his sideburns.

"Don't apologize. It's a great smile."

I felt his gaze on my face, but I kept my focus on the trimmers so I didn't do anything stupid like nick his ear or kiss him.

"Did you leave a boyfriend behind in Michigan?"

He made it hard to control my breathing in his

close proximity, and asking me personal questions didn't help the situation. "I left several boyfriends behind in Michigan, but I left them long before I decided to move back here."

"Do you like Colorado better than Michigan? Or did you want to be closer to family?"

I wanted to be closer to you.

"A little bit of both. I think I knew that if I didn't move back here, your beard would never get trimmed."

"Ha ha ..."

I stole a tiny glance into his eyes before resuming the beard trim. "I do love it here. And I missed my mom. We no sooner reunited after five years of separation while in prison, and she left for California. Not long after she returned, I went to Thailand. Then Michigan."

"It's crazy that I remember Rory but I don't remember her going to California."

"Well..." I used my finger to tip his chin up "...if you remembered her going to California, then you would remember me."

"True. What did you do in Thailand?"

I missed you. Developed feelings for another man. Gave away my virginity. Found my calling in life. And missed you some more.

"Mission trip. Originally, it was just going to be for six months. But the friend who convinced me to go, he wanted to stay for another six months. Best decision ever. I assisted a midwife. And that's where I fell in love with midwifery. So I went back to Texas after

Thailand, just long enough to have my grandparents help me get my tuition paid."

"So you owe this guy, your friend, a big thanks for convincing you to go to Thailand."

"I suppose I do."

And Fisher. I owed him a thank-you for helping me see just how terrible the timing was for *us*.

"That's pretty cool," Fisher said. "I like when fate does its thing. Had a friend of my dad's not given me a summer job with his construction company, I probably would have gone to college just to play sports. Who knows how that would have ended?" Fisher shrugged a shoulder. "Angie said she wanted me to play baseball in college. She thinks I would have gone pro." He chuckled. "Apparently, I've known her since we were six. Our moms had our wedding planned before we left elementary school."

"So ... you remember that you love construction, but you don't remember owning a construction company? And you remember your family, but you don't remember the girl you met when you were six? The woman who you proposed ... well, said 'yes' to?"

"Maybe it's a sign."

"A sign?" I tilted my head.

"Maybe it's a sign we need more time."

"Oof ... I hope you haven't said that to her." I turned off the trimmer, removed the guard, and blew on the blades before returning the guard to its place and setting it on the counter.

Fisher ran his hand over his closely trimmed beard.

63

"What if I don't remember her? What if I don't ..." He rubbed his lips together, his gaze averted to the floor.

"What if you don't what?" I took the towel from his lap and shook the whiskers into the trash.

"What if I don't fall in love with her again?"

I coughed a laugh. "Um ... you had sex with her last night." I couldn't look at him. I wasn't eighteen, but I also wasn't immune to the bathroom we were in or talking about sex with the naked fisherman.

He jerked his head back as if my statement made no sense. "Sex isn't love."

"It might be to your *fiancée*."

"She wanted it. And you suggested my dick might not be working properly, so I did it. Now she's happy. And Nurse Capshaw is satisfied too."

I shook my head and cleared my throat while tossing the towel in the hamper. "Please don't have sex with ... *anyone* to satisfy me. I'm just an old employee, your friend's daughter who you can't remember. And ..." I held up my arm to look at my watch, being very dramatic about it so he would drop the topic. "I need to run errands now."

"Where are you going?" He followed me out of the bathroom.

"I just said I'm running errands."

"Yeah, I'm not deaf. I meant, what errands?"

"Target and the uniform store to get some new scrubs."

"You should invite me."

As I reached his front door, I turned. "You think so?"

He shrugged, looking so handsome it made me want to cry. Stupid life timing. What I wouldn't have given for him to have stepped closer, to have made me melt with one look.

Are you going to kiss me?

I'm thinking about it.

"Give me thirty minutes to get home and make my list. Then I'll pick you up."

A slow grin worked its way up his face, warming my skin and forcing my heart to do some silly beat skipping.

CHAPTER EIGHT

"Never thought I'd see this day," I said as Fisher climbed into my vehicle.

"What day is that?" He fastened his seat belt.

"The day you jumped at a chance to go to Target and a uniform store because you're so bored."

"I'm not bored. In fact, I finished one of the crossword puzzles while waiting for you."

Tossing him a quick glance, my eyes narrowed. "You didn't. They weren't easy puzzles."

"Maybe not to you." He stared out his window and shrugged.

He left me speechless for a few blocks.

"I need gas." I pulled into a gas station. After filling the tank, I ran inside to get something.

Fisher eyed me and the drink in my hand when I returned.

"For you." I handed him the plastic cup filled with red liquid.

"What is this?"

"Iced tea and fruit punch." I handed him a straw too. "Your favorite."

He ripped open the straw and poked it into the lid. "It is? How do I not remember things I like and dislike? Do I have food allergies? Will shellfish kill me? I mean … I don't know." He took a sip. "But what I do know is this is really good. I clearly knew my shit."

I grinned, putting the car into *Drive*. "Easy partner. Your head's getting too big."

He took another long sip. "What else should I know about you?"

"Me?"

"Yeah. I know everything about that Angie girl because she's told me everything. She's AB blood type. Allergic to walnuts. Scared of spiders. And she cries easily."

I laughed. "Well, hmm … I'm O-positive. No allergies. You already know I don't like peanut butter. Spiders are okay. I like my coffee extra sweet. And I don't watch a lot of TV."

"I watch a lot of TV. It's a distraction from the stranger living with me."

"The *stranger* you had sex with last night."

"Yes, to prove that my dick worked and to get her to stop being so weird."

I giggled. "Weird? What do you mean by weird?"

"She's constantly watching me. It's creepy. And she's too … cheery. Not like you."

"Whoa … not like me?"

"No. You're selectively happy. Which is normal in my mind. Like you are who you are. You could hate puppies and rainbows and not give a shit what anyone thinks about it."

"I ..." I shook my head. Was that how he saw me? "I do not hate puppies. But rainbows are a little overrated."

His shoulders shook on a light chuckle as he sucked on the straw.

"I do like learning new things, and you taught me how to sand wood. Nothing too hard, but I asked you to teach me things, and you did. I still like hands-on things."

"I taught you things? Sanding?"

I nodded.

"In my workshop?"

Another nod.

"Huh ..." He seemed perplexed.

"Is that surprising?"

"I think so."

"Why?"

"Because I've been told by more than one person that I like to do my own thing. I hire people who already know what they're doing. I'm not much of a teacher. I don't have enough patience."

"Mmm ..." I nodded. "They might be right. And I said you taught me. I didn't say you were patient with me. I'm sure you indulged me just to be nice to Rory."

Fisher hummed. "Maybe," he murmured.

We pulled into Target. "Are you staying in the car?

I only have a few things to grab." Tampons. I needed tampons. And deodorant.

"No. I have my own list of things to get." He climbed out of the vehicle.

After we walked into the store, he grabbed a shopping cart while I plucked a basket from the stack.

"You can just put your stuff in my cart."

"Or you can get the stuff on your list and I can get the stuff on my list, and we can meet back here when we're done."

"What's the rush? I don't have to work. You don't have to work. We might as well walk the aisles and let the end displays tell us what we didn't know we needed," said the guy who dragged me in and out of an apparel store in record time when I needed boots and a hard hat.

Surrendering to the fact that I'd be making a second trip that day to get my tampons, I slid my basket back into the stack and followed Fisher's lead.

"So what are you getting?" I asked.

"What are *you* getting? Show me your list and I'll show you mine."

I rolled my eyes, despite my grin and complete feeling of bliss. "My list is in my head."

"Mine too."

I giggled as we strolled through the electronics aisles. "Then how are you going to 'show' me your list?"

"I assumed you could read my mind. You know ... since you guessed my favorite drink."

"I didn't guess." I playfully nudged his good arm as we crossed over into the cards and party stuff.

"Did you get lots of birthday parties when you were a kid?" He grabbed a big party hat from a tall stack and set it on my head.

I kept walking down the aisle with the hat on my head. "I got lots of parties since I was an only child, until Rory went to prison. Mostly Disney princess parties. What about you?" I snagged a funny pair of glasses that had a big nose and mustache attached to them. Then I slipped it onto Fisher's face.

"Oh yes. My parents have always celebrated everything. And I have a huge family, so even things that weren't a big deal seemed like one because fifty gazillion people were there, and that was literally 'close family.' You were at the hospital. Tell me the waiting room wasn't filled to capacity with my family."

I laughed as we continued to stroll, garnering funny looks from other shoppers since I still had on the hat and he wore the glasses. "Point made."

"Do you use an alarm clock?" Fisher picked up a retro looking alarm clock, the kind with an actual bell.

"I use my phone. Does anyone use an alarm clock?"

He pointed to the clock in his hands. "Someone does."

"Fake plants or real plants?" I buried my nose in a fake bouquet of decorative flowers.

"Real."

"Agreed." I nodded.

"Halloween. Best holiday ever or most annoying holiday ever?" Fisher asked when we crossed a main aisle to the seasonal displays. Lots of Halloween stuff.

"I'm inclined to say best."

He wrinkled his nose at my answer.

I turned to face him, holding onto the cart while walking backward. "And before you unfairly judge me, you have to know that after Rory went to prison, I didn't get to go to parties because my grandparents said Halloween was Satan's holiday, so my dad caved to their nonsense and didn't let me go. Then he died and I didn't have a prayer of ever going to anything fun like a costume party. So imagine my excitement when my roommates wanted to have a Halloween party my first year of nursing school."

He grinned, matching mine. "Let me guess, you dressed up as a naughty nurse."

"Pfft ..." I shook my head.

I totally dressed up as a naughty nurse. I also had sex with Batman that night. Good sex. Two beers, lowered inhibitions, and false confidence sex.

Naughty nurse ended up dating Batman for eight weeks.

Fisher eyed me through his funny glasses. "Then what was your costume?"

"Um ..." I glanced around as if I'd see something and use it.

"You were a naughty nurse."

"I wasn't!" I giggled.

"Liar."

I turned forward again, still giggling. He knew. And I could no longer hide it.

We spent an hour in Target. There was a lot one could learn about a person by spending an hour with them in Target, such as neither one of us cared that people were looking at us in our hat and glasses.

Fisher was a huge Star Wars fan.

I owned over thirty Barbies by the time I was ten.

We both loved big mirrors.

Fisher had never played pickle ball.

And I was a sucker for bookends in the shape of animals. Specifically elephants.

"Your list ... what did you need?" he asked as we approached the pharmacy area.

I sighed, no longer feeling like I wanted to hide my list and come back later. "I need deodorant and tampons. What do you need?" I quickly countered before he had a chance to react to the tampons.

"Mouthwash and condoms."

Gulp ...

He steered the cart toward the tampons first.

Figures.

"Applicator? No applicator? Regular? Super? These are made with organic cotton in case your vagina is eco-conscious."

And there it came ... that blush only Fisher could bring out of me so quickly. I snagged the box I needed and tossed it into the cart.

"So your vagina *is* eco-conscious." He grinned. "Noted."

Oh my gosh ... what exactly is he "noting" and why?

We grabbed my deodorant and his mouthwash, making our final stop in the condom aisle.

"I'm a little surprised Angie isn't on the pill." I fidgeted with the hem of my T-shirt. Old habits never died.

"Apparently, she went off the pill in preparation for getting pregnant."

I nodded. "So you're going to have kids right away. That's exciting."

He tossed a box of condoms in the cart. "I'm not sure if it's exciting, hence the condoms. I'm a little hesitant to make a child with someone if I'm not sold on the idea of marrying them yet."

I followed a few steps behind him.

"So you're just going to hump her and dump her."

He stopped so quickly I ran into his back.

"Oof ... why'd you stop?"

Facing me, he squinted and twisted his lips. "You don't think I should have sex with her if I'm not certain I want to marry her?"

With a tight smile, I lifted a shoulder. "I don't have a strong opinion on it. But I imagine she does. Maybe you should make sure you're on the same page. The intimacy might lead her to believe all is good between the two of you. That's all. It's the male brain versus the female brain."

Fisher waited until I felt a little squirmy before he responded with a sharp nod. "Good tip." Turning, he headed toward the checkout lane.

CHAPTER NINE

"It's like getting to wear pajamas to work," Fisher said, checking out the racks of scrubs.

"It sure is. And I can wear comfy shoes instead of work boots."

He glanced up at me, his hand resting on a pile of scrub tops. "Are you making a jab at me? Did I tell you to wear work boots? I should have. It's a safety issue."

"Yes." I picked out a top. "You took me to buy boots and a hard hat, but I wasn't wearing socks and that chapped you."

"Well, who doesn't wear socks to work?"

"Lifeguards," I said casually, moving a few steps to a different round rack. "I bet strippers don't wear socks either."

He tipped his head, pretending to be really interested in a pair of smiley faced scrubs. Then he chuckled. "They might wear fishnet stockings."

"Do you think you would have been okay with me wearing fishnet stockings with my work boots?"

Clearing his throat, he glanced around the store. "I'm dealing with some memory loss, so I can't say for sure where my head might have been in that moment." His lips twisted as his gaze landed on me. A tiny grin teased his lips. "I might have been okay with it."

"Well, that's shocking." I took my scrubs to the checkout counter and paid for them while Fisher waited by the door.

"Time to return you before your curfew."

"Curfew. Pfft." He rolled his eyes. "I was thinking lunch."

"You're milking this outing."

"I'm in a cast. Going crazy. Help a guy out."

"Help a guy out ..." I mumbled as we headed to the car.

I helped the guy out, as if my eternally foolish heart had a choice. We found a soup and sandwich cafe with whimsical decor and a quaint little booth in the back surrounded by snake ferns and hanging Pothos.

"Tell me all about Thailand," Fisher said after we ordered our food and drinks.

"How much time do you have?" I chuckled.

Leaning back, he stretched his good arm along the back of the booth. "I'm yours for the rest of the day."

Oh, Fisher ... you're no longer mine.

We spent the next hour and a half eating and talking all things Thailand. While it was my story to tell, Fisher asked lots of questions and seemed genuinely engaged and curious.

We laughed.

I got a little teary eyed telling him about a still birth that tore out my heart.

But for the most part, I shared my stories with enthusiasm, using my hands and making crazy expressions. He seemed to eat it up. Every word.

We ordered a slice of chocolate pie to share. Sharing our germs. Saliva swapping.

I didn't go into much detail about Brendon. Not our romance. Not our engagement. I never even said his name. Fisher was none the wiser. And not once did I think about the eighteen-year-old girl he didn't remember. I was too busy enjoying the moment—the moment he got to know the woman I'd become.

"Thanks for letting me tag along," Fisher said when I dropped him off at his house a little before three in the afternoon.

"Thanks for lunch. You didn't have to pay."

He ducked his head back into my car and grinned. "I invited myself. It was the least I could do." He winked.

THAT. That was almost too much. Tears came out of nowhere, sending me fumbling for my sunglasses.

"Well ..." I fumbled my words like my fingers fumbled my glasses. "Have a good rest of your day."

"I'll have a good enough day." He shut the door.

I made it out of his driveway and about ten feet

down the street before my tears escaped on a heavy blink. Why did he have to wink at me?

Why did he have to be so fun and goofy in Target?

Why did he have to be so interested in my trip to Thailand, so interested in *me*?

CHAPTER TEN

S<small>UNDAY MORNING BROUGHT</small> an unexpected guest to our house. I had just returned from my morning jog. Three long faces at the kitchen table greeted me.

Rory. Rose. And Angie.

"Hey," I said with caution.

"How was your run?" Rory asked.

"Fine," I replied slowly, filling a glass with water. "Is ... everything okay?"

"Fisher suggested Angie move out and they date again." Just Rose giving me the quick explanation made Angie cry. Again, I assumed.

"Oh." That was the best I had, but I dug deeper for more. "Well, I'm sure that's hard to hear. But he's not saying he doesn't want you. And it's impossible for any of us to put ourselves in Fisher's shoes. But I'd imagine he's feeling overwhelmed."

"And how do you think I'm feeling?" Angie cried.

Rory frowned at me like it was my fault.

"I imagine you're feeling scared. Grateful that you didn't lose him in that accident, yet you *did* lose him in many ways. It's like the family of someone with Alzheimer's. You realize that all the pictures and souvenirs from life mean nothing without the actual memories. You're a stranger to the person you love most in the world. And falling in love with someone is like offering a part of yourself to them. If Fisher doesn't recognize you, it's like you're missing a part of yourself. And you're questioning who you are or who you will be if you never get that piece back. But honestly, I'd imagine your biggest fear right now is that Fisher won't fall in love with you again." I pressed my lips together for a few seconds. I might have gone too far. "At least, that's how I would feel if I were in your shoes."

Angie blinked a new round of tears as her face wrinkled. "Y-yes … that's exactly h-how I f-feel."

Rose hugged her. "He'll come around. You're a beautiful, kind, talented woman. He'd be a fool to not fall in love with you again."

"W-what am I supposed to do…" she sniffled and wiped her face "…about the wedding? Do we cancel? We've put money down on a venue. A florist. I've bought a d-dress."

Rory looked to me, her silent plea for help. Just because I read her mind regarding her emotions didn't mean I had great advice for her wedding plans.

With wide eyes, I shrugged and turned my attention to the rest of the water in my glass, gulping it down. "I'm going to grab a shower. I hope it all works out how it should."

Sadly, I thought it should work out differently than she did.

My first day with Holly could not have been better. She was the midwife I wanted to be. Patient. Calm. Caring. Encouraging. The clinic was an old house with the rooms converted into 'exam' rooms, if you could call them that. They were decorated with a Zen theme. Nothing cold and sterile about them.

The midwives scheduled two hours with every person to give them the chance to ask questions and express concerns or fears about ... anything. One of Holly's clients was three months pregnant and stressed over what car to get for their growing family. Holly grabbed her computer and helped search for good options for safety, gas milage, best value, etc.

Who did that at a routine prenatal visit?

That was what I loved about Holly and the other midwives at the clinic. Nothing they did felt routine at all. Every client had their own birth plan, no two exactly alike.

Different needs.

Different inherent risks.

Different concerns.

She respected their decisions without judgment.

"How was your day?" Rory asked when I arrived home a little after six in the evening.

As if she couldn't tell from the grin on my face and the exaggerated bounce in my step. We spent the next hour eating dinner and discussing my first day.

"Enough about me, how was your day?"

"Interesting," Rory said.

"Understatement." Rose rolled her eyes as I grabbed her empty plate from the table.

"Do tell." I carried our dishes to the sink.

"Hailey called me on my way to work. Apparently, Angie unloaded on her too. Hailey asked me to talk to Fisher. *Then* Fisher's sister called me. Again, asking *me* to talk to Fisher. Then it hit me ... I must be his only friend. Why does everyone think that I can fix this? That he will listen to me? And I don't even know what I'm supposed to tell him because I *know* what it's like to not be in love with the person everyone thinks you should love."

My dad.

"Sorry, Reese," she whispered as Rose kissed the top of her head.

I leaned against the counter and crossed my arms over my chest. "Dad died ten years ago. I think you can officially retire from feeling guilty for not loving him the way you love Rose. Okay?"

She nodded slowly. "Thank you."

"As for Fisher, I think you can talk with him, but I'd listen more than preach to him. Think of what you wanted from people around you when you knew you were going to disappoint everyone for having feelings that only you could understand."

Rory gave me a look for a few seconds. I couldn't quite decode it.

"You sure have grown up. I'm so proud of you."

I wasn't sure how grown-up I felt. Experienced in love and heartbreak? Yes. So much more than Rory realized.

"Thank you." I couldn't help my grin or the warmth in my heart. Nothing compared to feeling a mother's love. That year in Thailand with the midwife made me appreciate Rory so much more. "I'm going to read for a while and then try to get to bed early. Holly has two clients due in the next two weeks, so I'm on call. It's usually a rotating call, but two of the other midwives are out. One is on vacation. The other one has a child going in for heart surgery. So this could be a crazy and exhausting two weeks, but I'm so excited!"

"We're excited for you. Goodnight," Rose and Mom said to me.

The next morning, I headed out for my run. Waiting at the stoplight stood a familiar figure with a casted arm.

"You're up early." I slowed to a stop at the crosswalk.

Fisher grinned so big. "Good morning." And just like the Fisher I remembered, he took a few extra seconds to slide his gaze along the full length of my body.

My long-sleeved running shirt.

My jogging shorts.

Pink running shoes.

Shoulder-length hair pulled into a short ponytail.

I was so close to calling him out on it, the way I might have done five years earlier, but I didn't want to make him uncomfortable, given his present relationship status. Also, I feared he might stop looking at me that way if I said something.

"How was your first day?" he asked as we got the light to cross the street.

"Amazing, even though no babies were born. I'm on call. Should be two babies coming into the world in the next two weeks."

He chuckled, giving me a quick side-glance when we made it across the street. "Too bad you're not excited about it."

I laughed. Yeah, I *felt* completely lit up when talking about it. I could only imagine what he saw when he looked at me and my impossibly huge grin.

I nodded to the right, knowing he needed to go left.

Fisher looked down at our feet for a few seconds with his own grin solidly affixed to his face. He nudged the toe of my shoe with the toe of his shoe. "Well ..." His gaze slowly lifted to mine. Fisher wasn't ten years older than me. He was a twelve-year-old boy with his first crush on a girl. And I ... was that girl. And that was a side to Fisher Mann I didn't get to see five years earlier.

I never got to see anything but his confident side.

"I've solved all your puzzles, despite the difficultly of filling in the boxes with my left hand."

My nose wrinkled. I never thought about that.

"So I might need a few more to get me by until next week."

"What's next week?"

"I'm going back to work, whether anyone thinks I'm ready or not."

"I've seen you shop at Target. You're ready."

Fisher nodded while laughing a little. "Exactly."

"I'll drop off some puzzles after I get home from work later today."

"Perfect."

"Okay."

We clogged up the sidewalk, people passing us on both sides, as we stood in the middle of it facing each other in our little bubble.

My smile faded. "Rory is going to talk to you about Angie. I don't know what she's going to say, but everyone has been asking her to talk to you, to convince you to rethink things with Angie." My words flew out a mile a minute. In some ways, it didn't feel like my place to say anything to anyone, yet I couldn't *not* say something. "But I think you need to do what's right for you. It's not Rory or your family marrying her. It's you. And..." a pang of guilt tightened my stomach "...Angie is a good person. That doesn't mean we fall in love with someone just because they're a good person. I'm just saying, even if she's scared of it, she deserves honesty. And..." I shrugged "...my opinion should mean nothing to you, so take this with a grain of salt, less than a grain of salt. I think taking a step back and seeing if you can fall in love with her again is a good idea."

Fisher's brow wrinkled as he nodded slowly. "Thanks," he murmured.

I found my tiny grin again and gave it to him. "Bye, Fisher." I took a step backward, shaking my head as his gaze made a second trip up and down my body.

Oh, Fisher ...

We were in trouble, and I think he knew it as well. "Have a good day," I said.

"I'll have a good enough day."

Wink.

Gah! That wink.

CHAPTER ELEVEN

DEAR LOST FISHERMAN,

I'm falling in love with you, again. But this time, you're earning it, even if it's not your intention. It's not that I ever fell completely out of love with you. Timing ... it really is everything in life. And I still struggle with all the things I was taught to believe. Are our lives predestined? Where does free will play a part? Are destiny and fate real? Or is it merely what we call events in life after we're willing to acknowledge them, even if we refuse to accept them? I just ... don't know.

In the meantime, keep the smiles and winks coming my way.

Ten across: Seven letters. Clue: Awakening.

Rebirth.

"Hey, Rose. Where's Rory?" I asked as I set my bag by the entry and slipped off my shoes after work.

Rose glanced back at me from the stove. "She's having dinner with Fisher. The talk."

I raised my brows. "Sounds intense."

"She's in an awkward position."

I nodded. Seeing her stirring pasta, I grabbed a jar of sauce and emptied it into a pot. "She should have told his family and even Angie that it's not her place to tell Fisher what to think or do."

"Is that your unbiased opinion?" Rose shot me a look.

I smirked. "It's been five years. I've had other boyfriends. Angie asked Fisher to marry her. Why would you think my opinion by this point would be biased?"

"Maybe because you were so easily able to articulate everything that Angie's feeling. Like you have or *are* in her shoes. Like you're in love with a man who doesn't remember you."

Keeping my chin down, gaze on the sauce as I stirred it, I shrugged. "Want to know what I think would be incredibly romantic?"

"I don't know, do I?"

I released a quick laugh. "Probably not, but I'm going to tell you anyway since you've managed to keep my and Fisher's secret all these years."

"Lucky me. Then do tell. What would be incredibly romantic?"

"A true second-chance romance. Falling in love with the same person twice. Each time, feeling brand new. No memories of the first time. Just ... something about that person that makes you fall in love with them. Every. Single. Time.

"That chilling kind of love that maybe does last more than one lifetime. The truest definition of soul mates. If I were Angie, I wouldn't want to marry Fisher unless he did, in fact, truly fall in love with me again.

"Nothing forced. No timeline. No expectations. Just the butterflies in the stomach and insane giddiness of new love. If Angie loved him the way she claims to love him, she'd see that he's not the same Fisher. She'd see the subtle changes in his personality. And she'd feel this indescribable excitement at the chance to get to know the new Fisher and fall in love with him all over again."

Rose turned off the burner and rested her hand on my wrist to stop me from stirring the pasta sauce.

I looked over at her, the lines of concern along her face and the intensity—the concern—in her eyes. "Oh, Reese, you're going to get hurt."

On a nervous laugh, I shook my head and continued stirring as her hand dropped to her side. "I don't know what you're talking about."

"You didn't see them. Before his accident, you didn't see them. They were in love. You can't be that person, the one who tries to steal another woman's man."

"Like you stole my mom?"

She deflated.

I shut off my burner and set the spoon on the small plate as I blew out a long breath. "Rose, I love you. I love you with my mom. And I think things turned out exactly how they were supposed to turn out *because* you didn't give up on her. You never thought you were taking something—someone—who wasn't yours because you knew, you just *knew* she was, in fact, meant to be with you. What if I know? What if he's meant to be with me?"

She gave me a sad smile. "What if he's not?"

I swallowed hard. I wasn't delusional, just hopeful. "Then he's not."

"And you'll stay out of the way?"

"If he falls in love with her, if he decides to go through with the wedding, then I will stay out of the way."

"I'm worried you're going to play unfairly." Rose frowned.

Coughing on a laugh, I shook my head. "It's not a game, Rose. It's real life. I don't even know how I could play unfairly. I'm not the one living with him. I'm not the one sleeping in his bed. I haven't told him that we were more than friends, more than employee/employer *because* I want him to fall in love with me, not a bunch of memories of an eighteen-year-old girl." There. I said the quiet part aloud. I wanted Fisher Mann to fall in love with me ... again.

Angie gave him her whole damn body, a million photos, a million memories and stories of life since they were kids. I was a huge underdog. All I gave him was cruciverbalist. So if that trumped everything Angie gave him, then I thought everyone needed to back the hell off and let the two geeky word peeps have our happily ever after.

If ...

I knew it was a big *if*. An unlikely *if*. Maybe even an impossible *if*.

But here was the thing (it was an important thing), if a fifty-micrometer sperm could join with a point-one millimeter egg and result in an entire human being, then two cruciverbalists could fall in love ... twice.

"It might be time to tell Rory."

I shook my head. "There's nothing to tell. The past is the past. And here in the present, there's still nothing to tell. But if anything changes and becomes *something* to tell, I will tell Rory."

"You promise?"

"Promise. Now, let's eat. I have to take some cross-word puzzles over to Fisher tonight, after Rory gets home, of course."

"Reese ..." Rose shook her head and rolled her eyes.

I grinned and shrugged. "Hey, he asked me to bring him more puzzles. No big deal."

"Angie packed a bag and has decided to stay with a friend. I think you visiting her fiancé will feel like a big deal."

"Well, then we won't tell her because they're puzzles, not nude photos of me. I'm saving the nude photos for closer to Christmas."

"Reese!" She playfully punched my arm as I giggled.

"How'd it go?" Rose asked the second Rory walked through the door.

I glanced up from my book, one of many books on birth Holly gave me to read.

"Dinner was great. Just me and my friend Fisher, enjoying pizza and beer. I talked. He listened. And he didn't seem the least bit surprised by anything I said. I'm sure he's been anticipating it since everyone else has talked with him already." She set her purse on the counter and plopped onto the sofa next to Rose, giving her a quick peck on the lips. "He wasn't angry. I think he's trying to put himself in Angie's shoes. I really do. But it doesn't change his feelings. And right now, she's a stranger. He thinks he enjoys spending time with her, but he also wants time to himself. I think she's still too much of a stranger to him to have her *there* so much. He wants space and time. He doesn't want to feel like he's the groom in an arranged marriage. Fisher wants to fall in love with his wife before he marries her." Rory shrugged. "And I can't blame him. He's having dinner —a date—with Angie this Friday night. So he's trying. He wants to date her. I say ... let them date. Let things happen naturally."

I nodded slowly with a tight grin. Rose gave me a quick evil glare in return. When Rory glanced at her phone, head down, I stuck my tongue out at Rose. She had to bite her lips together to keep from laughing.

"Well, if Fisher's home, I'm going to run these crossword puzzles over to him before I crash for the night. He asked for more. Isn't that crazy?" I closed my book and stood.

"That is crazy. But I love that you have someone working on your puzzles." Rory smiled.

"I do." I smiled back, ignoring distrusting Rose. "See ya after a bit."

Since it was getting late, I drove to Fisher's house instead of walking there. I may have also added a little makeup in the car and a dab of perfume to make up for the rest of my casual attire, jeans and a hoodie. I wouldn't have gotten away with anything dressier, not with Rose silently rooting for Team Angie.

"It's late. I assumed you weren't coming," Fisher said when he opened the front door. I stole a silent moment to take him in—always sexy in jeans and a tee. That messy, dark blond hair. The beard I trimmed for him.

"Rose told me you were having dinner with my mom, so I waited until she got home. If it's too late, I'll just give you these..." I handed him the pile of puzzles "...and head home."

"Too late for what? My roommate moved out. I'm officially free."

I frowned, following him into the house. "I heard Angie's staying with a friend while you *date* her. Big Friday night plans?"

He gestured to the sofa, and I sat in the middle while he took a seat in his recliner. "I don't know. What should we do? Dinner and movie? Just dinner? Do I bring her back here? Or is that too weird since I asked her to move out?"

"You don't remember the woman you're engaged to. I think worrying about weird at this point is an afterthought. Do whatever feels right."

Fisher ran his hands through his hair. "Ugh ... I don't know what feels right because I don't know how I'm supposed to feel about her."

"It's not about what you're *supposed to* feel about her. Ask yourself how you honestly *do* feel about her. Let that be your starting point. I think you've already done that to some degree. I'm sure it wasn't your family's idea for her to move out and the two of you date. That was you. Go with that voice."

"It's hard to go with that voice because I do have this other voice in my head, the one that tries to put myself in her shoes. I'm sure I would be really messed-up if I loved someone and they didn't remember me. I don't think I could just walk away without a fight."

Pulling my feet up and crisscrossing them, I formulated my response. He had no idea I was trying to see if I fit into his equation. "I couldn't ..." I smiled softly. "I couldn't walk away without a fight."

"You're so young." His lips turned into a pleasant smile. "How old are you?"

I chuckled. "What you mean is, how *young* am I? I'll be twenty-four soon."

"So you're twenty-three."

My eyes rolled upward. "Yes. I'm twenty-three."

"And have you ever been in love?"

Oh, Fisher ...

My mind immediately jumped back five years to the day on the playground.

"I'm trying so hard..." I whispered, my voice shaky in my chest and wobbly as the words fell from my lips "...trying so hard not to fall in love with you."

A few breaths later, he whispered back, "I know."

"Yes."

"Tell me about him. What happened?"

I laughed and cleared my throat, cleared the pain from the memories. *My* memories. Fisher didn't have memories of us. "Bad timing. I was young. And I was trying to figure out some things in my life. He had things in his life figured out quite well. So ..." I pulled in a shaky breath and shrugged. "It was just ... bad timing."

"Did he love you back?" Fisher wasn't the same man. The old Fisher wouldn't have asked me those questions.

"I think so." I couldn't look at him, so I fiddled with the hem to my shirt and kept my gaze on my lap.

"Do you know where he is now? Have you thought about finding him?"

More pain escaped my chest, disguised as laughter while I pinched the bridge of my nose. "Yes, I've thought about finding him."

"And?"

My head inched side to side as I continued to pinch the bridge of my nose. "And I'm not sure he's ready to be found by me."

"Why would you say that?"

My gaze lifted slowly to his. "Because he's found someone else." My lips fell into a frown as I lifted one shoulder like it was no big deal.

"Married?"

I shook my head. "No."

"Then he's fair game."

Barking a laugh, I glanced up at the ceiling again, gathering my hair in one hand and slowly releasing it as I made eye contact with him. "Fisher, you certainly have a liberal view of dating. You're not married to Angie, but you're dating her. So would you be okay with another guy making moves on her?"

Fisher shrugged, lips twisted. "If another guy made moves on her and she responded to his moves, then I think I'd have my answer about us."

"What happened to fighting for what you want?"

"I think fighting for something when you have an actual chance is different than fighting for second place."

"Stick to building houses, Fisher. I don't think you have a future in couples counseling."

"No?" He grinned. "I'm just saying, if you're still interested in the guy, knock on his door and say, 'Remember me?' Then at least you'll know."

"And what if he doesn't remember me?"

"Then he never loved you."

I swallowed hard and nodded. "Well ..." I scratched my chin. "That's harsh and a little heart-breaking."

"Life is harsh and heartbreaking."

I giggled. "Who are you? Because this is not the Fisher Mann I knew. Did your head injury awaken some deep philosophical part of your brain?"

"No." He stood and stretched his good arm above his head and his casted arm about half the way. His shirt lifted a few inches, revealing his abs.

My gaze stuck like sticky spider fingers, and when I tore it away, after he dropped his arms back to his side, Fisher was looking at me. I felt the deer-in-the-head-lights look on my face. His expression was more unexpected. Not the cocky one I remembered. It was more of a curious expression like he was in disbelief that I had been staring at his exposed skin.

That familiar blush crawled up my neck.

"I should go," I whispered, scrambling to my feet and brushing my hair away from my face.

"Thanks for the puzzles." His grin held so much satisfaction, his eyes filled with that familiar look he'd given me so many times before.

"You're welcome."

My phone vibrated and I pulled it from the pocket of my hoodie. "Oh my gosh ... oh my gosh! It's time."

"Time for what exactly?"

I glanced up from the screen, eyes wide, smile even wider. "Holly's client is in labor! I have to go. I'm ... I'm going to help deliver a baby. Eek!" I jumped up and down hysterically, and before I realized what was happening, I had my arms thrown around Fisher's neck, my body still doing its spastic jumping motion.

He rested his good hand on my back and chuckled.

"This is happening!" My hands went from his neck to his face, framing it, and I kissed him. It was quick, but ... *ugh!* It was on. The. Mouth. My excitement completely erased reality just long enough for my brain to fart.

Jumping away from him, my eyes widened even more as I covered my mouth with my hand. "I ... oh ... shit ... I'm so sorry. I ... oh ... shit. Fisher, I'm ..." I shook my head repeatedly.

When the shock dissipated from his face, he grinned. "It's fine."

I tucked my phone back into my pocket and turned toward the door. "I have to go. I'm so embarrassed. It was nice knowing ya." Flying out the door, I hopped into my car and bolted. I couldn't get miles between us fast enough.

CHAPTER TWELVE

I HELPED DELIVER a seven-pound twelve-ounce baby boy after twelve hours of labor. A water birth.

Then two days later, I did the follow up visit with the family to check on the baby and mom. She was glowing.

I focused on work and reading through the books Holly gave me, basically anything to keep from thinking about kissing Fisher. The weekend came and went. Rory and Rose hung out with Fisher on Saturday night, probably to get the scoop on his Friday night date with Angie. They invited me, but I declined, opting to just keep reading, just keep avoiding Fisher for approximately forever.

On Wednesday of the following week, I helped deliver a baby girl. Six pounds, eleven ounces. And perfect.

I loved every aspect of Holly's job. Wellness visits. Prenatal visits. Postnatal visits. Happy families. Tiny babies. Women feeling alive again after working with Holly to get their hormones balanced—to get their lives balanced again. Very rewarding work.

Holly and I had Thursday off to recoup from a long night of waiting for that sweet girl to make her way into the world. I was so tired and grateful for the time to get some sleep. After hours of not moving an inch in my bed, Rory woke me up.

"Are you having dinner with us?" She ran her hand through my hair.

I blinked my heavy eyelids open. "Um ..." I rolled onto my back and stretched. "Yeah. I think so. What time is it?"

"Six."

"Yeah, I'd better get up so I can sleep later." I sat up and rubbed my eyes.

"No rush, sleepy head. Dinner won't be ready for another thirty minutes if you need a shower or whatever."

I nodded. "Yeah, I need a shower, at least to wake up."

"Okay." She kissed my head and left my room.

I padded to the bathroom and stripped into my bra and panties. There were no clean towels on the shelf, which meant Rory probably hadn't taken them out of the dryer.

I opened the door and crossed the hallway to the laundry room. Sure enough, clean towels were in the dryer. As I crossed the hallway again, I made a casual glance to the side, seeing something move. Someone move ...

Fisher stood maybe three feet from me.

Me in my bra and panties.

Me holding the bath towel in my hand instead of covering my body.

He didn't hide his wandering gaze, not one bit. And I didn't hide any part of my body. After a hard swallow, he met my gaze. "I'll use Rory's bathroom."

"K," I whispered, wanting some tiny part of his lost memory to return upon seeing so much of my bared flesh. With no rush, I moseyed into the bathroom and shut the door.

Then I showered and touched myself while replaying Fisher's slow inspection of me. My hand pressed to the side of the shower, eyes pinched shut, jaw slack as I came, feeling weak in the knees.

Feeling empty.

Feeling impatient.

Feeling confused.

With wet hair, jeans, and a long-sleeved tee, I made my way to the kitchen. "Smells good." I smiled at Rory while taking a seat next to Fisher, the only seat left to take.

Rose passed me the dish filled with chicken and roasted veggies. "New baby?" she asked.

"Yes." I spooned food onto my plate. "A girl. Ivy Elizabeth. Tons of black hair. Ten fingers. Ten toes. And a strong, beautiful cry. When it was finally time, she pushed three times. It was a water birth. Fourth child." I laughed. "I'm not sure why we were there. The mom did everything. She knew when to push. When to rest. How to breathe. She grabbed the baby all by herself. Ivy cried. The mom put her right to the breast. It was ... beautiful." I realized I had tears in my eyes, and I quickly blotted the corners.

"Oh ... that sounds amazing, sweetie," Rory said, clearly not missing my emotions.

I refused to look at Fisher. What did he think of my sappy side?

"So ... how was everyone else's day?" I asked.

"Crazy, as usual." Rose laughed.

"How was your day, Fisher?" Rory asked him.

He wiped his mouth. "Fine. I've been playing catch-up this week, driving around to see where we stand on all the jobs. It's weird. So hard to describe. I don't remember the projects, but I know what to do. I have these skills that my brain does remember. And all I need are the plans and an update on where each project stands, and I magically know what to do. So then I met with new clients over lunch. And I spent a few hours this afternoon in my workshop. Who knew I had unfinished projects? I don't remember starting them, but again ... I know what needs to be done. When I get this fucking cast off, it will be easier to do things. I need to grow an extra hand to help hold things when I glue and clamp pieces together."

"When are you seeing Angie again?" Rory asked.

"Saturday. It's my dad's birthday, so they're having a get-together, and of course, she was invited."

I couldn't read him. Was he fine with that?

"Things going okay?" Rose asked while I kept my focus on my plate.

"I suppose. I'm trying, but sometimes I feel like she doesn't think I'm trying hard enough. She texts or calls me every day. And I think on the days I don't suggest we go somewhere or do something, that she's disappointed. Sometimes I don't answer her call because I don't know what to say. So then she texts me. And since I don't really *know* her yet, I can't possibly read her."

"Before Rose and I moved in together, we called or texted each other every day. I think it's normal for two people who are in love to talk every day. So you can't blame her for that." Rory did the best job of playing the middle ground. Trying to be the facilitator, the peacemaker.

Fisher nodded slowly. "Yeah, I suppose you're right."

Unless you don't love her. Do you love her?

"What do you need help with? In your shop? Because I'm up now. I won't be sleeping anytime soon. After dinner, I could help hold stuff for you."

"Just a corner shelving unit. And that would be great." He gave me a sideways glance.

I eased my head to the right just enough to give him a tiny smile, still unable to hold his gaze for more than two seconds. "No problem," I mumbled.

And just like that, we ended the Angie subject, and the mood lightened.

After dinner, I walked with Fisher to his house.

"Thanks for saving me," he said, playfully nudging my arm with his like I had done to him in Target.

Everything between us felt effortless and natural.

"Saving you?" I looked both ways before we crossed the street.

"All Rory talks about is Angie. I miss my beer drinking friend who used to tell me stories about her time in prison or her dreams of owning her own salon again."

"Rory has told you stories from prison? She hasn't told me any."

"I'm sure they're not stories she cares to share with her daughter."

I frowned.

"Speaking of stories, I love watching you come to life talking about your job."

My face filled with heat. "You mean when I lose my mind and kiss my mom's friend."

"You know..." he bumped the side of his body against mine again "...I don't have to just be Rory's friend. I can be your friend. The friend you kissed because you were so excited. I thought you might wet your pants." He opened his garage door.

"I wasn't going to wet my pants." I scoffed, following him down the stairs to his workshop. "But I did lose my mind. I was just so excited. So I don't want you to think I kissed you for any other reason than you just happened to be the only one in the room when I got drunk on an adrenaline and dopamine cocktail. I literally would have kissed anyone in that moment."

He eyed me over his shoulder, squinting as he flipped on the rest of the shop lights. "I'm not feeling quite as special at the moment. Why did you have to take that away from me?"

I laughed because it was funny, right? He wasn't serious. I didn't know how to handle him being serious about kissing me. Not yet.

As much as I wanted to steal back the naked fisherman, I didn't want to hurt Angie. But what if he didn't love her? If you loved someone, you wanted to hear their voice. Every text felt like a digital kiss. A wink of acknowledgment. That "hey, it's just me letting you know I think the world of you."

"Sorry," I said jokingly. "I'm sure you're really disappointed I didn't set out to intentionally kiss my *engaged* friend." And I added my signature eye roll to fully sell my innocent intentions.

Fisher seemed to let it all slide with nothing more than a grin. "I'm going to glue these two pieces, then you're going to hold them together while I clamp them. Okay?"

"Okay."

He glued. I held. He clamped.

We did this with a half dozen parts to the shelf.

"Perfect." He finished propping up the last two clamped pieces.

I ate up that look on his face, that look of satisfaction. I'd forgotten how much I missed watching Fisher do what he did best. Well, one of the things he did best.

"I am," he said, running his hand over the smooth board, his back to me.

"You are what?"

"I'm ... disappointed that you didn't intentionally set out to kiss your friend when you were overcome with excitement. And ..." He slowly shook his head. "I'm not proud of my feelings. Still, they're unintentional which makes them feel so very real. So here I am ... waiting for my memory to return so I can not only remember Angie but remember why I agreed to marry her. And maybe that's tomorrow. Maybe tomorrow I get my memory back, and it will make the feelings I'm having right this minute seem inconsequential. Nothing but the wandering mind of a crazy man." He turned, wearing a sad face.

"But what if my memory never returns? What if I spend months going on dates with Angie, dates where I'm not really thinking about her because I'm really wondering what Nurse Capshaw is doing. Is she working on crossword puzzles for me? Is she shopping at Target without me? Is she running in her sexy running shorts? Or is she delivering someone's baby and grinning from ear to ear? Is she so excited that she needs someone to kiss? And if I'm on a date with Angie, how can *I* be the one Nurse Capshaw kisses? And why is my thirty-three-year-old brain thinking about a woman ten years younger than me? Is it the accident? *Did* I permanently damage something? And after all these thoughts, my brain circles back around to the possibility that I might remember everything tomorrow. It's quite the quandary."

Yes. So many quandaries. I was in *quite the quandary* myself.

"Well ..." I inhaled and released it slowly. "I don't know how to respond other than to say that this Nurse Capshaw is a very lucky nurse. If she knew your feelings, I'm certain she would be flattered. And maybe a little sad too. Sad that you're feeling so tortured by your thoughts and the uncertainty of what tomorrow or a thousand tomorrows after that will bring. And I wish I had the answer for you. But I don't."

With several easy nods, he seemed to process my words. I was so ready to go knock on his door and say, "Hey, remember me?" But I knew he didn't.

"I finished your crossword puzzles. Do you want to see them?"

"You mean, do I want to check your work?"

"No. My work is correct. I mean, do you want to see them. I'm bragging, not looking for confirmation that I did them correctly."

I giggled. "So much confidence for someone who wasn't even sure he liked crossword puzzles."

"I still didn't say I liked them." He passed me and headed up the stairs. "I was just painfully bored."

Sure, Fisher ...

I followed him into the house.

"Beer? Wine? Water?"

"Wine would be great. I'm not on call for the next seventy-two hours."

"Wine it is." He pulled a bottle of wine from his wine rack, a corkscrew, and two glasses. "Let's go downstairs."

"Is that where your crossword puzzles are at?"

"Yes. I've framed them and hung them on the walls."

I laughed. "Sounds about right."

The puzzles weren't on the wall, but he flipped on my favorite globe lights and led me to the screened-in porch. So many memories.

The folders of puzzles were on the table along with several pens.

"Have a seat." He nodded to the chair where Rory used to sit.

I took a seat on the sectional, instead, in the exact spot we slept that night over five years earlier.

"You took my spot." He frowned, handing me my glass before trying to uncork the wine.

"Fucking cast," he grumbled, fumbling with the corkscrew in his left hand.

"Let me." I took the bottle from him.

He kept his frown pinned to his face; it only made me grin bigger as I easily uncorked it.

"And this isn't your seat." I poured myself a generous glass before handing him the bottle. "It's where I used to sit. And I know you don't remember that, but I do. So sit somewhere else."

He turned and started to sit on my lap.

"Fisher!" I held up my glass so it didn't spill.

On a hearty laugh, he adjusted his aim and sat right next to me. It was a little weird since it was a big sectional and there were two chairs as well.

"There they are. Read 'em and weep." He nodded to the puzzles.

"I don't need to read them. I have no doubt that you finished them. And I'm not a weeper." I sipped my wine.

"My cast comes off Monday."

"That's exciting. And nobody signed it. Not even Rory. Fisher, you need better friends."

"I'll second that. Here..." he leaned over me, putting way too much of his body heat and woodsy scent right under my nose "...you sign it." He handed me an extra fine-tipped Sharpie. That's how confident he was in solving the puzzles I gave him.

"You're getting it off Monday."

"So."

I shook my head, set my wine glass aside, and removed the cap to the Sharpie. Then I pulled his casted arm into my lap, bringing him close to me again. So close his breath brushed my forehead.

My heart screamed for me to do something more, but my brain unsheathed its own sword of common sense.

He was still engaged. I thought. Actually, I didn't know.

I lifted my head just enough that our mouths were sharing the same oxygen. Fisher's gaze fell to my lips for a breath, my lips that parted slightly. Then he met my gaze again.

"Are you going to kiss me?" he said.

He. Said. It!

It flipped my world on its head. Opposite world. A new kind of déjà vu.

I dipped my chin and pressed the tip of the Sharpie to his cast, making slow strokes, thinking extra hard to make each letter because I was writing it upside down so that he could easily read it when I was finished.

I'm thinking about it.

Keeping my chin tipped to my chest, I capped the Sharpie as he read his cast.

"And what exactly are you thinking?" he asked.

"I'm thinking about Angie. And I'm thinking about tomorrow," I whispered, tracing my finger along the letters on his cast. "If neither existed, I'd kiss you. Because ..." I released a long breath. "I *really* want to kiss you. Which means I should go home." On a nervous laugh, I stood and set the Sharpie back onto the table.

Fisher's good hand encircled my wrist. "Don't go. We still have wine to drink. And you haven't given stars or smiley faces to my completed crossword puzzles. And there's pool. Do you like to play pool? Or we could—"

In the middle of his desperate ramblings, his valiant effort to keep me from leaving, it hit me. No one had ever tried so hard to just ... be with me. And it felt amazing.

Pulling my arm from his grip, I turned and pressed my hands to his face, kissing him slowly while crawling on the sofa and straddling his lap, standing on my knees so it put me a little higher than him, so I felt in control.

Control of the kiss.

Control of the moment.

Maybe even the crazy illusion that I had control over what he did to my heart.

If he remembered Angie, that meant he'd remember me. He'd remember us. And I wanted that to be enough, but I didn't know what made him say yes when Angie proposed to him. If it was love, then I needed to keep my heart on a tight leash while we did … whatever we were about to do.

When I ended our kiss, I smiled over his lips and he smiled back. "You can have all the stars, Fisher. And the smiley faces too. But I'm going to kick your ass at pool, and I won't feel sorry for you when you *weep* like a baby."

"We'll see."

We'll see …

Oh the memories those two words brought back to me.

"But for now. Kiss me again." He lifted his head to capture my lips, but I pulled away. "No. That's it. That's all you get today. If you still want me to kiss you tomorrow, then I'll kiss you tomorrow. One day at a time, Lost Fisherman." I climbed off his lap and headed to the door.

"Lost Fisherman?" He stood.

"Yes. You are my lost fisherman. Waiting to be found."

"Who's going to find me?" He followed me into the house. "You?"

I grabbed two pool sticks. "No. I already found you." I handed him a stick.

"Then who?"

I racked up the balls.

"Angie?" he asked, eyeing me carefully.

"You, Fisher."

"What if I don't get my memories back? Does that mean I'll forever be lost?"

I grinned, shaking my head before taking the first shot. "I hope not. That would be tragic. You'll know when you're not lost."

He chuckled. "That makes no sense."

"When you're not lost, it will make perfect sense. That's how you'll know you're no longer the lost fisherman."

He continued to eye me with confusion, maybe even a little distrust, as we took turns making the balls disappear into the pockets.

After we each won a game, I nodded toward the stairs. "I do have to go now."

"I'll walk you home."

"No. Don't be silly. It's not that far. I'll be fine."

"Probably, but I'm still walking you home." He turned off the porch lights and followed me up the stairs.

When we stepped out the front door, he moved to my right side. I gave him a funny look. Then he took my hand. He had to move so his good hand could hold mine. We walked without any rush, taking twice as much time as necessary.

"I want you to date Angie. And do whatever you need to do to figure things out and to feel sure about the decisions you make. I don't want you to be impulsive or scared. Don't make a decision about your life unless you're certain it's the right one. Because these aren't small decisions, Fisher. And I know you can't even imagine what that feels like right now ... to make a decision and feel confident and certain about it because you're living with the fear of the unknown."

We stopped just before reaching the driveway. "I'm sorry." I released his hand and covered my face with both hands. "I'm rambling. I just don't want you to feel like I expect anything from you right now." I dropped my hands. "Okay?"

After a few seconds, his brow tightened and he nodded. "Okay. But I'm going to kiss you goodnight because I'm really confident and certain that it's what I want to do right now ... it's *all* I want to do right now."

"I said tomorrow."

He held up his good arm and tapped the screen of his watch.

12:14 *a.m.*

I twisted my lips as if I was contemplating it. "Sorry. No goodnight kiss for you."

His good hand slid around my neck, his fingers teasing my nape. "Why?" he whispered.

Biting my lips to keep him from stealing anything, I shrugged. "Because it's officially morning, not night."

Fisher grinned a second before kissing me.

Patient.

Soft.

Teasing.

Perfect.

When he released my lips, he whispered, "Good morning."

CHAPTER THIRTEEN

IF IT WAS FINALLY our time, why was it so hard to be with Fisher? Did our time have to include him losing his memories of me? Did it have to include a fiancée?

It definitely didn't have to include an invitation to his dad's birthday party. A party at his parents' house. A party with Angie on the invitation list. Yet ... it did.

"I don't think I'm going." I sulked into the living room, wearing old sweats, my hair in need of a comb.

"Are you not feeling well?" Rory asked.

Rose pressed her hand to my forehead. "No fever. You can go."

"That's not an accurate way to take someone's temperature." I frowned.

"She doesn't have to go." Rory finished wrapping Pat's gift from us.

I stuck my tongue out at Rose. She grinned and shook her head. I knew she only wanted me to go so I'd see Fisher and Angie in their element, surrounded by his family. A huge Team Angie party. But Rose didn't know about the two—scratch that—three kisses. The underdog was making progress. And I was doing it without telling Fisher about our past. I wasn't only playing fairly; I was playing with one hand *zip-tied* behind my back.

"I think Laurie is going to get Fisher to commit to sticking with the wedding date. June third." Rose gave me a tight grin, baiting me.

"Oh, I wasn't sure it was even still an option. So they're dating, but officially still engaged?" Rory asked.

I shared her surprised sentiment. "I'll shower." I grinned at Rose. "Give me twenty minutes."

She glanced at her watch. "Fifteen."

I got ready in thirteen minutes and a few seconds, saving my makeup for the car ride.

When we pulled into their big driveway, there must have been ten other cars there. It was more than family. I wasn't sure how that would play out for me. Would they all be friends who knew Angie? Probably.

One of the grandkids let us into the house filled with people. It was a cooler fall day in the foothills, so it forced the festivities inside.

"Welcome!" Laurie greeted us. "So glad you made it. There's a table for cards and gifts over there. Don't forget to sign the guest book. And help yourself to food in the dining room. Games and more seating downstairs. I don't know where Pat disappeared to, but you'll find him somewhere."

I followed Rose and Rory like a shadow to the gift

table. To the kitchen. In line for food in the dining room.

"Hey!" Angie appeared in tight black pants and a white sweater. Her curly black hair was softened into big curls. Perfect nails and makeup.

"Hi, hon." Rory hugged her. "You good?"

She nodded. "I really am. Things are going well. I think this party is exactly what I need, what *we* need." She glanced around. "Where'd Fisher go? He's probably in the garage trying to cut off his cast. He's been so unruly about it lately. It comes off Monday."

Angie nodded to my shoes. "Cute shoes, Reese. You always look so adorable."

I grinned without showing any teeth. Adorable. Exactly what I was going for.

Angie tootled away, the glowing bride-to-be. It had been forty-eight hours since I'd seen Fisher. Did something happen? Did he get his memory back?

We filled our plates with food and cake. We found Pat and wished him happy birthday, and I broke away from my mom and Rose, sneaking downstairs with the kids. All the kids.

And ... Arnie and Fisher. They were playing ping-pong with the kids as well as video games on the big TV.

Fisher missed the ball when he looked up at me.

"Champion!" Arnie declared, tossing his paddle aside and throwing his arms in the air.

I cringed, a silent apology for being a distraction and costing him the game.

Arnie looked over his shoulder at me. "Reese! Just in time. You're my next competitor."

"Me?" I laughed.

He snagged Fisher's paddle and handed it to me.

"Scat." He shooed Fisher away. "You lost. Go play with the kids."

Fisher shook his head, grin huge and eyes on me. I tried not to stare too long, afraid everyone would see right through me.

After I beat Arnie three times in a row, he tucked his tail between his legs and headed upstairs for more cake.

Fisher handed one of his nephews his controller and made his way toward me as I hung back behind the sofa a few feet, watching the games on the big screen TV.

"Hi." He grinned.

I rubbed my lips together, fighting to keep from showing him how thrilled I was to see him. "Hi."

"You killed Arnie. He'll never recover."

I laughed. "He'll manage."

"I wasn't sure you'd come." He stood right next to me and touched his hand to mine on purpose in a way that no one would notice, especially since we were surrounded by a bunch of distracted kids. "But I honestly had no idea who they invited. My mom called it a small, cozy gathering." He chuckled.

I laughed. "She might have missed the mark if that's the case."

"There you are." Angie peeked around the corner.

Fisher took a step to the side so our hands no longer touched. "What's up?"

She wrapped her arms around him, giving him a hug while kissing his neck. "Come upstairs with the adults. Everyone keeps asking about our wedding, and I don't know what to say. What do you want me to say?"

Without a word, I slowly drifted away, up the stairs and back in the shadows of Rory and Rose. A few minutes later, Arnie stood on a chair in the middle of the great room and whistled with his thumb and middle finger up to his mouth. It was a loud and impressive whistle that silenced the room.

"Rock star always has to be the center of attention," Shayla yelled, eliciting a wave of laughter from the room.

Arnie grinned, owning the truth. "Not today. It's our dad's big day. The man who showed us what it means to work from sun up to sun down. What it means to put family first. Patrick Mann is my hero."

Emotion filled the room when Arnie got a little choked up. "He's *my* rock star."

A collective "Aw ..." filled the space.

"And just recently," Arnie continued, "he once again showed us what a real man does. When my brother fell off his little bike and got a boo boo on his head ..."

Tears quickly turned into laughter. Arnie was a true artist. A true performer.

"Our dad was the voice of reason and the voice of

hope. He knew, no matter the outcome, our family would get through this. He stepped up and filled Fisher's shoes at work. He spent many nights at the hospital, right next to Fisher's bed. He worried about us, our mom, Angie ... just everyone more than himself. And as a side note, it is worth mentioning that we are *all* glad that Fisher came out with his life and at least part of his brain intact. And while he struggles to remember a few things like the girl he has loved since he was just a little boy racing to the potty before wetting his pants ..."

More laughter.

I told myself not to look, but I couldn't help it, I had to do it. Lifting onto my toes, I glanced at Fisher and Angie standing at the top of the stairs. She looked up at him so adoringly.

"We know it's only a matter of time. Angie's the girl schmucks like me write sappy love songs for. The love you've shared for nearly three decades is once in a lifetime. And you lived, Fisher ... so don't screw this up. Marry the girl and count yourself one lucky bastard every single day."

"Marry the girl!" Shayla lifted her glass.

Then Teena followed. Then another person. And another person. And it just went on and on like a herd of wild horses trampling relentlessly over my heart.

Then the clinking of silverware tapping glasses took over. "Kiss. Kiss. Kiss."

Angie lifted onto her toes and slid her hands

around Fisher's neck. And he relinquished the last few inches and kissed her.

I turned away, in the wrong direction. Rose wasn't looking at them like Rory was; she was looking at me. Not gloating. As much as I knew Rose didn't understand Fisher and me, I knew she loved me. She grabbed my hand and squeezed it. That "you'll be okay" squeeze. I couldn't blame Fisher. I thought of all the things I did to please my dad, to please my grandparents, to please God. There were so many times in life we did what was expected of us. A soldier putting their country before self. That room was Fisher's country.

I couldn't even hate Angie. Nope. She was kind. And she fell in love with Fisher when he was just a young boy. It seemed like the perfect example of fate and destiny. She'd lost her parents. She didn't have siblings. Fisher and his family were her family.

Maybe ... I thought just maybe ... it really wasn't our time. And that meant it would never be our time.

After Rose released my hand, I took slow steps in the direction of the front door, making sure no one was watching me, and I slipped outside into the crisp air. I hugged my arms to myself and walked toward the end of the drive to grab my jacket from Rory's car, but she'd locked it.

"Ugh! Rory ... no one's going to steal your car," I grumbled to myself. I gave the idea of going back inside a full three seconds of consideration before I headed down the gravel road, hoping my toes in my "cute" green suede boots wouldn't freeze right off. I picked up my pace, trying to warm the rest of my body—it was at least twenty degrees colder than in Denver that day.

Crunch. Crunch. Crunch.

I glanced behind me. "Don't. Just leave me alone." I started to jog.

"Slow down. I'm not a fan of jogging in a cast."

"Then go back to your family, Fisher."

"Slow ... the ... fuck ... down ..." He caught up to me and grabbed my arm.

I yanked it out of his grip, not because I was mad at him. I was just ... mad at life. Mad at the timing thus far in my life.

"It's cold." He shrugged off his jacket and wrapped it around me.

"I'm fine."

"Your teeth are chattering." He chuckled.

I threaded my arms through the sleeves while he zipped it. Maybe my arms were freakishly long, but his jacket was still an ocean on me.

"I'm mad too."

I glanced up at him, but I didn't say a word. He read my mind.

"I'm mad because the people who have known me the longest and should know me best don't seem to know me at all right now." He blew out a breath, a white cloud in the cold air. "And maybe it's not their fault. Maybe I'm not the same. So I feel like it's this cluster-fuck situation and no one is to blame. Yet no one knows how to navigate the way out."

My gaze dropped to our feet.

"I don't care if I remember these missing pieces or not. I really don't. I just wish someone could tell me for sure. Yes, Fisher, you're going to get your memory back in six weeks. Or no, Fisher, this is it. You will never remember. Because I can't fall in love with photographs. I can't fall in love with someone else's memories. I just ..." He shook his head. "Can't."

"What do you need, Fisher?" I lifted my gaze and looked into his lost eyes.

"Time. And space."

I nodded. "You followed me," I whispered.

"See, that's the problem. The people I need time and space from just refuse to give it to me. And the one person I need *more* time with and much less space from is the one who keeps running or driving away from me."

"I was running to keep warm. And the day I drove away, I had to help deliver a baby."

Fisher grinned while easing his head side to side. "That's your story?"

I shrugged. "It's the truth."

"My family thought I did a great job trimming my beard."

"As they should have. I did an impeccable job. But it's getting scruffy again."

"I'll make you dinner tonight if you come over and trim my beard."

"You get your cast off in two days."

"But I like it when you do it."

"Well, that's just lazy, Fisher."

"I'll let you help me finish the bookshelf in my shop."

"What time is dinner?"

He grinned and it was glorious. It was for me. All me. Fisher wanted to spend *time* with me. Fisher wanted as little *space* between us as possible. I let myself believe it wasn't about Angie, like Rory's relationship with Rose wasn't about my dad or even about me.

"Six."

"Fine." I acted like it was such a sacrifice.

A car drove past us, and Fisher waved to them as I turned my head so maybe they'd think I was Angie.

"Come prepared. I'm going to kiss you until your lips go numb."

I pressed said lips together to keep from grinning.

"I might even make a play for second base. Dress accordingly."

I snorted, no longer able to contain it. "Who are you?"

"According to you, I'm the lost fisherman. Just trying to find myself."

"And you think you'll find yourself on the way to second base with me?"

He glanced over my shoulder into the distance, head bobbing a little bit. "Maybe not on my way to second base. Third base ..." His lips twisted. "That's a much higher possibility. I think a home run would make me not give a shit if I found myself or anyone else for that matter."

"It's funny because you're talking, and I see your lips moving, but I'm still thinking about you teaching me how to build that shelving unit. Do you think I'll get to use more than just sandpaper? Like a hammer, a saw, or a screwdriver?"

Fisher eyed me, a tiny grin bending his full lips. "You're getting a little excited. Am I about to get kissed? Or fondled? Pinned to a pine tree so you can have your way with me?"

"What about that tool that drills the little holes for the shelf pins?" I ignored his questions. "Could you teach me how to use that?"

The more I ignored him, the more amused he seemed to get. And I loved it.

"A shelf pin jig?"

"Sure. Call it what you want. I just want to know if you're going to teach me how to use it?"

"I'm not calling it what I want. I'm calling it what it is." He shook his head. "I can't believe I ever agreed to teach you anything. I think you're lying about that."

"I'm not lying. And you're going to let me use the jig thingy if I'm going to let you explore second base."

Fisher eased his head to the side, that puppy dog head cock. Lips corkscrewed. Eyes narrowed. "Shelf pin jig it is. Six o'clock. Now we have to get back. Separately."

I shrugged off his jacket. "Here. You need to return as you left."

"You need to get back before you freeze to death.

How am I supposed to do *things* to you later if you're frozen to death?"

I laughed. "Your biggest concern about me dying is what that means for you getting to second base? Do you need me to grant you a special ten-second rule?"

"I'm listening." He tipped his chin up while glancing down at me.

"I die. You get ten seconds to fondle me before it will be considered perverse."

Fisher's eyebrows crawled up his head. "You're one sick chick."

"Is that a yes or a no?"

"It's a solid yes, but I just want it on record that it was your idea."

"Noted."

"Seriously, your lips are blue. Go. Run. I'll wait a few minutes before heading that way, and I'll go in through the lower door."

"Six." I grinned a second before turning and jogging toward the drive.

"Reese?"

I turned.

Fisher grinned before shaking his head and wiping his mouth to hide his grin. "Nothing. Just ... go."

I giggled all the way back to the driveway. My teeth hurt and my lips were frozen to my gums. A small group of people exited the house, and I used that opportunity to sneak back inside without drawing any attention to myself.

"Want to see Angie's wedding dress?" Teena whispered in my ear as I snuck a handful of chips.

I turned, eyes wide, wondering if she meant to whisper that in *my* ear. Of course she did. I was Fisher's best friend's daughter. A family friend. Fisher's ex-employee. Why wouldn't I want to see his fiancée's wedding gown?

"Um ..." I shoved a few chips into my mouth to buy time and feed my anxiety.

"She's in my parents' bedroom. We're not telling Fisher. It might freak him out. But it's stunning. You have to see it."

"Okay," I mumbled, barely audible over the chips. I might have even spit a few pieces into the air on my reply. And I didn't have that much of a choice anyway as Teena grabbed my arm and dragged me down the hallway and into the master bedroom filled with a handful of women, including Rory and Rose.

Angie stood in the corner, facing a full-length mirror, wearing a strapless white gown. Simple. Elegant. A perfect choice for her. She looked like a princess.

As she smiled, a tear trailed down her cheek, and she quickly wiped it away. "Sorry." She sniffled. "I just always imagined my mom being here to see me in my wedding dress." Another sniffle. "And I imagined my dad walking me down the aisle."

Well fuck ... (necessary use of the F-word)

She made my eyes burn with emotion, along with

everyone else in the room. I wasn't a total monster. She fell in love with Fisher when they were six. Six!

Rose shot me a tight grin. A "are you really going to try to take *Fisher* away from her too" look. I wasn't trying to take Fisher away from her.

I. Really. Wasn't.

Sure, I kissed him, but it was a complete lapse in all coherent thought. I would have kissed anyone standing in front of me when I got the text. Had Angie been there, I would have kissed her.

Really.

As for the kisses that followed that first kiss, they were mutual. Some might have even said they were Fisher's idea.

"My girl." Laurie hugged Angie. "We are your family. Always. You've felt like one of my own girls since as long as I can remember. And Fisher has loved you since his stubborn little heart knew what it meant to fall in love. And he's going to remember you. And he's going to feel like a fool for hesitating for one single second."

Oh boy ...

By that point, I had to wear a fake smile, not blink, and definitely not look at Rose. I had to lock up my most irrational feelings. The ones where my heart felt heavy because Laurie wasn't hugging me. Laurie wasn't saying how I was family. Laurie wasn't reminding me that I owned Fisher's heart.

To be fair, she had no idea that *I* was the one who Fisher invited to dinner. I was the one who took Fisher to Target. And I was the one (not that I was proud of it) who very inadvertently encouraged him to have sex with Angie. Basically, I was a superhero, and like all superheroes, nobody knew my true identity. I remained in the shadows being a do-gooder without an ounce of recognition.

So selfless.

CHAPTER FOURTEEN

"Where are you headed?" Rory stopped me as I failed in my attempt to sneak out of the house.

"I'm uh ... going to Fisher's to help him finish his shelving unit. Then I suppose we might order pizza or something. Just depends on how long it takes us to finish it."

"Sounds fun. I need to finish a couple loads of laundry. Then Rose and I will order pizza, our treat, and head over. I found a new beer I think Fisher should try. Will Angie be there too? She prefers something a little sweeter like a Riesling or a Moscato. I can pick up a bottle for her too."

There went our night, and there was nothing I could do about it. The smirk on Rose's face confirmed it as she thumbed through a pile of papers from school.

"Sounds great. Give us a couple hours."

"If we get there early, we're good with waiting for you two to finish," Rose said.

"Absolutely." Rory nodded. "Tell Fisher there's no rush."

"Mkay." I nodded, sulking out the door to my car. I would have walked, but the duo of Terrible Ideas and her sidekick Even Worse Ideas butted in on our night. I wasn't putting it past them to call Angie just to make sure she'd be there too.

"Hey. Good timing." Fisher opened the front door and grinned.

"No. Nothing about us is good timing." Too bad he didn't know just how much truth I packed into that statement.

"Uh oh ... what happened?" He stepped aside.

"Rory saw me leaving and asked what I was doing. And the next thing I knew, she was inviting herself and Rose over for pizza and beer. Maybe Angie too. I'm not sure." I frowned.

"And you're upset why?" He shut the door and leaned against it, his good hand in his front pocket.

With a long gaze, I remained silent. Was he really going to make me say it?

"I mean, for me it sucks," he started. "I've been thinking about second base all afternoon. But for you wanting to learn how to use the shelf pin jig, I don't know how additional company will affect that. Are you worried that everyone else will want to learn how to use it as well, and you don't want to share the experience with them?"

I'm afraid that Angie is the love of your life and

you're just too confused to see it. I'm afraid our time is limited and I'm only postponing the inevitable heartbreak.

"I'm reneging. If I die, you will not get ten seconds to fondle me."

"That's a little harsh. You're acting like it's my fault you did such a terrible job of sneaking out of the house. So now we're down to only two options."

I crossed my arms over my chest. "What two options?"

"Either you don't die, or I fondle you now."

Stupid Fisher. There he went again, making me laugh. Indulging me in ridiculous behavior and even more ridiculous conversation. Did he talk about fondling dead bodies with Angie? I couldn't see that. She seemed a little too sophisticated for that. I thought ninety-nine percent of the world's adult population was likely too sophisticated to talk about fondling dead bodies. And the other one percent was probably in prison or on a Most Wanted list.

"What if I don't die *and* you fondle me now? Why does it have to be a choice?"

Fisher grinned. "See, that's why we work. Two great minds." Pushing off the door, he took three steps, slid his good hand behind my neck, and kissed me.

I giggled into his kiss. The kiss lasted longer than I expected, his casted hand idle at his side and his good hand on my neck. Fisher was killing it at first base. It was everything, but not nearly enough. Not when I knew what it felt like to have Fisher sliding into home plate but falling a few inches short.

My hands rested on his T-shirt clad chest for several seconds before heading south.

"Oh ..." He pulled back, a single brow lifted as he glanced down at my fingers making a move on the button to his jeans. "Second base is everything above the waist."

Above the waist. Was he kidding? That left chest and abs for me. Not that Fisher didn't have a great chest and abs, but men had nothing forbidden above their waist. Second base was clearly defined by a man.

Or ... and this thought was the most disturbing ... Fisher Mann was *never* going to have sex with me.

Not. Ever.

We were destined to be professional flirters who dabbled in foreplay, an occasional dry hump. The players who never reached home plate.

"I don't trust Rory and Rose. They could show up any minute. Let's get to work on that shelving unit and showing me how to use that jiggy thing." I brushed past him and around the corner to the garage door.

"Whoa ... whoa ... whoa ..." He followed me. "Are you mad? Did you think *that* back there was me rejecting you?"

My feet made fast work taking me down the stairs. I so badly wanted to turn around, ball my hands, and tell him how I'd secretly felt rejected by him for more than *five years!* But that day, I saw Angie in a wedding gown that she picked out to marry the boy she fell in love with before she could ever imagine her life as a biologist, her life as a woman, her life as an orphan. My problems seemed petty at best. I needed to settle into the fact that Fisher would not be all mine for a while, maybe ever. That meant I had to decide what my heart could handle. Did it have the strength and patience to go the distance for the slim chance that it would be me? That *I* would be the person he loved with or without the memories of us or of Angie.

"I'm only going to feel rejected if you don't show me jiggy action."

"I'm not buying it. Here. I was stupid. I wanted to wait until my cast came off before I suggested more, but I'm clearly the world's biggest idiot."

When I turned to assure him he wasn't the world's biggest idiot because I had already taken that title years earlier, I stumbled on my words and nothing came out.

He stood at the bottom of the stairs with his shirt off and his jeans pushed down to his ankles over his work boots. Just black briefs and a killer grin. "Forgive me?"

After my eyes got their fill, after my tongue made a half dozen swipes along my lower lip, I nodded. "Put your clothes on."

"Are you sure?" He waddled toward me, taking tiny steps restricted by his jeans at his ankles. Fisher was the sexiest duck I had ever seen.

"Stop." I giggled. "Just … put your clothes on."

"Now *I* feel rejected."

"Then we're even." I laughed.

"I knew it!" He pointed a finger at my face. "So you did feel rejected."

My smile faded and I curled my hair behind my ears. "No." I shook my head slowly before hunching in front of him and pulling his jeans up his legs.

Fisher's breaths kicked up a notch, maybe in anticipation of what I was doing, maybe from my proximity to his erection pressed against the black cotton.

I watched my hands, as did he, while I buttoned and zipped his jeans. "Today I saw Angie in her wedding gown. Spoiler alert: she looked stunning. And emotional. She looked like the girl who had dreamed of one boy and only one boy her whole life." My fingers traced the scars along his abs and chest; they tightened even more under my touch.

"I'm not saying that you should marry her. And anything short of wearing that dress for you will cut her deeply. So I'm also not saying that I think my walking away will change how you feel about her or how she will feel if you don't marry her. But I need perspective, Fisher." I lifted my gaze to his.

Concern lined his beautiful face.

"I'm not in this to destroy a woman's dreams," I said. "I'm not in this for a quick lay. It's not a game, even if every moment with you feels exciting and filled with so much life. So thank you." I found a small and easy smile for him.

"For what?"

"For stopping me. For rejecting me. It's easy to lose perspective when I'm with you."

"No." He shook his head. "Again, I didn't reject you. And you are never allowed to thank me for stopping us from getting naked. Just … no. I won't allow it."

"Put your shirt on. We have work to do." I took a step backward.

He snagged his shirt from the floor and pulled it over his head, threading his arms through it slowly. I turned and ran my hand over the wood pieces we glued two nights earlier.

"I'm sorry," he whispered, pressing his chest to my back and kissing the top of my head. "I'm sure seeing Angie in her wedding gown was not easy for you. I wish I knew with certainty how this story will end." He bent lower and kissed my neck as his good hand slid around my waist. "I know how I want it to end right now. But I'm so fucking scared of the plot twist because there are just too many chapters left. And I no longer trust life and its plot twists."

If only we could've just packed a couple of bags and left with one-way tickets to someplace far away and never returned. But we weren't running from Rory and Rose or even Angie and his family. We were running away from his lost memories.

I turned in his arms and snaked mine around his neck. "Let's not read any further." I grinned. "Let's go back to the beginning and reread—relive—our favorite chapters, like this one."

"This one?" He narrowed his eyes a fraction.

I pulled him to me, lifting onto my toes as my lips brushed back and forth over his. "Yeah," I whispered before giving his mouth a slow kiss. My right hand reached for his left hand, and I guided it under the hem of my shirt.

Up.

Up.

Up.

"This is the chapter where the lost fisherman makes it to second base."

Fisher grinned before I kissed him again. His hand cupped my breast, and his thumb slid under the fabric and grazed my nipple.

We knew it wouldn't go past that. So we took our time kissing, like sipping coffee on a lazy Sunday morning.

The naked fisherman wouldn't have had that much self-control, neither would have that scatterbrained, hormonal eighteen-year-old girl. We knew time and patience were our only options, our only hope.

I didn't know how long it would last, how long *we* would last, but I loved the new version of us. Fisher didn't take my virginity because he wasn't sure he deserved it, and he wasn't sure I was truly ready to give it to him.

Five years later, we were in the same situation, but this time it wasn't my virginity. It was my heart. And like five years earlier, I trusted Fisher explicitly to take what he felt he deserved and leave anything he might hurt.

"Fisher ..." I whispered in his ear as he kissed along my cheek.

"Hmm?"

"Teach me."

"Teach you what?" His knuckles ghosted along my other cheek.

"Everything."

CHAPTER FIFTEEN

Fisher showed me how to use the jiggy thing. He showed me how to get things prepped to stain the pieces which we would do at a later time. He even took me through all his tools, giving me a brief explanation of what they did and examples of when he used them. He did have patience, maybe only with me, but that was all that mattered.

Fisher wanted to be with *me*.

"Hello?" Rory called down the stairs just as we were sweeping the floor.

Fisher squatted to hold the dustpan as I swept the small pile into it. "Down here."

Tap.

Tap.

Tap.

Rory made her way down the stairs. "Pizza's here."

"Okay. We're done." Fisher stood and dumped the sawdust into the trash.

"Maybe you should have been a trim carpenter instead of a midwife." Rory eyed me as I dusted off my jeans.

"Fisher's pretty amazing at what he does, but he hasn't pushed an entire human being out of his vagina. So I'll stick to my new job."

"Aaannnd ... we're done down here." Fisher flipped off the lights, leaving only the light on above the stairway.

Rory laughed and headed back up the stairs with Fisher and me right behind her.

"Hey, babe." To no one's surprise, Angie was in the kitchen, setting out plates and napkins.

I really needed a game plan. One that involved telling my mother that she was *ruining* my life. It was a speech I didn't get the chance to give her before she went to prison. Rory had no idea, so was it fair to blame her? I wondered if she'd have felt bad had I told her. Or would she have been way too upset with Fisher and me to care about her role in keeping Angie's hopes and dreams alive?

"Hey." Fisher had no problem switching roles, maybe because Rose reserved her distrusting scowls for me.

I pulled his pants up, Rose. I pulled them up! Zipped. Buttoned. That was all me.

Angie hugged Fisher and gave him a quick peck on the lips. I'd signed up for *The Bachelor*. Oh the joys of sharing one guy.

"Reese, you're setting the bar pretty high for our

future kids." Angie poured herself a glass of wine while Fisher opened a bottle of beer and took a long swig.

"Oh?" I said with caution as I poured a glass of red wine for myself. Just what I wanted to do, talk about their future kids.

"Your mom said you love working in Fisher's shop downstairs. I don't go down there. It's too dusty. But I'm sure he dreams of teaching our kids his skills someday. If they show no interest, he'll wonder why he didn't get a child like you."

I choked on my wine, and Rose came to the rescue, slapping my back a little too hard while Rory jumped into the conversation. "Reese has always been curious and hands-on with things. Even as a little girl, she wanted to do everything she saw her dad and me doing."

"Oh ..." Angie's nose wrinkled. "That sounded weird. I'm sorry." She slapped her palm to her forehead. "I wasn't implying you're a child. That ... just ..." She set her wine down and buried her face in Fisher's chest.

He held his good arm, the one holding the beer, out to the side so as not to spill it on impact.

"It's been a long day." She chuckled, rolling her forehead against his chest as his casted arm rested gently on her back.

Every thirty seconds I had to remind myself that Angie's mind remembered everything about Fisher Mann since he was six years old. She felt comfortable in his presence and in his embrace. Not just as a lover, but as a friend of nearly thirty years.

"It's fine. I knew what you meant."

Nope. I had no idea what she meant. It was the craziest comparison. But I wasn't in the business of making people feel bad or uncomfortable. If Angie and I wouldn't have been competing for the same bachelor, we might have been better friends. I related to her being an only child and losing a parent. For the three years between my dad dying and Rory getting out of prison, I felt like an orphan. Angie loved a good glass of wine and pretty dresses. So did I. And she loved Fisher Mann ... and so did I.

I didn't hate her.

In many ways, I was her.

"I turned on the porch heater. Let's go out there." Rory handed Rose her beer and grabbed the two pizza boxes.

Fisher and Angie snagged the plates and napkins while I carried my wine out with two hands like a good little girl.

Fisher's main level porch was a three-season porch with nice furniture and lots of plants. Rory deposited the pizzas on the irregular shaped wood coffee table before taking a seat next to Rose on a love seat while Fisher sat on the opposing love seat with Angie right next to him, her back partially molded to his chest like she was his stuffed animal to cuddle.

That left the light gray bean-bag-like chair for me. Its back and arms were more structured than a bean bag, which made it the most comfortable chair in the house. That seemed fair since I drew the fifth-wheel spot for the night.

"Well, someone has a birthday in two weeks." Rory sipped her beer and eyed me.

I returned a tight-lipped grin and focused on not spilling my red wine on Fisher's light gray chair.

"If you're not on call, we should go camping."

"Sounds cold." After taking a slow sip of my wine, I shot her a toothy grin.

"Campfire. Warm sleeping bags. Wool mittens. We'll be fine. We never went camping when you were younger. Your dad wasn't a camper. But Rose and I bought camping gear several years ago. And we think it would be fun to go as a group."

"A group?" I discouraged my curious mind from steering my gaze toward Fisher as I hoped her group reference was to a group of people from her work or some camping group they joined. If that was even a thing.

"Us. Your village." Rory circled her head, signaling to the room. "What do you two say? Are you in for camping on Reese's birthday?" she asked Fisher and Angie.

"Sounds fun. I haven't been camping in years. I think Fish has plenty of gear from all the camping he's done with his family. Right, babe?"

Fish. Babe.

I had no nicknames for Fisher. At least none that I could use in front of anyone else. Just like I couldn't kiss him or hold his hand in front of anyone else. Five years changed everything ... and nothing. We were both in a better place, but the timing was still wrong. I wanted to close my eyes and nod my head like a genie and skip ahead a year so I would know.

I would know if he fell in love and married Angie. If his memory returned. If my heart survived all the *ifs*.

Fisher nodded. "I have a lot of camping gear between the basement and what's at my parents' house."

Happy birthday to me, I thought, while putting on a brave face. For my special day, I would get to freeze my butt off in a tent, probably by myself, while the lovers snuggled in for the night in their tents after a romantic evening by the campfire.

"Say yes, sweetie. Take a chance. I think you'll love camping. You said you love the mountains. What could be better than spending the weekend there with good friends and family?"

Jabbing my eyeballs out with an ice pick. Removing my fingernails with pliers. Eating cockroaches. Wiping my butt with sandpaper. So many things would be better than Rory's group camping idea.

I wasn't on call that weekend, but I considered lying. With my luck, Rory would have seen Holly at the salon. Poof! Outed!

"Sounds amazing." I shoved nearly half a piece of pizza into my mouth. It was time to eat my frustrations. "Oh!"

It happened. *Of course* it happened.

I spilled my wine all over me and his amazing chair.

"Shit. Er ... shoot. I'm ... I'm so very sorry."

And embarrassed. I couldn't look at anyone, least of all Fisher, as I scrambled to get out of the chair and blot the red wine with a wad of napkins.

"It was an accident. No worries, Reese. We'll take care of it if you want to go get yourself cleaned up." Angie jumped to the rescue as everyone else tossed their napkins onto the pile to save the chair from as much wine soaking through to the filling as possible.

I pulled the wet fabric of my T-shirt away from my skin as I ducked my head and sped my way to the guest bathroom, shutting the door behind me before staring at myself in the mirror. After a good two minutes of internally scolding myself for being so clumsy in my flustered state following the camping topic, I took off my shirt and ran the stained part under water.

Two soft knocks tapped the door.

"I'm good. Just give me a minute."

The door opened because I hadn't lock it—because who opens a closed bathroom door uninvited?

Snatching the hand towel from the counter, I held it to my chest as Fisher peered through the crack he made with the door.

"What?" I tipped up my chin, fighting the urge to have a mini-emotional breakdown.

If he looked too long into my eyes, he would have seen me teetering on the edge of losing it.

"Shirt for you." Opening the door just enough to squeeze his hand through, he handed me a T-shirt.

"It will be huge on you, but it might also cover the stain on your pants."

I nodded slowly as my gaze dropped to the T-shirt in my hand. "I'm really sorry about your chair. I'll pay for any damage or a new chair." Turning my back to the door, I dropped the hand towel and slipped on his shirt.

"Angie is drinking too much wine tonight. I can't let her drive home. So she'll stay here."

I turned. "I wasn't talking about Angie's level of sobriety. I was talking about your chair."

"Well, I don't give a fuck about the chair."

After clenching my teeth for a few seconds, I fired back. "Well I don't give one if she stays here or not. I'm not stupid. I know you're having sex with her. You told me, *and* I was with you when you purchased condoms."

There was no other way to describe that moment other than to say, I had super fucking (necessary use of the word) hero bravery to say those words to him without my heart exploding through my chest and shattering onto the floor. The thought of him having sex with Angie ... it was unbearable. My chest felt physical pain that worked its way up my throat, twisting into a tight knot that made every word a struggle to get out of my mouth.

Burning eyes.

Racing heart.

Nauseous stomach.

But the bravest of faces.

Because ... *because* I loved Fisher, and even if my chances of happiness with him were less than one percent, he was worth it.

Fisher deflated a little like I had disappointed him. I wasn't trying to disappoint him or anyone for that matter. That was why I agreed to go camping. That was why I kept my feelings about Angie and him locked up tightly.

"It was a box of twelve. The box is unopened. All twelve are there now. All twelve will be there in the morning."

My gaze remained averted out of self-preservation, and I shrugged. "Whatever." I wadded my dirty shirt in my hand and opened the door, brushing past him. As soon as I noticed Angie, Rose, and Rory still hard at work on the stained chair, using some bottle of special cleaner, I turned back around. My hands landed on Fisher's chest, catching him off guard as I pushed him down the hallway to his bedroom.

I didn't turn on the light or shut his door. I guided him through the room, to his bathroom, stopping in his closet. A slow dance lit only by some moonlight filtering through the window shades and skylights.

Dropping the wet shirt to the floor, I crumpled his shirt in my fists and pulled him to me, pressing my lips to his—giving him all my unspoken emotions in that one slow kiss.

His good hand tangled in my hair, deepening the

kiss, and I softly moaned. I loved our bubble, but I hated the fate of it, like the fate of every bubble. Eventually, all bubbles popped.

Pulling back, I released his mouth but kept my hold on his neck so he kept his lips close to mine as I whispered, "I'm in. I'm in as long as you want me to be in your life. Even on the days it hurts like hell. I'm in."

He rested his forehead on mine and blew out a slow breath. "Can I tell you something truly terrible?"

I grinned, lifting my chin and brushing my lips against his as I giggled. "Tell me."

Fisher dragged his mouth along my cheek, depositing small kisses on his way to my ear. "The only memories of my past I want to get back ... are the ones of you."

There was no way out of *whatever* it was that all of us were in together. And I knew it wasn't *if* things fell apart in the most tragic fashion ... it was when.

Rory would be hurt, angry, and disappointed in me and Fisher and Rose too.

And either Angie or I would be left alone. Fisherman-less. Undeniably heartbroken. And even if other feelings like resentment or anger played a part, the only thing that would last forever would be the Fisher-sized vacancy in someone's chest.

I should have had the advantage of knowing that he had a choice to make. And it should have prepared me. But there was no way to prepare for losing *the one* you loved more than any other.

As he started to release his hold on me, I tightened

my grip on him. "Ten more seconds," I whispered, nestling my face into his neck and taking a deep inhale.

Fisher counted down from ten.

"Ten."

Kiss on my head.

"Nine."

Another kiss.

All the way to one.

When he released me, when we released each other, I had all I needed to make it another day, another round. Another mile in the marathon.

CHAPTER SIXTEEN

THAT FIRST CRY.

There really was nothing that signified life more than a baby's first cry. It was like she announced her place in the world. As equal and deserving as anyone else.

Life would be hard.

Life would be beautiful.

And she would have to fight to find the courage to keep that voice, not be silenced by guilt or circumstance. She would have to make difficult choices—sometimes choosing her own happiness over someone else's happiness.

Who did we die for?

Who did we live for?

Was there a right answer?

"Oh ... my ... gosh ..." I breathed the words in astonishment.

"You're witnessing a rare moment." Holly glanced

over at me and smiled as she delivered a baby en caul—in an intact amniotic sac.

A peaceful little girl with one hand on her head and the other hand at her mouth. A firsthand glimpse at what a baby looked like in the womb. She was outside of her mother, but not really born yet.

"It's my first." Holly got teary eyed as we observed the phenomenon with the stunned parents, doula, and birth photographer.

"Is she okay?" the dad asked, his voice a little shaky.

"She's perfect," Holly whispered, running her finger along the thin sack, touching the baby's foot.

"What do you do?" the mom asked.

Holly shrugged. "I can remove the sac now or we can let her be for a few more minutes if you want to take in the moment a little longer."

After delivering hundreds of babies, Holly still treated each birth like she, too, was experiencing a miracle in her own life. I felt that as well.

The photographer took a slew of photos of the rare moment. One in eighty-thousand births. I knew I might never witness it again.

When Holly and the mom released the baby from its sac, I laughed, but it was more of a sob as tears fell in relentless streams down my face.

"I SAW A BABY BORN EN CAUL!" I ran into the house at eight on a Thursday night. I didn't know if anyone was home. I hadn't talked to Rory or Rose in over eighteen hours. And I hadn't seen Fisher since Saturday night at his house—the wine incident. "Hello?" I ran down the hallway.

Nobody.

I ran downstairs.

Nobody.

I checked the garage.

Rose's car was gone.

Too much adrenaline ran through my veins. I had to tell someone, so I ran over to Fisher's house in the dark. When I got there, more air deflated from my lungs. I wanted to cry because all I needed was a person. Anyone at that point to share my day. But Angie's car was in the driveway. Despite my complete lack of peppiness by that point, I gave myself a pep talk.

If I would have been his clear choice, we would have already been together. No secrets. No guilt. But he hadn't made his choice because on one side there was me, on the other side was Angie and his entire family. It wasn't that his family didn't like me, but there was no way they were going to shrug and kiss Angie goodbye then turn to me with open arms.

No way.

One of the many reasons I loved Fisher was *because* he had such a close-knit family, something that unraveled in my own life when I needed it the most.

"She's out of town."

I turned, standing at the end of his driveway as Fisher walked toward me in his jogging shorts and a hoodie.

He pulled out his earbuds. "She asked me to take her car to get the oil changed if I had time." He shrugged. "Seemed like the nice thing to do."

Yet another reason to love Fisher Mann.

"One in eighty thousand babies is born en caul. That means it comes out of its mother's body still in the amniotic fluid sac. It's the most amazing sight. I ..." I shook my head. "I can't even describe it. But I saw it. I. Saw. It!"

He grinned, a gleam visible in his eyes under the street light. "Do you need to kiss somebody?"

My smile nearly cracked my face in half as I shook my head. "Not somebody. I need to kiss *you*."

"Then what are you waiting for?"

I giggled, threw myself into his arms, and kissed him with my hands pressed to his scruffy face. He grabbed my butt with both hands. That was when I released his lips and turned to look at his arm.

"You got your cast off. How does it feel?"

"Better on your ass." He grabbed my butt again and pulled me back to him. "Are you coming inside? Or did you just come over here to stare at my house?"

I rolled my eyes. "Nobody was home at my house. And I had to tell someone, so I ran over here."

"So I *am* just somebody?"

Grabbing the neck of his hoodie, I tilted my head

back. "I share you, so *you* have to share me and my enthusiasm. If you must know, I was looking for my mom and Rose first because occasionally I value self-preservation. And I was reminded of that when I got here and saw Angie's car."

"Come trim my beard before I get into the shower."

"Your cast is off."

He grinned slowly, taking my hands away from the neck of his hoodie and pressing them to his face and the beard he wanted me to trim. "Come trim my beard before I get into the shower." Fisher's signature expression always seemed to be mischievous, but only with me. I never saw it quite the same way when he looked at other people.

Not his friends, Rory and Rose.

Not his sort-of fiancée.

Not his family.

Just me.

"I have to get home soon. I'm still on call for the next few days."

"Come trim my beard before I get in the shower."

I laughed at my lost fisherman stuck on repeat. A one-track mind and the most convincing smile.

"Remember what I said about self-preservation?"

Turning his head, he kissed my palm. "I would never hurt you."

Oh, Fisher ... I'm already hurting in ways you can't even imagine because you don't remember.

"What do you want for your birthday?"

I laughed, pulling my hands away from his face.

"To not go camping with you and your fiancée. I realize you can't say you're sick because you're never sick, but you could make up some excuse."

"How do you know that I'm never sick?"

"Because you told me."

He frowned. "I don't remember that."

"I know you don't. Trust me ... I know."

Taking my hand, he pulled me toward his front door.

"I'm going home." I made a weak attempt at pulling away from him.

"Eventually," he said.

"Fisher ..."

"Nurse Capshaw, queen of the veiled birth."

As the door closed behind me and he started to release my hand, I squeezed my grip on him and yanked him to stop. "Veiled birth?"

"It's another term for en caul."

I nodded once. "I'm aware. But how do you know that?"

He shrugged. "Probably a crossword puzzle or something."

"I haven't put that in my puzzles."

Fisher shrugged a second time and tried to turn away from me.

Again, I tugged his arm. "Fisher Mann ... you like crossword puzzles. You liked them before I made them for you."

He eyed me for a few seconds with the most

contemplative expression. "Are you genuinely asking me or are you testing me?"

"What do you mean?"

"I know so much about Angie that there are some days I don't feel like I've lost memories of her. I start to wonder if the events in my head are my memories or things I've been told because I've been told *everything*. The only test I have with her is my feelings. I don't remember how I felt about her. But with you it's different."

"Different how?" I released his hand, feeling the shift. Now I was the one being interrogated, not him.

"I feel like you've given me bits and pieces, on a need-to-know basis. My story with Angie makes sense in my head. Childhood friends. On and off again relationship when we got older. Me doing my thing. Her doing her thing. Our families keeping us connected. She comes back to town for her mom. We rekindle our romance. Even if I don't *feel* it now, it makes sense to me."

"Well, that's good." I gave him a tight grin as I fiddled with the hem of my shirt.

"From everything my family has told me about who I was, I don't think I would have taken a part-time employee to my workshop. I wouldn't have showed her how to sand anything. Yet that's your story."

"You thought a lot of Rory. I'm sure it was a favor to her. And I was relentless. You probably just did it to shut me up."

With his brow drawn tight, almost cemented in

place, he inched his head side to side. "Why were you so certain I'd like crossword puzzles?"

Another half shrug. "I wasn't. Why are you being so weird? Have you remembered something? Memories can return slowly, and they can cause confusion as you try to piece them together and make sense of them."

"Do you know an attorney named Brendon?"

I swallowed hard. "What? Why?" It barely made its way past the constriction of my throat.

"Because I saw him yesterday."

"Where?"

"At my therapist's office."

"You have a therapist?"

Fisher nodded like it wasn't a big deal.

"Since when?" I asked.

"Since yesterday."

"Why?"

"We're not talking about me."

"We are. Why?"

"Because I was in an accident. I'm missing part of my memory, and I have a fiancée and maybe a girlfriend." He shook his head like talking about it bothered him. "And it's not my point anyway."

"What's your point?"

And did you tell your therapist about me?

"Brendon recognized me. He must be a patient at the same office. He was leaving when I arrived. He said hi. Of course, I had to apologize for not knowing him and give my quick spiel about my accident."

Brendon was in therapy. I cringed a little, wondering if I was the reason? Gosh ... I hoped not.

"How is he?"

"Why do you ask?"

"No reason. I mean ... I haven't seen him in years. We used to go to the same church, not too far from here."

"So you were church friends?"

I nodded, completely gambling on the hope that in such a short encounter, Brendon didn't back up the dump truck and unload onto Fisher.

"Just church friends?" He knew something.

"Brendon was the one who convinced me to go to Thailand. He's actually the friend who went with me."

"He's the one, isn't he?"

"Yes, I just said he's the one who went with me to—"

"No." Fisher shook his head. "That's not what I'm talking about. He's the one you loved. The one we talked about. You said he's with someone else, but not married. I told you to go knock on his door."

It was such a game. Playing one card at a time, neither one of us knew what was in the other one's hand. I so badly wanted to lay down my hand and show him every card.

It's you, Fisher! Everything is you.

My heartstrings were so tangled in Fisher, I could barely breathe. Every move seemed to create a new knot. When we got too close. When we were too far apart.

"Why do you think it's him?"

"That's not an answer."

"It's not him."

"Fuck ..." He rubbed his temples with his thumb and middle finger. "I didn't see that answer coming."

"Why?" A twinge of frustration gripped my words, making them tight and clipped.

He chuckled. "Well, because he casually mentioned having not seen you since you agreed to *marry him* and broke off the engagement all within twenty-four hours."

Well fuck. (Mandatory use of the F-word)

"I told him you were back in Denver. He said to tell you hi. So ..." Another chuckle. "You were going to marry Brendon for two seconds, and he's not the guy you were talking about? This other guy must be quite something if he's the one you think about when you think of being in love instead of the guy you said yes to marrying."

On a slow deflate, I whispered, "He is."

"Is he the reason you broke up with Brendon?"

My eyes narrowed at the floor while I thought about my answer. The truth. "No. I ... I only said yes to Brendon because he asked me in front of a group of people, and I didn't want to embarrass him. The reason I didn't marry him was because I still hadn't done anything for myself. And I wasn't ready for Wife and Mother to be my new titles and full-time profession, which was funny because I had been watching all these babies come into the world. And I was longing for a husband like the men holding their wives' hands. The love. The family. I wanted it, just not yet. And I didn't want it with Brendon. And that truly sucked because he was ... I'm sure still *is* an amazing, kind, smart, and loving man. Just not the one for me."

"What if I can't live up to him? Will I be the next Brendon?"

Oh my lost fisherman ...

"No. You won't be the next Brendon because he got a parting gift, I suppose."

"What was that?"

"My virginity."

Fisher's head jerked backward. "You loved someone else, but Brendon from *church* took your virginity?"

"*Took* might be a strong word. I gave it to him. Persuaded him to take it." I curled my hair behind my ears and risked a glance up at Fisher.

"Why didn't you give it to the guy you loved?"

Such a fantastic question, Fisher. Thanks for asking.

"He didn't want it."

His eyes widened and his jaw dropped. "What?"

"He knew the timing wasn't right for us. And he knew, at the time, that I had mixed emotions about my V-card. After Rory going to prison, my dad dying, and attending a Christian academy while living with my ultra-conservative grandparents ... Jesus, God, and every chapter of the Bible haunted me."

"But you wanted to have sex with him?"

The hint of a smile twitched my lips. "Yes."

"I rescind what I told you about him. Don't go knock on his door. He doesn't deserve you. If he didn't have the balls to man the fuck up when you chose him, then he didn't deserve it or you. He choked, and that's pretty pathetic."

I laughed. "Yeah, well ... I didn't look at it like that. So let's not stone him for his decision. Besides, you have some things in common with him."

He crossed his arms over his chest. "Such as?"

"You weren't going to let me go past second base."

"Fuck. Stop. Just ... no." He shook his head. "We are never talking about that again. It was a joke. I would have hit the damn home run and you know it."

I brushed past him, moseying down the hallway toward his bathroom. "Sure. Sure. That's what *he* said."

"He's an idiot."

I giggled. "Sometimes."

Fisher peeled off his shirt and tossed it into the hamper. Then he sat on the vanity bench. I draped the towel over his legs and grabbed the trimmers. He spread his legs wide, unlike the previous time, and pulled me between them with his hands on the back of my thighs.

I laughed as the towel on his lap fell onto the floor. He didn't care. I turned on the trimmers, and he buried his face in my chest.

"I've missed you," he mumbled.

"It's only been five days." I ran my free hand through his hair.

"And nights." He lifted his head. "Nights too. Don't forget nights."

"Because we've spent so many nights together?" I made my first swipe with the trimmers.

"You're with me every night. In my dreams. You're naked, except for my tool belt. You're always wearing my tool belt."

I laughed. "Sounds interesting. Am I building something?"

He frowned. "No. You're always just teasing me."

"Funny. In my dreams, you're always a baby with an adult head, sucking a pacifier."

"Not funny." He tightened his grip on the back of my legs.

I jumped, holding the trimmer away from his face. "Careful." I continued to trim his beard. "And it's actually quite funny."

He said nothing more while I finished, but I felt his eyes on me the whole time.

"Perfect. As usual." I set the trimmers on the counter. "Well, my trim is perfect, considering what I had to work with."

Fisher remained a little subdued, not as quick to jab back. In fact, he didn't take the bait at all.

"I'll grab the vac hose to sweep up the mess."

"Leave it." He pulled me closer to him again.

I smiled, running my palms along his face. "So handsome."

He closed his eyes and took an audible breath,

releasing it like it carried some pretty heavy stuff with it.

"Did you tell your therapist about me? I know it's none of my business, but—"

"Yes." He opened his eyes.

I nodded slowly, pressing my lips together.

"I told her I'm engaged to a woman I've known nearly my whole life. But I'm in love with a woman I've known for a breath, maybe two."

Drawing in another one of those breaths of time, a shaky one, I blew it out with a whisper, "You love me?"

He shrugged. Of course he shrugged. It was Fisher. "I'm assuming that's what this annoying feeling is."

"Annoying feeling?" I narrowed my eyes.

"The increased heart rate I get just from thinking about you. Oh ... and that. The *constant* thinking about you. The stupid smile that I can't seem to wipe off my face because I'm thinking about you *all the damn time*."

He seemed so annoyed. It made me grin, but I fought it by biting my lower lip.

"The dreams. The driving by your house just to see if your car is there. Lack of focus on anything or anyone but you. It's ..." He shook his head. "It's bad." His gaze met mine. "What about you? Do you have any feelings toward me? Or do you just want into my pants? Be honest ... am I the girl in this relationship?"

"Fisher ..." I whispered. His humor didn't completely mask his nerves. How did two people fall in love so quickly? Then how did they do it twice? Just as quickly, just as passionately? And with terrible timing *again?* I pressed my lips to his.

We kissed.

Fisher loved me. *Me ...*

So we continued to kiss because that's what people who loved each other did.

He unbuttoned my jeans and eased down the zipper. Then he kissed my exposed skin just above my panties.

My fingers laced through his thick hair. "I love you, my lost fisherman."

He stilled for a second before his gaze lifted to mine. Those blue eyes. That heartbreakingly lost look in his eyes.

"This is so messy." I gave him a cautious smile.

"That's how we know it's real." He slowly stood, taking my shirt with him.

I lifted my arms, willingly surrendering.

He dropped my shirt onto the floor and kissed me again, easing my bra straps down my shoulders as I reached around and unhooked it.

Maybe our future was uncertain, at best. But not his touch. I knew ... I just *knew* he didn't touch her like he touched me.

The slide of his warm tongue.

The brush of his thumb over my nipple.

And the hum, almost a tiny growl, like he was a little angry that everything had to be so damn complicated.

That slow kiss took us all the way to the bed. I

wasn't the nervous girl anymore. And knowing he wasn't getting my virginity didn't make it feel any less special.

I wasn't a used sanitary napkin.

I was the woman who put myself first, who loved myself first. I was the girl who left the love of her life to *find* a life.

There were mistakes.

Lessons to learn.

Tears to cry.

Intimate moments with other people.

Risks to take.

And I did it all.

I did it not because I thought it would lead me back to Fisher; I did it for me. The only gift I cared to give my future husband was the most confident version of myself. A full heart and a humbled soul.

As I leaned back on the bed, Fisher pulled my jeans down my legs. "Not even death will take this memory away from me." He grinned.

As his mouth made its way up my body, he stopped briefly to tease the sensitive flesh between my legs while sliding off my panties.

"Fisher ..." I closed my heavy eyelids, and my hands fisted the bedding, my hips lifting from the mattress looking for absolutely anything he would give me. When I opened them, he was discarding his jogging shorts and briefs.

That grin ... so sexy.

The slow prowl, bringing every inch of that body to

me. I'd never felt so alive. My legs spread wider. My fingers feathered his chest, his abs, and the hard muscles along his back.

Settling between my legs, teasing me like he did to the eighteen-year-old virgin, he kissed my breasts, my neck, my ... everything. Fisher had always been the patient one with me. And that night was no exception. He guided me onto my stomach and kissed along my back and the curve of my butt like an artist admiring every detail of a fine work of art or ... a lost fisherman exploring Target with the woman he was destined to fall for every single time.

I liked that analogy best.

And that smile ... the grin I felt every so often when he kissed my body.

Fisher was happy.

Happy with me.

"What ... do we have here?" He angled my butt toward the window and the sliver of streetlight coming through it.

Oh ... I forgot about that.

"A tattoo? You have a tattoo?"

I craned my neck to look over my shoulder as he held me firmly in place, closely inspecting my butt cheek.

"Callipygian," he said slowly.

"I was drunk, hence the hidden tattoo on my butt. It means—"

"It means you have a shapely ass. Alcohol makes

you confident and a little vain." He chuckled before biting it.

"Ouch!" I wriggled out of his grip and rolled onto my back. "How do you know that word?"

He guided my knees apart. "Because I have the same word tattooed on my ass."

I giggled. "You do not."

He dipped his head between my legs.

"Stop teasing me," I pled my case with my hands claiming his hair as he tried to set up camp down there.

"Don't hurry me."

I smiled as his mouth made a lazy exploration up to my lips, making several stops along the way. He didn't understand my rush because in his mind, he'd been waiting weeks for this. I'd been waiting years.

He seemed pretty proud of himself when he made a production of getting a condom from the *unopened* box.

"Wipe that grin off your face." I rolled on top of him and pinned his arms next to his head.

Our mirrored smiles faded as I lowered my head and kissed him. He guided my hips over his erection.

I sat up just enough to let him push into me the whole way. Drunk on the feeling, I couldn't move. I just wanted to stay in that exact position forever. I'd imagined that feeling so many times, and despite the other men I'd been with, there was no comparing them or anything I'd done with them to Fisher being inside of me.

Him sitting up and kissing me.

Him rolling us again and again.

Arms and legs tangling together with the sheets woven every which way.

The look in his eyes when he moved inside of me—so intense. His strong hands all over my body, laced with my fingers, and tangled in my hair as he kissed me.

The whispered promise of never forgetting that moment—so heartbreaking.

The focused expression and taut muscles in his jaw and face when he made sure I came before he did, but only by a few seconds. So many emotions flooded me in that moment.

I had *never* felt so vulnerable in my life, a permeating fear that I just gave him something so much greater than my virginity.

After long minutes of stillness with him collapsed on top of me and still inside of me, he rolled to the side. "My therapist is going to be really pissed off with me."

I shifted toward him, finding my new favorite place —my naked body molded to his. My face in the crook of his neck, his in my hair, and his hand on my butt. "Why?" I asked.

"Because she told me to take a step back, to not get distracted by the physical part of my relationships."

"I'd get a second opinion. Because in my humble opinion, we should do this again ... maybe even a lot."

Fisher chuckled. "I second that opinion." Kissing my head, he moved to sitting on the edge of the bed. "I'm going to take a shower. You should join me."

I sat up, hugging his back and teasing his earlobe with my teeth. "I'm going home. You distracted me with sex, but I wasn't done telling the world about the birth I witnessed."

He turned his head to look at me. "Are you saying the birth was more memorable than the sex?"

I hopped out of bed and dressed quickly. "I'm saying it's my constitutional right to not answer your question."

"You can't plead the Fifth on this." He grabbed his shorts and sauntered into the bathroom.

I slowed my hands as I hooked my bra, taking a few seconds to watch his callipygian figure. "Did you hear me say that birth was one in *eighty thousand?*"

Seconds later, he appeared around the corner in sweatpants and a tee, leaning against the wall, hands crossed over his chest.

"Tonight, you were one in a billion ... times infinity. But if I didn't live up to one in eighty thousand, then I think we're done here." Fisher didn't even smile. He simply bowed his head.

"Tonight, *you were one in a billion ... times infinity.*"

If Fisher didn't pick me, fall eternally in love with me, if he got his memory back and it brought with it an unmatchable love for Angie, I knew I would be the one in therapy for the rest of my life.

"You're right." I squeezed past him, ignoring his pouty face, and grabbed my shirt from the bathroom floor. I shook the hair off it and pulled it over my head.

"Angie has been giving you everything. She wants you to remember how you felt about her. And if I were wearing a diamond ring you gave to me, I'd probably be doing the same thing. Retelling our story to you a thousand times in a thousand different ways. But for me, it doesn't matter if you loved me then, it only matters if you love me now."

He turned.

"Just ..." I whispered. "Love me today."

I saw it in his eyes. And I thought he would say it, say something like "I'll love you every day," or "I'll love you always." And what woman in her right mind wouldn't have wanted a man to say that to her?

Me.

So either I was the exception or I wasn't in my right mind.

Fisher got lost. I got lost. And nobody could help me find my way. It was something I had to do myself. In my own way. In my own time.

I couldn't ask for more from Fisher than I was willing to give myself. If that meant he had to risk losing me to find himself, then I would accept that.

"I love you today," he said.

That was his reply. The perfect reply.

I nodded toward him. "Thought you were going to shower."

"After I drive you home."

I grinned, taking two steps to him then taking his hand and pulling him toward the front door. "You're one, Fisher."

"One in what?"

I opened the door, and he closed it behind us.

"Not *in* anything. Not one in eighty thousand. Not one in a billion times infinity. You're just one. *The one.*"

CHAPTER SEVENTEEN

"Where have you been? I messaged you and tried calling you," Rory asked before I got both feet in the house.

I missed that message, which wasn't good since I was on call. Retrieving my phone from my pocket, I checked for messages or missed calls other than Rory's.

She glanced over my shoulder as I started to shut the door while slipping my phone back into my pocket. "You were with Fisher?"

"Um ..." I locked the door. "Yeah. I was looking for you and Rose when I got home because I've had the Best. Day. Ever! And I was dying to share it. So I ran to Fisher's house on pure adrenaline, thinking you might be there. But you weren't. He was. So I told him all about my day. And he gave me a ride home." I toed off my shoes.

"It's eleven, sweetie. What time did you get home? And why didn't you just call me? Rose and I went out with friends. I didn't know when you were going to be home."

"It's fine." I headed into the kitchen for a glass of water, feeling a little parched after my unexpected workout with Fisher. "Hey, Rose." I smiled as she sat in her robe at the kitchen table with her laptop in front of her.

"What time did you go to Fisher's?" Rose asked, looking at me over her reading glasses. They made her look sixty instead of forty-eight. And I loved the way they made sure I knew the time, like I was fifteen and past curfew.

"What?" I narrowed my eyes just before gulping down the water.

"What's your great story? It must be a long one since you're just now getting back from Fisher's." Rory seemed concerned about the length of time I spent at Fisher's too.

"Well, it's late. So you're just getting the abbreviated version of the story because I'm tired." And I didn't want to play Twenty Questions about my time at Fisher's house.

"Holly delivered a baby, an en caul baby. That means the baby was born in an intact amniotic sac. It's a one in eighty thousand occurrence. It was the coolest thing I have ever seen. I mean ... the baby was basically still in the womb, calm and content. And we just watched it, in total awe for close to five minutes."

"That's incredible." Rory shook her head. "I didn't know that was even possible."

I yawned. It had been a long time since I'd slept. "Rare, but possible. And that's my news. Sorry, I acted way more excited about it earlier, but now I'm dead tired."

"So you just told Fisher and then he brought you home?" Rose ... she was such a little devil.

"No. We talked about some other things. He's seeing a therapist, but don't say anything in case I'm not supposed to share that information. He saw Brendon the other day, so he mentioned that because Brendon recognized him. Then we talked about other random stuff, and I trimmed his beard."

"You trimmed his beard?" Rory laughed, locking the door to the deck.

"Yes. Another secret you have to keep. I did it once before too, but he wanted everyone else to think he'd done it so he didn't look incapable of doing it. You know how he can be."

"Yeah, but he got his cast off. Why did he need you to do it again?" Rose's eyebrows peaked with too much curiosity.

I shrugged. "I don't know. He asked. I had nothing else to do, so I did it. You know, some guys get their beards trimmed professionally. Maybe it's easier for him to let someone else do it. Maybe the cast is off but his arm has lost some muscle and it needs to build up strength again. Maybe he was just using me because he's too lazy to do it himself."

"That was nice of you, sweetie." Rory kissed my

head and shuffled down the hallway. "I'm going to bed, ladies. Shut off the lights."

Rose slowly closed her computer.

"Night." I tried to make the same quick escape that Rory made.

"Reese," Rose said.

No escape for me.

"Yes?" I turned slowly, already deflated from the speech she hadn't yet given me but knew it was coming.

"Is there *something* to tell?"

I promised I would tell Rory if the day came that there was something to tell.

"Not yet."

Her head tilted to the side. "Are you sure?"

After several seconds, I nodded slowly, but I couldn't hide what she saw on my face—worry and fear.

"Night." I sulked to my bedroom and shut the door. As I sat on the end of my bed, my door opened slowly. Rose squeezed through the partially opened door and softly closed it behind her.

I blinked and the tears escaped. "I love him," I whispered as Rose kneeled in front of me, resting her hands on my legs.

"Does he love you?"

I nodded.

"Are you sure?"

"Yes."

Rose didn't ask me how I knew; she simply gave me

several slow nods, tiny crevices of concern etched into her forehead.

"Do you think he loves Angie?"

I wiped my face and sniffled. "I don't know. I think he cares about her. But he doesn't love her like he loves me."

"And if he gets his memory back, will he love her the way he loves you?"

A billion ... times infinity.

"No," I whispered like it wasn't my brain answering her. It was my soul whispering its truth.

That seemed to bring out an additional dose of worry. Rose looked at me like I was in love with a movie star. An infatuation that had gone too far. "How can you say that?" she whispered.

"Because what we have is effortless. It just ... happens. What we have doesn't care if it's right or wrong. It doesn't care about timing. It doesn't care about age. And it doesn't need memories to live or survive. Fisher doesn't have to remember that he loves me. It's simply that he does, whether he makes a conscious choice to do it or not. I think he loved Angie because he'd convinced himself it made sense. And if his memory comes back, I think he's going to realize that, and then he's going to realize it no longer makes sense."

Rose shook her head, gaze pointed at the floor, at my feet.

"I know you're Team Angie. It's fine. She's great. If I wasn't heart and soul in love with Fisher, I'd be

Team Angie too," I said with a little defeat to my voice.

"Oh, hon ... I'm Team Reese. Always." She lifted her gaze. "I love you like my own daughter, which is precisely why I'm so protective of you. And it's nothing against Fisher. I love Fisher too. But I saw him with Angie. It wasn't one sided. He loved her. It wasn't pity love. It wasn't a second-choice love. And I know what that looks like because I was married to the wrong person for too many years. So as much as I want to feel as confident as you do that this will all work its way out in your favor ... I'm not as sure."

After a long pause, I nodded. "It's okay. I don't know if it's going to work out in my favor either, but I know this ... if he gets his memory back and chooses her, I will understand. And it won't change my love for him. And when he waits for her at the altar, he will find me in the crowd of people, and we will share a look." I wiped a few more tears from my eyes. "That look that says we know he loves me more." I shifted my gaze to Rose. "The way you knew my mom loved you more than my dad."

With a sad smile pulling at her lips, she nodded several times.

CHAPTER EIGHTEEN

I took my en-caul-birth-and-sex-with-Fisher high and rode it for days. It didn't matter that Angie came home and dominated Fisher's time that weekend. I knew he wasn't having sex with her.

The following week, I stayed busy with work, reading books for work, morning jogs, and crossword puzzles. Rory and Rose went over to Fisher's one night to have dinner with him and Angie. I was invited, but I declined. My heart needed more time to prepare for that awkward moment—seeing him again with Angie after what we did together.

That moment came all too quickly. My birthday weekend. Camping. Party of five. A fifth wheel on my own birthday.

Not cool.

"Rory's running late," Rose announced when I got home from work Friday afternoon. "She had a client who had a fender bender but apparently 'needed' her hair highlighted before leaving town tomorrow. So I'm going to wait for her. And you'll ride with Fisher and Angie to get everything set up before it gets dark." Rose moved food from the fridge to a cooler, shooting me a wrinkled nose smile. "Sorry."

"Or we can leave in the morning."

Rose shook her head. "Nope. Your mom wants you to wake up in the mountains on your birthday. Pancakes on the camping griddle. And a hike before lunch."

"I'm telling her about Fisher. I'm just telling her. And she can figure out how to deal with it. I'm tired of her unintentionally sabotaging my love life and now ruining my birthday by inviting my boyfriend's fiancée for a weekend camping trip."

Rose chuckled, shaking her head. "Just stop for a second and think about how insane that sounds. Your *boyfriend's fiancée*."

I frowned.

"Go get ready. Fisher and Angie will be here to get you in less than an hour."

Dragging my feet, I made my way to my bedroom to change my clothes and finish packing a few things including a warm jacket, boots, gloves, and a hat. There was a slight chance of snow in the mountains for my pre-Halloween birthday.

After zipping my bag and grabbing a jacket, I took a few deep breaths and let them out slowly just as there were two quick knocks on the front door.

"Hello?"

Fisher's voice.

I should have been happy to hear his voice, but it just meant I had to put on a fake smile. I had to be the odd woman out, sitting in the back of his truck for several hours while Angie fiddled with his hair, talked about their wedding, and in general made me sick to my stomach.

"She should be ready. Reese?" Rose called.

On another deep breath, I pulled back my shoulders and played the part of the happy birthday girl as I trekked to the front door.

It was a chillier day in Denver, and it was the first time I had seen Fisher in a beanie. I wanted to cry. He looked so sexy. Sexy for her, not me.

"Hey." He grinned too big, said *hey* with too much enthusiasm.

I managed to return two raised eyebrows and a closed-lipped smile.

"Let me take your bag. I'll meet you in the truck. No rush."

I relinquished my bag.

"Hopefully, we'll only be an hour or two behind. Did you get our gear that I set by the garage?" Rose asked.

"I did," Fisher said just before shutting the door.

"No pouting. It's not the worst thing ever." Rose handed me a thermos. "Hot chocolate for the road."

"Thanks." I took it.

"See you in a few hours?"

"Yup." I went out the front door.

Fisher's truck was backed into the driveway. I wasn't going to sit behind Fisher and have Angie glancing at me every two seconds, so I walked around to the passenger side so my view would be of Fisher.

I opened the back door. "Um ..." I glanced up front to the empty seat. "I thought you picked Angie up already." I climbed into the back.

"Get your ass up here." He glanced at me and grinned.

I narrowed my eyes.

"Happy birthday."

"It's not my birthday until tomorrow."

"Yes, but I'm giving you your present now."

"My present is riding in the front seat? I'm not ten. And Angie riding in back is just weird."

"But Angie's not going, so it's only weird if you ride in back."

"What?" My eyes widened.

"She's not going. Just get up front before Rose comes out here because she doesn't understand why I'm still parked in the driveway."

I hopped in the front seat, and Fisher wasted no time pulling out of the driveway.

"Is she okay?" I didn't want to accidentally smile or squeal with joy if something was wrong with Angie. I wasn't a catty bitch by nature.

"She's fine. Just a little headache."

"She stayed home for just a little headache?"

He shrugged. "I suggested she stay home."

"Why?"

With a contemplative expression, he kept his gaze forward. "Because I love you today. And I think there's a high probability that I will love you tomorrow—on your birthday. Loving you means making your birthday as special as possible."

"Pull over."

"What?" He shot me a quick glance. "You feeling okay?"

"Pull over now."

He veered off the road just before we reached the interstate.

I unbuckled and crawled over the console.

"Whoa ... what are you—"

With one leg still on the console and my other leg pressed between his legs so my knee was on the seat, I grabbed his face and kissed him.

It took him a second—two at the most—to get past the shock of my sudden need to kiss him, hug him, *love* him. One of his hands found my waist and his other hand palmed my backside.

"I love you." I moved my eager mouth from his lips to his cheeks, showering him with kisses. "I love you so much."

"Yeah?" He chuckled. "I picked the right present for your birthday?"

"Yes."

Kiss.

"Yes."

Kiss.

Fisher laughed a little more. I couldn't stop kissing

him. It had been over a week since I'd seen him. And he exceeded my expectations in every way possible. I pulled off his beanie.

"Hey, that's my hat."

I slowly ran my hands through his hair and brought our noses together, closing my eyes for a brief second as I exhaled. "I just ... need to feel you everywhere I can," I whispered. "It's how I know you're mine. It's how I know it's *real*."

Fisher brought his chin up so our lips pressed together again, kissing like he kissed me the night in his bathroom. Then he pulled back, hands sliding up my back, gaze sweeping across my face. "If we waste too much time here, we won't get to the campsite in time to set up and do ... *things* before Rory and Rose get there."

I grinned, slipping his beanie back onto his head. "Things? What kind of things do you plan on doing to me?" A jolt of excitement shot through my veins.

"All the things."

I swallowed hard. "Well, why didn't you start with that?" I pushed him away, as if he were the one who forced me onto his lap, and I scrambled to get fastened into my seat. "Go. Don't wait for me. Go! Go! Go!"

He laughed, shaking his head while pulling back into traffic. I synced my phone with his truck so I could control the music. John Legend's "Wild."

I knew Fisher hadn't heard it because he wore a slight scowl on his face when the song started. But as the lyrics flowed through his speakers, his scowl turned into something resembling ... *lust*.

Next, I played Josie Dunne's "Good Boys."

Fisher shot me a smirk. Who were we kidding? He wasn't a good boy even if he didn't remember all the crude things he said to me. I remembered.

James Bay's "Wild Love."

ZAYN's "It's You."

HRVY's "Me Because of You."

Song after song.

I sang them all. All the lyrics. Serenading my lost fisherman.

By the time we pulled into the campsite, I was only a few verses into "Natural" by The Driver Era.

Fisher jumped out much faster than I did. He pulled the tents out of the back of his truck. "Do you know how to put up a tent?"

"I think so."

"Great. Get moving." He tossed one of the tents at my feet.

I laughed. "Okay."

He finished putting up the two bigger tents by the time I had the smaller tent assembled.

With my hands on my hips, I stared at the small tent and frowned. "This is mine, isn't it? Big tents for the couples. And birthday girl gets the smaller tent with nothing but a sleeping bag to keep me warm at a night."

Fisher didn't seem interested in my pity party for one. He unloaded a cooler, sleeping bags, his backpack and mine.

And I just stared at the small tent. Was he going to keep Angie warm? Probably. Why wouldn't he have?

"What the fuck are you doing?" He stepped in front of me, blocking the view of my tent and bending down so his face was level with mine.

"Just thinking about how things could have gone," I said in a monotone voice.

"*That's* what I figured. When are you going to start trusting me?"

I lifted a shoulder. "I don't know. I trust you ... just not your memory."

"Well, that makes two of us." He grabbed my hand and pulled me toward one of the bigger tents, squatting down to untie my shoes for me before unzipping the door. "But I remember what you felt like and what you tasted like. That's all the memory I need. So get your ass in the tent."

Still feeling too pouty for a nearly twenty-four-year-old, I stepped into the tent and moved to the middle of it where I could stand up. He already had two open sleeping bags and extra blankets and pillows spread over a big pad. Why was I so bothered by a small tent? Why was I so bothered by "what if" should Angie have come too? It was stupid. A big what-if did not matter at all. I guess we all had triggers. Who knew a tent would be mine?

I jumped when Fisher's hands landed on my hips, but he wasn't standing behind me; he was kneeling, his lips finding their way under my fleece jacket and my shirt to the skin along my lower back.

Tiny kisses.

Hands sliding to the button of my jeans.

Unbutton ... unzip ...

I closed my eyes, trying to shake off the negativity. Fisher peeled my jeans down my legs.

So ... very ... slowly.

As his hands took charge of my jeans, his teeth took care of my panties. And that did it ...

Fisher removing my panties with his teeth was the most erotic thing ever.

Really. *Ever!*

Angie? Angie who?

Little tent? What little tent?

I let Fisher undress me and do *all the things*. He kissed me in places only he could kiss me and make it feel sexy, make me feel beautiful and desired. When he touched me, it didn't feel like my body. It felt like an extension of him, and I just got to experience him giving me a thorough tour of it.

Every touch was a silent whisper, all the things he said to me by *showing me*.

This is how I make you moan.

This is how I steal your breath.

This is how I make you beg.

This is where you make me feel like a god.

Because I don't remember you, but I know you.

I. Know. You.

Nestled between two open sleeping bags, we made love, we made noise .... and we made new memories.

CHAPTER NINETEEN

"What did you say to make Angie stay?" I asked while piecing myself back together. There was no time left for cuddling. Rory and Rose would be there soon.

"I said that my therapist wanted to make sure I was setting aside time to think, time to be alone, but not just at work. Since she had a headache, I suggested this weekend be that time." He zipped his jeans, still on his back so that I could have the tallest part of the tent.

Yeah ... he loved me.

"I said you, Rory, and Rose would probably do some things without me. Or maybe not want to take the same hikes I take, so I'd have time to be alone with my thoughts. And she agreed." He sat up and pulled on his thermal waffle shirt and his beanie.

"And you did it for me?"

Staring at me in silence for several seconds, he nodded. "Yes. For you." Then a tiny smirk hijacked his serious expression. "I mean ... I might have done it a little bit for me too."

"Yeah?" I trapped my lower lip between my teeth.

"Don't give me that look." He shook his head and crawled toward the door to the tent. "It will lead to *things*, and we are out of time. They'll be here soon. And I need to get a fire made."

I giggled, following him out of the tent with my pillow, backpack, and a sleeping bag and extra blanket. After tossing everything into the smaller tent, I helped Fisher make a fire and set up the camping chairs around it. Shortly after we started roasting hot dogs, Rory and Rose arrived.

"I texted Angie to make sure you had everything and that we didn't need to stop on our way out of town, and she said she wasn't coming. Why didn't you tell us?" Rory asked Fisher.

I kept my gaze on the fire and the hot dog at the end of my stick.

"Spaced it, I guess. After I took Reese's stuff to the car and loaded the equipment, I didn't go back inside."

"Angie said she had a headache. I told her to take something for it and come with us. But she said no. I asked why, and she said to ask you?" Rory had Fisher in the hot seat.

I glanced up at Rose as she walked past me to put their bags in their tent.

Yes, Rose. We planned this. And while you were driving through the winding mountain roads, I was having the best sex EVER!

I wasn't sure if she got all that from my tiny smirk, but I knew she wasn't stupid. And I don't think she was mad either. Her silence said as much. Before our little heart-to-heart, she was the first to call me out on everything.

I mean ... even with my hat on, I must have had a terrible case of sex hair that stuck out in all directions beneath my hat. Fisher put me in every position imaginable, often grabbing my hair until I submitted by bending, spreading, or opening at his command. My cheeks filled with heat just thinking about it.

In return, Rose lifted a single brow and shook her head. She knew I was thinking about *things* that would have made Rory shudder, shattering her naive little world, at least when it came to me.

"It was kind of my therapist's suggestion," Fisher said to Rory.

"What does that mean?" Rory took a seat as Fisher handed her a stick and the package of hot dogs.

"It means, while I sort out my situation and consider all possibilities ... meaning the possibility of getting my memory back as well as the possibility of not getting my memory back ... it's important for me to have time to clear my head without the influence of outside opinions."

"So we're not allowed to give you our two cents this weekend?" Rory grinned, putting her hot dog over the fire.

"Correct. No Angie talk. No accident talk. No wedding talk. We can talk about you or Rose or the birthday girl." Fisher gave a resolute nod, clearly proud of his little speech.

"Okay. Let's talk about the birthday girl." Rory grinned at me from across the fire. "One of the other ladies who works at the salon has a brother that I think would be a perfect match for you."

My gaze shifted to Fisher for a split second, but he kept his attention on the fire, jaw a little tighter than usual.

Rose sat next to my mom, shooting me a tiny grin. Yeah, I needed to find a way to tell Rory everything.

"What makes him a perfect match for me?"

"He's a third-year resident in pediatrics." Rory's smile could have crossed the Grand Canyon. Really, she thought she hit the jackpot for me.

I chuckled. "That makes him perfect for me?"

"He loves traveling, reading, *puzzles*, animals, all sports, and he's a Christian. Oh ... did I mention he is incredibly hot? During his undergrad years, he did bodybuilding competitions. He's not like over-the-top bulky with massive, hard veins popping out of his skin everywhere. Just extremely fit."

But would he peel my panties off with his teeth while kneeling behind me?

"I'm sure he's great, but he's also a resident which means he lives at the hospital. And I'm starting my master's next year which means I won't have a lot of free time either."

"Reese, stop waiting to find love. The timing will never be perfect. You can't pass up opportunities.

When the right person comes along, you should grab him. Nothing would make me happier than you finding love. Like I found with Rose." She reached over and squeezed Rose's leg. "Like Angie and Fisher. I want the people who mean the most to me to have the best life has to offer."

"What if she just wants to work and finish school?" Fisher said. "What if she wants to live freely like I did at her age? What if she doesn't want one man? What if she wants a different guy every night because ..." He shrugged. "Why the fuck not? Why rush into anything?"

I wasn't sure who was in more shock, me or Rory. On the one hand, he was kind of sticking up for me. On the other hand, *did* he believe the things he said to her? Did Fisher think I was still too young? Was that our fate? Our reality?

When I was seventy, was he still going to play the age card?

"Reese, you might have a little arthritis, but wait until you're eighty and you can't get out of bed in the morning without a handful of pain meds consumed with a stiff drink."

Rose did a commendable job of taking Rory's hot dog from her and getting it on a bun with ketchup and mustard, acting like it wasn't the most uncomfortable conversation.

"Is that what you want, Reese? Just ... random hookups? Have you completely left your religious morals behind?"

"Well ..." I wasn't sure how to answer that. How to make the whole conversation end or shift the focus to someone besides me. "Maybe there's something between marriage and sleeping with three guys a week. Maybe I can just focus on my job and let my love life happen organically without being fixed up right now." I took a big bite of my hot dog. "But thanks," I mumbled over the food in my mouth.

Rory was just looking out for her daughter. And a few months earlier, I would have been really excited about Dr. Awesome.

After another hour of fire, beer, and marshmallows, Rory and Rose escaped into the woods to do their business.

As soon as I felt confident they were out of earshot, I kicked Fisher's leg.

"What was that for?" Fisher narrowed his eyes at me.

"You think I should be with a different guy every night?"

"I think I hate asking you to wait for me to get my life straightened out."

That wasn't the answer I wanted. "I'm going to catch up with them." With a flashlight in hand, I stomped my way into the woods.

"Reese ..."

I didn't respond.

By the time we returned to the campsite, Fisher had extinguished the fire and returned the chairs to the back of his truck.

"Fisher? You ready for bed?" Rory called.

"Yup," he called from inside his tent. "I went potty and brushed my teeth. Thanks, Mom."

Rory laughed. "Okay. Night."

I started to unzip the door to my tent.

"Night, sweetie. See you in the morning, birthday girl." Rory hugged me and so did Rose.

"Night." Turning on the lantern light for my tent, I paused on my knees just before zipping my door shut. My sleeping bag was laid out along with an extra blanket and my pillow at the top with a note on it.

I'll ask anyway ... wait for me.

Taking the note, I hugged it to my chest, then I changed into my thermal leggings and matching long-sleeved shirt before crawling into my sleeping bag and shutting off the light.

It took me forever to get to sleep, probably because Rory and Rose were up so late playing mancala. Then a little after two in the morning, I woke from the cold, tossing and turning, unable to get warm. After letting my teeth chatter for nearly another half hour, I wrapped the blanket around me, shoved my feet into my shoes, and tiptoed to Fisher's tent.

He didn't move when I unzipped his tent nor when I zipped it shut. Peaceful Fisher nestled into his sleeping bag, curled onto his side ... happy birthday to me, I thought.

Until ...

The most jarring sound blared out.

I nearly wet my pants.

Fisher shot up. "What are you doing?"

"Oh my god ... Fisher?" Rory called.

I dove out of his tent, but not before Rory and Rose were out of their tent with flashlights shining on both Fisher's tent (and me) and his truck with its alarm blaring.

It stopped when Fisher stepped out of his tent, holding the key fob.

"Jesus, was it a bear?" Rose asked.

"Reese, what on earth were you doing in Fisher's tent?" Rory didn't seem to care about the possibility of a bear setting off Fisher's truck alarm.

I tightened my grip on my blanket, still shivering, even more so since my body was in shock from the alarm sounding. "I ... I was f-freezing. And ..." I needed to think fast, but it was hard because I was so cold and feeling terrible for waking everyone, and it was technically my birthday, and yeah ... I started to cry.

"She just poked her head into my tent to ask for my truck keys because she was cold and wanted to sleep in the truck, but when she crawled next to me to wake me up, she hit the key fob and set off the alarm." Fisher for the save.

Rory eyed me, shining the stupid flashlight in my eyes. "Sweetie, your lips are blue. Oh my goodness."

I sniffled and quickly wiped my eyes, feeling so stupid and terrible for everything as Rory hugged me.

"Get in our tent. We'll keep you warm."

Shooting Fisher a quick glance, I followed them to their tent.

CHAPTER TWENTY

My attempts to get warm next to Fisher failed miserably. However, his attempt to come up with a good excuse for me being in his tent was a total success. Rory didn't think twice about it.

Then I, the lucky birthday girl, got to wake up nestled between Rose and Rory instead of nestled into the naked chest of Fisher. Twenty-four was already an unforgettable birthday.

"I have to pee," I whispered, peeling myself out of the middle.

"Okay. Happy birthday, sweetie," Rory mumbled. It was still early. "I'll go with you." She sounded half awake at best.

"I'm good. Really."

"Sure?"

"Yep."

"I'll get up and start breakfast soon."

"No rush. I'm not hungry yet." I escaped their tent with Rose still sleeping and Rory likely on the verge of going back to sleep.

After I got dressed, Fisher greeted me at the opening of my tent with a thermos of coffee, handing it to me.

"Th—" I started to thank him, but he held a finger to his lips.

Then he smiled while ducking his head to my ear. "Happy birthday."

With my free hand, I gripped his fleece jacket. He dragged his mouth along my cheek to my lips and kissed me, using his hands to hold my face.

I wasn't sure if the absence of Angie was my gift or the sex in his tent the previous night ... or the coffee? The kiss? Or was it the huge grin he gave me after the kiss as he nodded to the right and took my hand?

Fisher was the gift.

He took the thermos from my hand and set it by the tent before taking my hand again and pulling me toward the woods.

"Where are we going? I have to pee," I whispered.

"On a hike. We'll find you a rock to pee on."

I laughed as he led us out of earshot from Rory and Rose. "Why a rock?"

"It's the more eco-friendly place to pee. It dries. Nothing is harmed. And I know you're an eco-friendly girl." He glanced back and smirked.

The organic cotton tampons.

"What about Rory and Rose?" I asked.

"I don't know what tampons they use."

Rolling eyes, I shook my head. "I mean, what happens when they wake up and we're gone?"

"I'm going with alien abduction. Rose is a real conspiracy theorist. And I know she believes in aliens."

"She does?"

"Fuck. I don't know. I'm just making shit up to entertain you. Are you entertained?" He shot me a sideways glance as I caught up to him.

I didn't want to grin, but I did. He squeezed my hand as we made our way up the incline. I wondered if he had meaningless banter like that with Angie. And by meaningless, I meant it was everything. It meant we made each other laugh. It meant he enjoyed being with me as much as I enjoyed being with him.

And I wanted it to mean that we were meant to be together—that we *would* be together.

"I'm always entertained by you. And ... I still need to pee. We're passing a lot of good rocks."

"Sorry." He released my hand and pointed to a rock just off the trail. "That one should work."

I glanced in both directions. There didn't seem to be anyone close by us. "Okay." I maneuvered my way to the rock and turned toward the trail, hands starting to unbutton my jeans and pull down my zipper. "What are you doing?"

He stood on the trail, arms crossed over his chest. "What do you mean?"

"I mean, why are you standing there, staring at me?"

"I'm keeping a watch out for you."

"But you're staring at me. I'm not going to pee with you staring at me."

"I've seen you naked."

"And I've seen you naked, but I don't want to watch you pee."

"I didn't say I *wanted* to watch you. I said I'm keeping a watch out for you."

"Turn around."

"Just hurry up."

"I can't hurry up! I have to remove my boots and my jeans."

"Why are you removing your boots?"

"Because I have to remove my boots to take off my jeans."

"Why are you taking off your jeans?"

"Because I don't have a penis!"

And then ... a middle-aged gentleman made his way down the trail, hearing me loud and clear, a tiny grin pinned to his face as he glanced over at me with my jeans unbuttoned and unzipped.

"Morning." Fisher smiled and gave the guy a little chin nod.

I dropped my face in my hands. "Kill me now," I whispered.

"I'll turn around." He chuckled.

There was most likely an art to squat-peeing

without removing one's jeans, but I wasn't trained well in that technique. I knew my attempt would have led to my jeans being doused in urine. So yeah, I removed everything below my waist before angling myself to pee on the rock.

"Someone's coming. Hurry up."

"What?"

"I said someone's—"

"I heard you." I cut my pee off midstream.

"Then why did you say *what*?"

"I meant it like WHAT!"

"Like what the fuck?"

I rolled my eyes and scrambled for my panties, but they were caught in my jeans because one of the legs to my jeans was inside out.

"What are you doing?" He turned around, and I didn't have time to care.

"My jeans are messed-up!" I stabbed my arm in the inside-out leg.

Beanie.

Thermal shirt and fleece jacket.

And socks. That was it. All I had on.

I glanced to the right. The couple coming up the hill were getting closer.

"Fisher!"

That stupid smirk slid onto his face as he took his time trekking toward me. I wadded my jeans in front of me to cover as much as possible as Fisher stood in front of me, facing the trail and angling his body to keep me as hidden as possible when the couple passed us.

"Morning." He shared another friendly greeting as I pressed my face into his back to hide from ... life at the moment.

"Gah! I should have gone farther off this stupid trail. How embarrassing!" I fought with my jeans to free my panties. Then I dressed as fast as I could. When I glanced up while buttoning my jeans, Fisher had his lips trapped between his teeth while he adjusted himself. "Are you ... turned on?" I asked in disbelief, feeling a little irritated that he had the nerve to find my unfortunate situation sexy.

He lifted one shoulder. "I'm not ... *not* turned on."

"Screw the foliage or eco-friendly etiquette. I should have just peed in the brush." I stomped my way up the hill, keeping a good six feet ahead of him.

"Are you mad at me?" he asked.

"No."

"Sounds like you're mad at me. Is it because I have a penis and you don't? Because I didn't ask for a penis. It just came with my body."

"Stop it," I tried to say with a completely serious tone, but it was difficult.

"Stop what?" He took a few long strides to catch up to me.

"Stop talking."

"Why?"

"Because you're trying to make me laugh, and I don't want to laugh. I want to be mad."

"It's your birthday. You can't be mad on your birthday."

I stopped and faced him, hands balled at my sides. "I can be mad on my birthday because I froze my ass—my butt off last night! And when I tried to warm up, your stupid truck's alarm went off. And then I spent the rest of the night sleeping between my mom and Rose. And they both snore. And ..." I started to run out of steam.

"Were you going to ask me to warm you up?"

"No. I wasn't going to ask you. I was just going to wedge my cold body next to yours in your sleeping bag."

"Naked?" His eyebrows lifted.

"I ... I don't know." I shook my head, feeling irritated that he asked me that. And feeling irritated that he wouldn't stop grinning.

"That would have been the only way to really warm you up. Both of us naked. You're a nurse. You should know that."

I started to speak, but I had no great reply to his gibberish.

His head cocked to the side. "You were ... you were going to get into my sleeping bag naked. You were going to get warm and then try to get some. Am I right? A little early birthday delight."

It hurt the muscles in my lips too much to not smile. I had to grin. I had to giggle.

Fisher refused to let me be anything but happy. And wasn't that the whole purpose in life? To find one's happy place and stay there as long as possible? He was mine.

Bliss.

Smiles.

Giggles.

"There she is." His already ginormous grin managed to swell a little more. He tugged my beanie down a fraction of an inch, a playful, teasing gesture.

"Can I ask you something?" My smile faded a little.

"Of course."

"What do you fear most? Is it your memory returning and you suddenly knowing what you felt for her and why you felt it? Is it disappointing your family if you don't marry her? Is it making the wrong decision?"

He tucked his hands into my back pockets and kissed my forehead. "It's losing you while I attempt to do the right thing."

"What is the right thing?"

"That's..." he shook his head slowly as creases formed along his brow "...just it. I'm not sure. I feel like a nearly thirty-year friendship deserves something ... even if it's just a little more time. And while I don't remember loving Angie, I'm not immune to her feelings now. I'm not immune to my family's feelings either. And they still have this great hope that I will get my memory back. And this huge part of me, the part that loves you, doesn't care to remember the past. But this other part feels like I can't end this planned future without remembering my past."

"And what if you never remember? I mean ... I'm

here. I'm here for you. And my heart is firm on this ... I'm in it for as long as I'm *in* it. But my brain will eventually try to override my heart in an effort for self-preservation. You haven't canceled your wedding. If you don't remember by then ... then what? You marry her?"

"No. I don't marry her. I ... I ..."

He didn't know. How could he?

"I postpone it."

"You postpone it?" My jaw dropped. "You postpone something you want to happen, just at a later date."

"What do you want me to say? What would *you* want me to do if you were in Angie's shoes?"

"I'd want you to love me. Love me now. Love me without any yesterdays. And if you couldn't love me like that, then I'd want you to let me go."

He nodded slowly. "Then I'll let her go."

I couldn't believe he said it. He said it without hesitation. He said it with such absolution it made my heart pause for a second.

So why ... why did my paused heart hurt so much in that moment? Was I asking too much? It hadn't been that long since his accident. We fell in love so quickly. And maybe that did mean everything. But did I say what I said because it was really how I would have felt in Angie's shoes? Or was it easy to say that because I already had his love?

Why did it have to be so hard? So messy?

Closing my eyes, I shook my head. "Give it ...

202

give it more time." I opened my eyes. "But draw a line. Like two months, six months, a year, whatever. Just draw a line so when we get there, we know it's over. Whatever *over* means at that time. Then let yourself *live*. Because you are alive with or without the past."

"January first."

"January first," I repeated. Just over two months away.

"If it doesn't come back by then, I move forward without trying to look back anymore. I let her go. I let my family know I can't marry someone I don't love."

"I can do January first." I nodded several times. After five years and a handful of months without Fisher, I could survive two more months if it meant we would be together. "So ... I'll just keep my distance while you do your part to remember things and keep your family happy for as long as possible."

His eyes narrowed. "Keep your distance? It's going to be hard for you to keep your distance with my dick inside of you at every possible chance."

There's my crude naked fisherman. I've missed you.

I started walking again, my face revisiting its eighteen-year-old version of itself—flushed cheeks and neck. "And when do you think your next possible chance might be?"

"Can't say." He took my hand again.

"Why not?"

"Because it's your birthday. And birthdays are for surprises."

"So you're going to surprise me with your dick?" I giggled.

"You'll never see it coming."

"Well, I won't if it's inside of me."

He laughed.

I laughed.

And we spent the next hour hiking the trail that circled back around to the campsite. A few yards before the clearing, he stopped and pushed me off the trail, my back hitting a tree trunk.

He kissed me with a hunger that I felt in my bones. And as quickly as he pulled me off the trail and attacked my mouth, he ended the kiss and returned without me.

He nodded toward the clearing up ahead. "Coming?"

I peeled my back off the tree and fixed my beanie and straightened my jacket. "What was that?"

"What was what?" Fisher tucked his hands innocently in the pockets of his jacket.

"See ... told you they didn't get eaten by a bear," Rose said to Rory as we made it back to the tents.

Rory rolled her eyes. "I didn't think that."

"You said it." Rose eyed Rory flipping pancakes on the grill.

"Well, I was just kidding ... sort of. Why didn't you wake us up to go with you?" Rory asked.

"I thought I'd take the kiddo for a walk while you two had a little alone time." Fisher gave them a suggestive grin. "Since she crashed your night with the truck alarm, blue lips, and chattering teeth."

Rory and Rose laughed, but then they shared a look that said they *did* take advantage of their alone time. Which ... made me think of the time I saw them in the shower. Yeah, that image was eternally burned into my brain.

"Take the kiddo for a walk?" I scowled at Fisher. "You make me sound like a five-year-old ... or a dog."

"If the leash fits." He grabbed a bottle of orange juice out of the cooler.

I nudged the back of his knee, making his leg bend unexpectedly, throwing him a little off balance as he shut the cooler.

"Watch it." He gave me a narrowed-eyed expression.

"Watch what, old man?"

"Listen to you two ... it's just like old times. Fisher, you and Reese used to fight and banter all the time, just like two siblings," Rory said, handing me a plate of pancakes.

I took a seat in one of the camping chairs, and Rose poured syrup onto my stack of pancakes, pressing her lips together for a second before murmuring, "Siblings my ass," so only I could hear her.

I winked at her, one of those cocky Fisher-style winks.

"No mancala for you two tonight," I said to my mom and Rose. "You're too loud. Too competitive."

"Sorry." Rory cringed. "Did we keep you up?"

I held up my thumb and forefinger an inch apart. "A wee bit."

"Mancala? I love that game," Fisher said. "We should play it tonight."

"It's only a two-person game," Rory said, handing Fisher his plate of pancakes.

"Well, you two played it last night, so I'll play it with the birthday girl tonight." Fisher took a bite of his pancakes and grinned at me. "Do you want to play with me tonight, Reese?"

My chewing slowed. He said that. Yes, he sure did. Rory paid no attention to his comment. But Rose choked on a bite of her pancake.

"You okay, babe?" Rory asked her.

Rose patted her chest several times and nodded. "F-fine."

After swallowing my bite, I smirked at Rose while answering Fisher. "That sounds fun. I'd love to play with you tonight."

Rose's face looked like a ripe red apple, and there was nothing she could do to stop us. And Fisher had no idea she knew. He thought our innuendos were solely between the two of us.

"I'm not going to go easy on you. I'm pretty competitive. I like to be on top at the end."

Again, Rose coughed and Rory handed her a bottled water. "Drink. And chew your food better." Rory shifted her attention to Fisher. "Don't get too cocky and underestimate Reese. She has a competitive streak too. I can see her winning ... being on top instead of you. So no pouting tomorrow."

By that point, Rose had her head bowed, fingers pinching the bridge of her nose. I felt certain she was silently chanting, "Make them stop!"

But all that mattered to me was Fisher and I were going to play.

CHAPTER TWENTY-ONE

Before I left Texas to reunite with Rory, I knew three things.

One: I wasn't ever going to drink or do drugs.

Two: No sex before marriage.

Three: I would think about God first in all my decisions.

At twenty-four, I knew nothing.

After another group hike, lunch, and taking a million pictures, we started a fire for dinner, and then we drank too much. The conversation took a turn because of me. Someone should have cut me off earlier.

"Have you ever told Fisher how he loved Angie?" I asked, picking at the label to my beer bottle. I didn't even like beer that much—that was how much I'd had to drink.

"What?" Rory said.

"I mean ... everyone says how much he loved her. Maybe if someone told him why they thought that ...

like … what specifically did he do to make you think he loved her? Then he might remember."

I had no idea alcohol could spark a self-destructive case of jealousy. Yet there I was … intoxicated and jealous.

Rory glanced over at Rose. "He sent her flowers."

Rose nodded. "They were cuddly …" She laughed, buzzed like the rest of us. "Is cuddly a word?" Rose laughed more.

"He took her to lunch a lot," Rory added.

"Sometimes you took her for rides on your motorcycle." Rose shifted her attention to Fisher.

I glanced over at him.

He nursed his beer, gaze on the fire as if he wasn't hearing any of the conversation.

"The four of us spent so many nights in the screened-in porch just talking about life. Fisher said he wanted two kids. Angie wanted four. They compromised on three." Rory grinned at Fisher.

Still … he showed no response other than to narrow his eyes a bit as if he was trying to make sense of what they were saying about him.

Did it still feel like someone else's life? A biography that wasn't his?

"And after Angie's mom died, Fisher just … did everything. He helped take care of her mom's property. He practically planned the funeral. Moved Angie into his house. Cooked for her for … weeks while she grieved her mom. I wish you could remember, Fisher. I really do." Rory frowned.

Fisher stood. "I'm going to bed." He didn't look at me or anyone as he tossed his bottle into a bin in the back of his truck before wandering into the woods to pee.

Rose shook her head. "I don't think we jogged his memory. I think he's miserable."

Rory stood and stretched. "Miserable? That's a strong word."

"It's not. It's the right word, trust me." Rose started to collapse the chairs.

I helped her load them into the truck.

"You two still going to play mancala?" Rory handed me the game. "It's late." She laughed. "And we've all had too much to drink. But whatever ..." She hugged me. "Happy birthday, sweetie."

"Thanks," I murmured.

"It's been a good day. Love you, birthday girl." Rose hugged me and kissed my cheek. Then she whispered in my ear, "He's not in a good mood. Let him be tonight."

I didn't say anything. I just gave a single nod to let her know I heard her.

After they found a spot to pee and retired to their tent, I planted my ass on the ground by the fire. When Fisher returned, he sat next to me, both of us with our knees bent and our arms resting on them.

"If it's January ..." I whispered. "Then we wait for January. I can't ..." I shook my head slowly. "Do this ..."

I couldn't sneak around with another woman's

fiancé any longer. If the alcohol imparted a sense of jealousy, then sobering up imparted a sense of regret.

"I know," he whispered back. "I'm going to fix this."

"Fix this?" I had trouble keeping my voice lowered. "How are you going to do that?"

"Do you trust me?"

I grunted a laugh. How many times had he questioned my trust in him? And where had it gotten me?

"I told you. I trust you. I just don't trust your—"

"Yeah, yeah ... my memory. Fuck my memory." He stood. "Come on." He held out his hand.

I took it. "I can't do anything with you." My inflamed conscience showed up to be the party pooper at my birthday party.

"We can play mancala."

My head canted as I eyed him.

"For real. Mancala." He tugged my hand.

We sat across from each other in his tent and played mancala for almost two hours, and it was fun. Everything with Fisher was fun and happy. He was bliss. And I couldn't imagine my life without bliss.

"I'm going to ..." I motioned toward the tent door. "Go to bed now."

"You'll be cold."

"I know."

"You could sleep with me." He set the game aside.

"I said I'm not—"

"Sleep. Just sleep."

"What about Rory and—"

"I'll kick you out before they wake in the morning."

I shook my head. "I don't think it's a good idea."

"Can't control yourself?"

"Full. Of. Yourself."

His grin faded, gaze averting to the space between us. Confusion replaced all amusement. "Full of yourself," he whispered before lifting his gaze to meet mine. "You've said that before. At my office. You ..." He shook his head. "You were mad at me. Do you remember?"

It took me a few seconds to realize what was happening. "Do *you* remember that?"

"Yes. No. I don't know. It's like déjà vu. You said that and it was too familiar, like we've played this out before, but not here."

I wasn't entirely sure when I said that to him. It was over five years earlier. Those were words I could have used on multiple occasions.

"I don't know. What else did I say?"

Fisher continued to shake his head. "I ... I don't know. But if it's a memory ..."

I nodded. "Then you might be getting your memory back or at least your brain is trying to make some connections again."

"Maybe." He nodded slowly, confusion still veiling his face.

Was it time to tell him about us? He had fallen in love with me, without those memories, without telling him about us.

He reclined onto his pillow. "So weird ... I see you

with your hands on your hips. You're angry. Do you remember being angry with me?"

I chuckled. "Sorry. I was mad at you on lots of occasions. You're not narrowing it down much."

"Maybe it's the beer." He sighed, closing his eyes.

"Maybe." I shut off the lantern light and curled up next to him, covering us with the top of his sleeping bag and a fleece blanket.

"You're staying?" he mumbled. So much exhaustion in his voice.

"I'm staying." I hugged his body and kissed his neck.

CHAPTER TWENTY-TWO

THE NIGHT in the tent was the beginning of what felt like the end, even if I wasn't sure what the end really meant for me. For us.

I immersed myself in work and read absolutely everything Holly gave me to read.

Halloween.

Early November snow.

And no Fisher.

Was I avoiding him? Yes.

Did he know why? Yes.

However, it was nearly impossible to avoid him until January, as I found out three weeks after my birthday. On my way home from a birth around noon on a Saturday, I stopped for gas. As I waited for it to get filled up, Fisher's work truck pulled in the opposite side of the pump.

My heart crashed against my chest. *He's here!* And my conscience said to chill out. Stay calm. No big deal.

A crazy big grin stretched across his face as he climbed out of his truck in jeans, work boots, and a dirty hoodie. "Hey."

My heart won. I matched his grin, maybe even upped it a notch. "Hey."

"On your way to work or heading home?" he asked, leaning against the beam next to the pump.

"Home. See the bags under my eyes?"

"Did you help bring a tiny human into the world last night?"

"Seven this morning. Little boy. Grant. Eight pounds exactly. How about you? Working today?"

"Just finished installing shelves in a pantry."

I returned the nozzle to the pump and took my receipt. "Well, I'm going home to crash for a few hours."

"Reese ..." He studied me for a few seconds. "We're not strangers. And I've been biding my time for three weeks. Sorting these memories as they come back. But I miss you. And I'm not going to let you get in your car and just leave with a friendly smile and tiny wave."

"What memories?" Rory and Rose hadn't said anything.

"Come here."

I shook my head. "What memories?"

"Come. Here." He wet his lips.

I tried not to look at his lips, but they were right there, full and recently touched by his tongue. I took a few steps closer.

He pushed off the beam and slid his hand through my hair. "I love you today."

"Fisher ..."

He kissed me. And I couldn't stop him because I didn't want to stop him. His proximity fed my soul. His lips awakened my heart with possibilities.

Then it ended.

It was just a kiss. We had control.

Until he kissed me again.

Harder. Longer.

His hands slid to my butt, and he moaned, gripping me hard. "Fuck ..." He pulled his mouth away from mine and buried his face in my neck. "Follow me to my house. Please just ..." His desperation fueled my need.

I was so tired, and it weakened my resolve because there was nothing I wanted more than to go home with Fisher. Let him make me feel *good*. And fall asleep in his arms.

As another car pulled in behind my car, I broke away from Fisher's hold and cleared my throat. "What memories? You said your memories came back."

He sighed, adjusting himself. "I remembered Angie. Well, one memory of her. Of us."

"What memory?"

"A party at her parents' house. Her twenty-first birthday."

"What triggered that?"

He glanced over my shoulder, off into the distance. "I'm not sure."

"Where were you when you remembered it?"

His lips twisted as he continued to stare off into … the past? "She came over last week for dinner. And we were talking about her cousin's wedding. And she said her cousin just found out she's pregnant."

I nodded slowly. "Was her cousin at Angie's birthday party?"

"No."

"Hmm. That's weird. But it's a memory. That's good right?"

Fisher seemed anything but feeling *good* about his recent recalled memory. "I'll let you get home to sleep."

He went from insatiable to listless in a matter of minutes.

"Are you okay?"

He returned a single nod, more of a tiny drop of his chin. Then he stared at me for a long moment before a sad smile tugged at his lips. "I miss you."

"I miss you too."

"Bye."

That was it. A sad goodbye.

That sad goodbye ate at me as I drove home. Instead of pulling into the driveway, I kept going and made my way to Fisher's house, arriving just as he pulled into his driveway.

I walked across the street as he hopped out of his truck. "What aren't you telling me about your memories?"

"What do you mean?" He didn't stop to address me face-to-face. He kept walking into his garage.

I stopped right behind him as he bent over to

unlace his work boots. Then I followed him into his house.

"You know what I mean. When you told me about the party memory, you looked frightened or maybe in complete shock. Why? Did that memory of her bring back feelings for her?"

He grabbed a beer from the fridge and opened it. After a long swig, he blew out a slow breath. "At her party, Angie pulled me aside and told me she was pregnant."

Did *not* see that coming. Neither did my delicate heart.

"I couldn't remember what happened after that. Angie said she miscarried two weeks later. Then ... I could. That's all she had to say, and I remembered what happened."

"What happened?" I whispered past the lump in my throat.

"We were supposed to meet for dinner after I finished working. But she showed up at the apartment I was living in at the time, and she was in tears. She'd miscarried. But ..." He glanced up at me. "I had a ring. I was going to propose to her that night."

"But you didn't."

He shook his head and took another pull of beer.

"Why?"

"Because I didn't want to get married. Not yet. I was doing it because it seemed like the right thing to do."

"So she never knew?"

"I don't think so."

"Did you tell her? When your memory came back, did you tell her about the ring?"

"No," he whispered.

Then it hit me. What he said to me five years earlier when I freaked out at the possibility of being pregnant.

"What if ..." I cleared my throat. *"Hypothetically, what if I were pregnant."*

"No." He grunted. *"No. We are not doing this. If you come back to me in a few weeks with a positive test, we'll have this conversation. But I'm not having it now."*

"Why?"

"Because I'm not."

"I think it's irresponsible to not at least have a plan."

Fisher was hard and standoffish. That was why. The last thing he wanted was another pregnancy scare when he wasn't ready to be a father or get married.

But things changed ...

Rory and Reese said as much when they said Angie and Fisher had discussed kids. Three kids.

"It's interesting that Angie told you everything about your past together, but not this."

His head eased side to side. "I think it was too tragic for her. She got pretty emotional when I told her about my memory."

After a long moment, I crossed the kitchen and wrapped my arms around him, resting my cheek against his chest so I could hear his heart. I never thought about Fisher's memories coming back in tiny pieces. And I didn't think about those tiny pieces cutting so deeply.

"I invited her over for dinner that night to tell her we needed to cancel the wedding."

My gaze shot up to his as I released him. "What? Are you ... are you serious?"

He frowned. "Then the memory came back. Then she started crying. And I couldn't add more to her that night. So it turned into a total disaster because she had me backed into a corner. And while her eyes were still puffy, she asked me to go to her cousin's wedding with her."

I took another step backward.

"And she started crying again thinking about how her mom wouldn't be there. So I told her I'd go with her."

"Okay ..." I drew out the word with caution. "So you go to a wedding with her. No big deal."

"It's in Costa Rica."

Not okay. That was *not* okay.

"We'll be gone for four days. It will be fine. Maybe it will be a good chance for me to really talk with her, express my feelings or lack thereof for her."

It sounded logical coming from him. He presented it like it really wasn't a big deal. But it felt like my bachelor was taking another woman to the fantasy suite instead of me. And they were just going to "talk."

"Tell me you're okay with this."

I backed up another few steps and shook my head. "I'm just really tired. I don't have the mental or emotional capacity to feel anything right now."

"Reese ..." He set his beer bottle on the counter and followed me to the back door.

"I'm going to crash. I'm over twenty-four hours with no sleep."

"Then crash here."

"It's not a good idea." I shoved my feet into my shoes and opened the door.

Fisher pressed his hand above my head to the door and shut it on me. "It's the *best* idea I've ever had."

I turned and shoved his chest.

He lifted an eyebrow and smirked. "You can shove me as much as you want, but it still doesn't change what I want."

I coughed a laugh. "What you want? What *you* want? What about what I—"

In a blink he was all over me.

Lips.

Tongue.

Hands.

A fisherman tornado.

My jacket ... his hoodie ... gone.

Three steps toward the hallway ... shirts discarded.

Several more steps ... the tie to my scrubs yanked undone while I made haste with the button and zipper to his jeans.

Several feet from the bedroom door, he pushed my back to the wall and kissed down my neck while shoving the straps of my bra down my arms, exposing my breasts.

"Fisher ..." My fingers dove into his hair as he licked, sucked, and bit my nipples.

"Hello. Hello. Hello ..."

Rory.

We froze, but there was no time to run or hide. No time to gather the trail of clothes from the door to our exact spot, which happened to be in plain sight of Rory and her unnaturally wide-eyed expression, hand cupped over her mouth.

I closed my eyes and cringed.

Fisher stood tall and buttoned and zipped his jeans before taking my shoulders and guiding me toward the bedroom and shutting me inside.

I fixed my bra and pressed my ear to the door, but it was hard to hear past my rapid breathing.

"Rory ... ever heard of knocking?"

"What in GOD'S NAME is going on?"

I flinched. I couldn't remember a time in my entire life when I heard my mom's voice sound that angry.

"I love her."

Dead. Fisher just slayed me. Lassoed my heart. And locked it up in his castle where it will take an army or an act of God to steal it from him.

"That is not an answer! *That* is my daughter. What the fuck are you doing with my daughter? She is *ten* years younger than you ... and YOU ARE ENGAGED!"

There was an uncomfortable silence for a few seconds.

Then Fisher spoke. Calm. Controlled. Matter-of-fact.

"I love her."

Tears burned my eyes, and I couldn't take it any longer. I opened the door.

"Stay in the bedroom, Reese," Fisher said with his back to me as Rory stared me down.

My hero. Protecting me. *Loving me ...*

Tying my scrub pants, I slowly shuffled my feet down the hallway.

Rory's jaw clenched, readying for whatever she might have thought I was about to say.

Plead my case?

Apologize?

Beg for forgiveness?

None of the above. I came out of the bedroom for one reason and one reason only. Turning to face Fisher, I blinked and the tears fell in heavy streams as I lifted onto my toes, pressed my palms to his face, and whispered, "I love you, my lost fisherman," before kissing him.

Soft and slow.

No regard for Rory and her audible gasp.

When the kiss ended, he smiled and wiped my cheeks, looking at me so adoringly like Rory wasn't there. Like we were in our bubble.

Then I turned and gathered my shirt and jacket, slipping them on as I made my way to the garage door where I shoved my feet back into my shoes. "Let's go home, Mom."

Mom.

I rarely, if ever, called her that, but that day I was leaving Fisher's house with a full heart, going home to tell my mom everything.

It was one thing to hear someone tell you they love you. It was something entirely different, infinitely more special to hear them say the words to someone else like it was a three-word explanation for their existence.

I love her.

I was the luckiest *her* in the world.

CHAPTER TWENTY-THREE

I MADE it home a few minutes before Rory. She might have stayed to give Fisher a few more pieces of her mind.

"Hey, you look exhausted," Rose said as she glanced up from her computer at the kitchen table. Then she narrowed her eyes. "Have you been crying?"

I nodded, setting my bag on the floor by the hallway. "Rory will be here any minute. I need to talk with her alone. Can you work at a cafe or the library for a while?"

Rose kept her concerned expression for a few seconds before nodding. "Is it time?"

Feeling another round of tears, I simply nodded. "Past time," I managed to eke out.

"She knows."

I nodded.

Rose stood and closed her computer. "Oh boy ... it's going to be a rough weekend." She slipped her computer in her messenger bag and hiked it onto her shoulder just as Rory entered the house.

They made eye contact. And it was like Rose coffered her part with one look.

Rory slowly shook her head and grimaced. "Un-fucking-believable."

Rose stopped before going out the back door. "Remember forbidden love?" She leaned over to kiss Rory's cheek, but Rory pulled away.

She wouldn't make eye contact with Rose, let alone acknowledge her comment. Rose nodded several times in acceptance as she bowed her head and headed out the door, gently closing it behind her.

"What have you done?" Rory whispered.

"I moved to Colorado to reunite with my mother after she got out of prison. Then she left me for a month. She left me alone in a new state, in a house with a stranger, and with complete trust in said stranger to watch out for me. And I did what you asked me to do. I trusted him. And then I fell in love with him."

Rory slowly lifted her gaze, a map of confusion distorting her pretty face. "W-when ..." It was like I'd knocked the air out of her lungs for a second time. "When did this start? Did this start *then*? Has this been going on for *years*?" She started to get worked up again.

"We haven't been together for *years*. So, no. It hasn't been going on for years. It wasn't the right time for us then. So I left. I pursued my dreams. And I let him go. I never imagined coming back here to him this way. Him not remembering me, not remembering us. And I never imagined the side note to the tragedy would be him having a fiancée who he also doesn't remember."

"Jesus ... Reese ... were you ... were the two of you ..."

I shook my head. "Don't. Don't ask that. The answer isn't so black and white. And the truth that you don't want to hear is that whatever we did, we did as two consenting adults. He didn't take advantage of me."

She wiped her eyes before her tears fell. "Did he h-hurt you?"

I gave her a sad smile. "No. Well, just my heart. He hurt my heart, but only because I was too young and stupid to guard it a little better."

"When did you tell him?" She made her way to the kitchen table and eased into a chair as I remained propped up against the wall by the fridge.

"Tell him what?"

"Well, he didn't remember you. So when did you tell him about the two of you? About *whatever* went on between the two of you five years ago."

On a tiny head shake, I murmured, "I haven't told him."

Rory squinted. "You haven't told him anything?"

I shrugged. "I told him that I lived with you in his basement for a while. I told him I worked for him. I told him we were friends. When you were in California, we went to one of Arnie's concerts. I met up with a friend from school and her boyfriend. Fisher went and took Angie because she was in town and his family insisted he take her to the concert. A triple date of sorts."

"Who was your date?"

"Arnie."

"Were you and Arnie also—"

"No." I chuckled. "It was a front because Fisher and I couldn't tell anyone because we knew nobody would understand or approve, least of all you."

Rory started to say something, then she clamped her mouth shut. She knew I was right. She threatened something along the lines of castration if Fisher so much as looked at me the wrong way.

"And Rose?"

"She was in the wrong place at the wrong time, depending on how you look at it. She walked in and saw Fisher and I *close*. Maybe kissing. I honestly don't remember. She gave me a huge lecture and told me to end it. And we agreed it would be best not to tell you ... especially if there was no longer anything to tell. Unfortunately, she's been caught in the middle yet again. And for that, I truly am sorry. I don't want what's happened between Fisher and me to affect your relationship."

Rory ran her hands through her hair and blew out a long breath. "Reese ... Fisher fell back in love with Angie during those five years you were gone. And they got engaged. Yes, he had an accident and has temporarily lost his memories of her, but that doesn't mean he won't get them back. And when he remembers her, I don't know what it will mean for you."

It was like she hadn't just heard Fisher profess his love for me.

I love her.

He didn't say, "I love her too," like he loved Angie and me equally. No, he loved me.

But he was going to Costa Rica with Angie.

"He does remember her. He remembers her twenty-first birthday party. He remembers her telling him she was pregnant."

Rory's head jerked backward.

"And he remembers buying a ring to propose to her two weeks later. But she miscarried the baby. And he didn't propose because he didn't really want to marry her."

And he didn't want to have a baby with me and marry me five years ago either.

My mind did a spectacular job of building my hopes up ... Fisher Mann, King of my Heart. Then it just as quickly tossed a grenade of doubt on everything.

Poof! Gone.

And once again, I was left in a rubble of confusion.

"He told you that?"

I nodded.

"And Angie knows he remembered that?"

Another nod.

"That must have dug up some painful memories for her as well."

Yes, Angie had been dealt a few bad hands in her

life. She lost a baby and lost her parents. Her fiancé was in an accident and couldn't remember her. Did that have to mean that she deserved Fisher more than I did?

"And the night he remembered that, Angie was having dinner with him, and he was going to tell her that the wedding's off."

Rory frowned. "He didn't ..."

I rolled my eyes. "No. He didn't because she was too emotional. But he was going to, which means he will when the time is right."

"Rose said Fisher and Angie are going to her cousin's wedding in Costa Rica."

Averting my gaze for a few seconds, I nodded. "He told me that too."

"And you're okay with the guy you supposedly love going to Costa Rica for a week with the woman he agreed to marry? You realize they'll be staying at a hotel in the same room, probably with one bed, right?"

"I don't know what the sleeping arrangements will be, but I trust Fisher."

She didn't have to tell me that. I hadn't let my brain go there yet. Now it was *there*.

He could sleep in the same bed as her without having sex. They'd done it before, except for that one time they did have sex.

She bounced out the door that day, skipping on clouds and sliding down rainbows. And he kissed her back. It wasn't a one-sided peck. He kissed her back.

Because he enjoyed the kiss.

Because he probably enjoyed the sex.

Of course he enjoyed the sex! It was sex!

My mind lurched into action, a malfunctioning amusement park ride, flinging riders into the air plummeting to their deaths.

"If you trust Fisher, why is he still engaged to Angie? Is he stringing her along? Stringing you along? Having his cake and eating it too?"

"I think if anyone is to blame for this situation, it's me and Angie. We know the details, even if we've chosen to not share all of them with him. We know he essentially met us for—in his mind—the first time just months ago. So for either one of us to play the victim here, it's laughable. You and I cringe at what I'm doing because we see the big picture. I'm involved with an engaged man who's been 'in love' with his fiancée for nearly thirty years. That sounds terrible. And if or when Angie finds out, she'll play the devastated fiancée role, and everyone will feel sorry for her.

"But in Fisher's mind, it's not like that. In his mind, he met us both a few months ago, and he fell in love with me. And everyone told him he was in love with Angie. It would be like me grabbing some stranger off the street, bringing them here, and telling you that you love them ... now act accordingly. Is that all it takes? Would you just embrace that stranger? Love them? What if I said you love this person more than Rose? Would you fall in line? Would you trust me and just ... *love* this stranger? Commit to forever with this stranger because I said, 'Trust me. You love her.' No. You wouldn't because it sounds utterly preposterous because it *is* utterly preposterous! And the fact that Fisher has fallen in love with me *twice,* all on his own, without any recollection of our past or anyone telling him he should love me ... *that* means something. No—" I shook my head. "That means everything."

Rory nodded several times, lines of deep thought trenched into her forehead. "It's a good speech, Reese. Very persuasive. But it doesn't change reality. Fisher isn't with you. To ninety-nine percent of the world, he's with Angie. Engaged to Angie. Childhood sweethearts who are destined to be together. And he hasn't done anything to change that. Why is that? Is it because he hasn't really made his decision?"

"No. It's because he does remember his family. He does remember his friends Rory and Rose. And that *does* mean something to him. It means he trusts all of you. So when you tell him how much he loved Angie, it makes him question himself. It makes him fearful of what might come from his memories if he does get them back. And he's not a monster, despite what you might think now. Even if he doesn't remember his life with Angie, he accepts that it happened and that it meant a lot to a lot of people, maybe even him. Clearly him too since he agreed to marry her. So it's not about *stringing* anyone along. He's not having his cake and eating it too.

"This isn't some party or game for him. He's simply in love with me. He wants to be with me because that's what his heart tells him. But his brain won't let him be anything but beholden to his past until he gets his memory back or at least enough of his memories to properly explain to Angie and everyone else why he doesn't love her the way he loves me. And it's cruel for anyone to judge him for living in real time, for having feelings in real time.

"He could have been injured worse. He could have been confined to a wheelchair for the rest of his life, and nobody would have told him to just get his ass up out of the chair and pretend to walk simply because he used to be able to do it. It would make all of us feel better if he would just be the exact same person he used to be. We have to accept that his mind and his heart may never feel or love the same way as before the accident."

There. I drew my own sword and fought for Fisher the way he did for me. Only I had to use way more than three words, and I still wasn't sure Rory was ready to surrender.

"Why doesn't he tell Angie?"

"Because she will be devastated. He's getting pieces of his memory back. And if I were to take a guess, I think he wants to end it with her, having some true recollection of how he felt about her. I think he needs to feel a little emotional pain too." My voice broke and tears burned my eyes. *I* was living in real time, not only convincing Rory of everything, but also convincing myself. "I'd imagine it's like losing someone and having no body, not true proof of death, but having a funeral anyway. There's not the same kind of closure.

I think Fisher doesn't merely want to end things; I think he wants closure."

"And if he doesn't get it? If he doesn't get his memory back ... his closure ... what's he going to do?"

I shrugged. "He's giving it until the end of the year. Six more weeks. And if he still doesn't have enough memories to remember why he fell in love with her..." I cringed because the analogy sounded terrible, but I'd already put it out there "...then he'll bury the empty casket."

That made Rory flinch. It started out as such a great analogy, but it ended rather morbidly.

CHAPTER TWENTY-FOUR

RORY WASN'T HAPPY. Not with me. Not with Fisher. Not with Rose.

It surprised me, and I think Rose too, that Rory struggled to accept the situation. After all, she went to prison and lost her marriage (and her daughter for five years) because she fell in love and that love caused a lot of damage. Rose speculated it wasn't what had happened as much as Rory felt like everyone knew but her. Everyone that mattered.

The following weekend, I got a phone call while cleaning the bathroom.

"Hello?"

"Hey. Just found your name in my contacts. Who knew I had your number?"

I grinned, flipping the toilet seat down and taking a seat. "Hi. Who knew?" I hadn't seen or talked to Fisher since Rory caught us in the hallway. We were trying to do things right, if there was such a thing as right. And it was clear that being together always led to situations like me half naked and tossing all intentions for human decency aside. All morals. Everything to make room for Fisher and only Fisher.

"Whatcha doing?"

"Cleaning the bathroom. What are you doing?"

"Thinking you should let me take you to lunch."

Biting my lip to hide my grin as if he could see me, I told my eager heart to chill. "I have to help clean the house. My grandparents are coming for Thanksgiving this week."

"Rory's parents?"

"Yeah. My dad's parents would not be caught dead having Thanksgiving here."

"Why?"

"Because their ex-daughter-in-law not only went to prison for growing marijuana, she also kissed a girl."

"And she liked it."

I giggled. "She did."

"Well, you need to eat. Give me an hour."

"I shouldn't."

"Fifty-nine minutes and not a second past."

I laughed. "Rory *just* started talking to me and Rose again. Not more than a few words, but it's something. I think lunch with you would take me back ten steps with her."

"Then don't tell her. Say you're running to Target for something."

It was a dumb idea. I needed to act a little more

grown-up. I needed to actually *be* a little more grown-up.

"Fine." There was always tomorrow to be grown-up.

"Where do you want to meet?"

"McDonald's on the corner."

"Okay. Ten minutes?"

I nodded before answering, my grin ready to break my face. "Ten minutes." I quickly combed my hair, brushed my teeth, and reapplied deodorant. My ripped jeans and tee would just have to be good enough. "I need a couple things from Target. Do you need anything?" I yelled down the stairs.

"We're good," Rose replied.

They'd been downstairs for quite a while. I had a feeling they were doing more talking than cleaning. Talking about the big five-year deception.

Fisher was already at McDonald's when I pulled into the parking lot. I walked around to his driver's door and opened it.

"What are you doing? Get in." He eyed me with such a bright gleam in his eyes. It did all kinds of things to me.

"Thought we were having lunch."

"We are. But not here. I just thought we'd meet here so you could leave your car and ride with me."

I stepped onto his running board so I could lean into the cab and get my face up in his face. "Do you love me today?" I grinned, our mouths a breath apart.

He smiled. "I do."

I kissed him and his hand snaked around my waist as he kissed me back. "Then buy me a burger and fries and tell me about your Thanksgiving plans. Tell me how your week's been. Tell me anything." I bit his lip and tugged it.

Fisher grabbed my ass. "We could get it to go. Drive back to my place. Eat and still have time to do other *things*."

I ran my hand along his extra scruffy beard then my thumb traced his bottom lip. "Things, huh? You and your things."

He bit at my thumb. "You like my things."

I giggled. "I do. Too much, really. So let's grab a table and a couple of Happy Meals and stay out of trouble for one day."

His gaze swept along my face once before he dropped a final quick kiss on my lips. "You win."

I hopped down and he followed me. Then he took my hand and led me inside. I wondered what he would do if he saw someone he knew ... saw someone who knew he was engaged. My hand in his hand.

"What are you getting?" he asked as we approached the next open register.

"Duh, we're getting Happy Meals."

He chuckled. "Um ... we are?"

"Yes. Hi. We'll take two hamburger Happy Meals with apples, one with juice and one with a chocolate milk."

"No fries?"

I glanced back at Fisher and his confusion over not

having fries. Then I turned back to the guy at the register. "And a small order of fries."

He laid down a ten. I handed it back to him.

"My treat." I winked. Yup. Big spender for our under-seven-dollar meal.

We took our Happy Meals to a booth by the window. As I unpacked my stuff, including the Avengers toy, I noticed Fisher was staring into his sack but not pulling anything out. A confused look stole his face.

"What's wrong?"

After a few slow blinks, he gazed at me. "You bought my work crew Happy Meals."

As I'm sure Angie did with the slow return of Fisher's memories, I waited for him to reveal just how much he knew before I rushed to fill in the blanks. Did he remember a piece? A chunk? Or everything?

"I did. Well, technically you did. I used a company credit card."

Fisher continued to stare into his bag. "Why? Did you do it to be funny? Did I tell you to do it? Was I cheap?"

I giggled while unwrapping my burger. "No. You weren't cheap. Had you been cheap, you wouldn't have taken food to your crews at all. You were very generous. And I wasn't trying to be funny. I was collecting toys for Rory. She used to collect Happy Meal toys before she went to prison. So I continued her hobby for her."

Fisher glanced up at me again. "Do you still collect them?"

"No." I grinned with a slight head shake.

"Then why are we eating Happy Meals?" He pulled out his sandwich and apples.

"Because I thought it might jog a memory. And it did."

It was possible the memory I was trying to jog involved his workshop and zip ties. I so badly wanted to just tell him, but the part of me that wanted him to remember on his own was stronger. Maybe I would mention zip ties another day.

"Huh ..." He relinquished a tiny grin. "Thank you."

Tapping a sliced apple on my bottom lip, I grinned. "You're welcome. So how was your week after Rory lost her head?"

He shrugged, shoving a wad of fries into his mouth. "Uneventful. Just work. I tried calling Rory several times, but she's not taking my calls."

Chewing my apple slowly, I nodded. "What about Angie. Am ..." My nose wrinkled. "Am I allowed to ask you if you saw her this past week?"

Fisher eyed me suspiciously for a few seconds before nodding. "You can ask me anything." He slid his leg forward so it rubbed against mine. "Yes. She came over Tuesday night. She brought pizza and cake samples."

My eyes widened. "Cake samples?"

"They were good. I didn't really have a favorite.

She assumed I'd like the chocolate with peanut butter. But it was my least favorite."

"Cake samples for Thanksgiving? Christmas? New Years?"

He smirked, gulping half the bottle of chocolate milk. "Wedding," he said, wiping his mouth with the back of his hand.

I cleared my throat, unable to read him. The smirk. The casual mentioning of cake. Was he baiting me? "Whose wedding?" Two could play his game.

After an exaggerated pause, his expression swelled with amusement, a little pride for his worthy opponent. "*Whose* indeed. She casually suggested she move back in with me, and I countered with calling off the wedding."

The hamburger dropped from my hand, an unexpected *thunk* on the tray like the unexpected *thunk* of my heart halting, paralyzed with disbelief.

My nose wrinkled. I felt Angie's pain. Fisher didn't need to say another word. I knew where the story was headed. At least, I thought I knew. But why ... *why* did I feel so bad for Angie? We were in love with the same man. On different teams, but at the same time, we were Team Fisher.

"What did she say?" I managed to say just above a whisper.

"She got a little emotional."

Annihilated. Fisher annihilated her heart. If Angie kept herself from telling him about the miscarriage until he remembered it on his own, she knew how to toss her heart into a bunker so he wouldn't see her true suffering. I knew this because it was what I would have done. It was what I *had* done with Fisher on more than one occasion.

"Then she asked me to think about waiting at least until after the holidays since I'm slowly getting pieces of my memory back."

"Well..." there was still a hoarseness to my voice, a crippling of emotions "...that's what you wanted too."

He leaned back and ran his hands down his face. "No. I mean ... yes. I did. But I don't anymore. I want *you*. And I can't for the life of me imagine what I might remember that would change how I feel about you. There's no way I had stronger feelings for her." He shook his head slowly. "A stronger feeling doesn't exist. It's just not possible."

After a pregnant pause, I compelled my reluctant gaze to meet his. Love never looked so tortured.

"I think about you a lot and touch myself."

Fisher's eyes flared as he eased his head to one side and then the other, checking for anyone who might have heard me. Speechless Fisher was such a rare sight.

"Where ..." He held his fist to his mouth and coughed. "Where did that come from?"

I shrugged. "What you said, I never expected it. So raw. So honest. And it reminded me of all the reasons I think about you ..." I grinned. "And touch myself."

"Fuck you," he whispered with a grin, "for giving me a hard-on in McDonald's, three feet from the PlayPlace."

I giggled. "I had to lighten the mood. It's hard to love you and yet feel sorry for another woman who loves you too."

He cringed, scratching his jaw. "Right? If Angie were a terrible person, this would be so much easier."

"It's not that long. And I don't blame her for not wanting you to call off the wedding right before the holidays. Her first Thanksgiving and Christmas without her mom. That would be pretty terrible of you. But then I think of what Rory walked in on last weekend, and that was pretty terrible of you too. It could have just as easily been Angie popping by. Then what? Can you imagine explaining that to your family? Nothing says happy holidays like a S-E-X scandal."

Fisher laughed, glancing around us again. "You realize half of these kids can spell, right? And who doesn't love a good S-E-X scandal?"

"The person not getting any S-E-X."

The woman at the table next to us cleared her throat and scowled at us.

"Let's go." Fisher gathered our trash and we took our PG-13 conversation out of the G-rated play zone.

"Are you still going to the cousin's wedding?"

Fisher unlocked his truck and turned toward me as he leaned against the side of his truck, kicking his foot back onto the tire. "Afraid so." He fiddled with the key fob in his hand, chin tipped to his chest.

"When is it?"

"The weekend after Thanksgiving."

I nodded. "It's Costa Rica. You'll have fun."

Glancing up, he shot me the hairy eyeball. "Fun?"

"She's your friend. It would be sad for that to change since you've known her since you were six."

"I don't know her."

I frowned. "But I think you will. You made a baby with her." That came out sounding much different than it did in my head. "I'm just saying, that has to give you a second's pause. Right? If someone brought a stranger to me and said I didn't remember them, but I made a child with them, even if the child died, I'd need a moment to process what that meant."

"It was hardly a child. She was only two months pregnant."

"Well, I was raised to think of a child at any stage of life after creation as being alive ... a *life*. And maybe I've changed my views on a lot of things over the past five years, but that hasn't changed for me. So yeah, I know I've thought about the baby you made with her. And my mind has run in so many directions ... like what if she wouldn't have miscarried? Would you be married to her? Would you have other children with her? And then, had you been in the same accident and not remembered her, would you have fought harder to get back that life ... those feelings?"

Nobody ... not Rory or Rose ... not his family ... not Angie ... nobody was allowed to say I swooped in and stole Fisher. Even when it didn't benefit me and my interests, I went the extra mile to make Fisher really think about his decisions. Probably because he made me think about mine five years earlier. He made me consider more than our selfish desire to be together. And because of that, I left.

Did I want him to choose Angie? No. I wanted him to choose me with all his memories of her. I wanted him to find happiness with me without any fear or self-doubt.

"Are you in that scenario?" he asked.

"Does it matter?"

"Maybe. I think I would have still fallen in love with you. But I would have felt a greater responsibility to my wife and kids. The kids more than my wife. So you can spin this any way you want to spin it, but it doesn't change my current situation. And I'm not married. I don't have kids. She *did* miscarry the baby. *That's* my reality. Playing the what-if game is just stupid. I'm not going to do that. So stop trying to make me fall in love with her."

Collapsing into his chest, I lifted my head and kissed his neck. "Fall in love with *me*."

He grabbed my face and kissed me. "Done."

"And do it again tomorrow."

He grinned. "Tomorrow? Thought you only ever wanted today."

My hands slid behind him, worming their way under his jacket and shirt, caressing the warm skin along his back. "You make me greedy."

"Greedy? Is that the best word you've got?"

I grinned. "Delirious?"

"You can do better." He nipped at my lips as his hands covered my butt.

"Wanton?"

"Now we're getting there." He kissed my neck. "Keep going ..."

I giggled, sliding one hand just beneath his waistband, my nails pressing into the hard muscles of his glutes. "Brazen."

"Move your hand to the front of my jeans ... then you can be brazen."

"That would be more inappropriate."

"You think?"

I gasped as his hand made a swift transition from my butt to diving into the front of my jeans and panties.

In. McDonald's. Parking. Lot.

"Titillating. Salacious. And maybe a little indecent." He rubbed me in slow circles.

"Provocative?" he whispered in my ear.

"F-fisher ... s-stop."

"I did."

I felt the curl of his lips along my cheek, a triumphant grin. He had stopped. It was me moving against his idle hand.

Yanking his hand from the inside of my jeans, I took a quick step backward, flushed and a little breathless.

After biting back his smile for a few seconds, he eyed the family climbing into their minivan parked on the other side of my car. "I think about you a lot, and then I touch myself." He slid his gaze to mine and added the most mischievous grin.

My cheeks flamed.

His lips twisted for a beat. "Not as good as you touch me, but it suffices."

Dirty talking in the parking lot of McDonald's. Who did that?

We did.

It wasn't something you could put on a dating app. The things that really made two people click were not something anyone would ever even think to put on a dating app.

"Twelve across. A bird's wishbone."

Fisher blinked once. *Once!* "Merrythought."

"I hate you." I turned and stomped my way to the driver's side of my car.

His soft chuckle followed me, and before I could shut my door, he planted his body in its way and ducked his head, putting his big, arrogant mug in my face. "Nine down. Extravagant boasting."

I didn't know, so remained silent so he'd think I didn't care.

"First letter is G, fourth letter is C."

I still didn't know.

"Gasconade." He kissed my mouth, but I didn't kiss him back. "I liked you. Five years ago ... I liked you."

My anger subsided, being replaced with curiosity. Why did he say that?

"You knew I liked crossword puzzles. That's why you mentioned it. You were trying to jog a memory. But I hadn't forgotten about my love of crossword puzzles. I also hadn't forgotten that I didn't tell people about it. But you knew. That's why you made them for me. That's why you tease me with twelve across. I liked you. That's the only reason I would have told you. I liked you a lot. I wouldn't have told you had I not liked you a lot. Because Angie knows I won spelling bees, but she's never mentioned the puzzles. She's oblivious to it, which means I never told her. So ... the question I have for you is ... did you know I liked you?"

I met his gaze that was just inches from mine. "I wasn't in Denver that long. And I knew Angie. We went on a triple date. Remember? I told you that. And I met Teagan. She was an orthodontist. Remember her?"

He shook his head, eyes narrowed.

"Well, you slept over at her place more than once."

"Then there was Tiffany the interior designer. Remember her? Rose fixed you up with her."

Another slow head shake.

"I met your harem. I knew you enjoyed your women. So what do you think? Do you think your friend's daughter, the eighteen-year-old virgin living in your basement, knew that you liked her? Do you think you took time out of your sex life to bond with her over crossword puzzles?"

"Yes." He nodded slowly.

He was *so* close to remembering. I just wanted him to do it. I wanted to be there when he remembered more about me than my Happy Meal deliveries. I wanted him to say "I loved you." I didn't want to tell him that he loved me. So I gave him the inch he was searching for, maybe the inch, the nudge he needed.

"I was having a rough day. You took me to your parents' house and showed me your boxes of crossword puzzles. Nerd status on full display. So if that meant you liked me ..." I shrugged. "Then I guess you liked me."

Fisher did that squinting thing, a painful expression. His brain tried so hard to remember, to repair the connections, to bring back the images and the emotions that went with them. "I liked you so much ... I hate that I can't remember that feeling. But it's the only explanation. I must have been scared out of my mind to tell you. Or maybe it was Rory. She would have killed me. We've seen that."

I bit the inside of my cheek while returning a single nod, trying to hide my disappointment.

He liked me a lot.

Was that emotionally a step above getting Angie pregnant? Puzzles over a baby?

"I'm going to go home and think about this."

"Okay." I drew in a breath and held it along with all my emotions.

"If I don't get to see you before Thanksgiving, have a good one."

"Yeah, thanks. You too."

"Love you."

I nodded as my heart ached.

Tell him!

It was such an agonizing predicament. Tell him

and feel heartbroken when he didn't remember. Don't tell him and drown in the anxiety of *wanting* him to know. Angie told him everything or nearly everything and she received zero satisfaction in return.

"Love you." I slid my hand into his hair and leaned forward, pressing my lips to his.

CHAPTER TWENTY-FIVE

I HAD to make an actual trip to Target after McDonald's with Fisher so I didn't show up empty handed. It wouldn't have mattered. Rose and Rory had a much better distraction sitting at the kitchen with an open bottle of wine and three glasses.

"Hey," I said with fake enthusiasm after preparing myself when I saw her vehicle.

Three women in yoga pants, sweaters, and fuzzy socks. Three women with their hair in various ponytail positions. And not a speck of makeup.

"Join us. I'll grab you a glass. Angie just needed a little girl time." Rory's hard gaze was a little more intense at the moment. Angie's visit resurrected her anger. Rose nervously chewing her lips confirmed it.

"How have you been?" I took a seat, feeling overdressed in jeans and damp panties from Fisher's hand down them. Yes. I absolutely thought about that while smiling at his fiancée. Ironically, I found it easier to feel sorry for her when I wasn't in the same room, except the wedding dress day. I fell victim to that trap like everyone else.

"I've been better." She rolled her eyes.

Maybe Rose and Rory thought I'd feel uncomfortable. Guilt-ridden. It wasn't my fault that Fisher loved me.

"Oh?" I curled my lips between my teeth and smiled at Rory when she set a wine glass on the table and slid the wine bottle toward me.

"Fisher wants to postpone the wedding. And I don't know what to say. I've done everything I can to help him remember me, remember us. And he is getting some memories back, but it's not enough to give him the bigger picture, to make him feel what he felt before the accident."

"I'm sorry to hear that." I felt Rory's judgmental gaze on me, but I didn't give her a single glance. My brain was caught on the word "postpone." Cancel and postpone were not the same thing. So who was telling the truth?

"He's just been really distant with me. I moved out. We agreed to 'date.' We were intimate. Things were back on track. Then it all came to a sudden stop. It's hard to fall in love with someone when you never see them."

They were intimate? Once? Right? Just once?

"Absence makes the heart grow fonder." I tried that on for size. It received three out of three frowns.

"I think I need to try a different tactic. I've

requested a room with a king bed instead of two queens on our trip to Costa Rica. And I've scheduled a couple's massage the day before the wedding. Maybe the issue is I've been trying too hard to get him to remember how he used to love me and not enough time making him fall in love with me now. You know?"

Yes, I knew. That was my MO. Except I didn't try to make him love me. He just did. It was effortless and inevitable. Was that enough to thwart temptation on his horizon?

"I shopped for all new lingerie for the trip. Maybe spice things up a bit? He can't say no to lace and satin, right?"

Rose cleared her throat just as I opened my mouth to speak. I had a lot to say on the matter.

"Just don't set yourself up to be disappointed. I really don't think the issue has anything to do with physical attraction. You're beautiful. What man wouldn't be attracted to you?"

Rory slid her gaze to Rose, and I had to stifle my giggle. Rose was taking it too far, making Rory a little jealous.

What woman wouldn't find you attractive?

Angie nodded. Of course she knew she was attractive. No need to show even a little bit of modesty.

"Have you considered the possibility of there being someone else?"

I eyed Rory with caution. Where was she going with that? She didn't look at me like I was supposed to fall to my knees and confess. Maybe she was gently preparing Angie for what I'd hoped would be the inevitable. And I kinda loved my mom for that.

"Wow ..." Angie's eyes widened like two brown saucers.

Nope. She hadn't thought about that.

"No. I mean ..." She shook her head. "No. That's not Fisher. He wouldn't do that. Did he say something to you?"

Rory shook her head. "No. He's never said a word to me." I didn't miss the hint of bitterness in her tone. "But if he doesn't remember his past with you, he might not feel..." Rory pressed her lips together, searching for the right word "...committed."

"No." Angie didn't care for that possibility. "Not Fisher. We've been friends for too long. He knows this has been my dream. And before the accident it was *our* dream. Besides, who would it be? Nobody. He goes to work. Comes home. Hangs out with you guys. No."

"Maybe he's on a dating app. Just hooking up. Meeting his needs without the pressure of remembering his past or leading you on." I grunted and flinched when Rose kicked my shin.

"What?" Angie seemed to find that possibility even more appalling than the idea of him simply being with someone else.

I personally viewed a random hookup for sex much less threatening. That was just sex.

I, however, wasn't just sex to Fisher. Angie should have wished for that. Instead, she was going to lose Fisher to the adorable and cute girl she never saw coming. The way she never noticed our magnetism on the triple date to the concert or her complete unawareness that while she slept in Fisher's bed that night, he had the head of his cock pressed between my legs on the pool table.

They were destined to always be friends (if she was lucky) and we were destined to always be lovers, no matter how destructive and shameless our path to each other ended up being.

Man ... I sure hope that's our destiny.

"I don't think you know Fisher very well." She scoffed.

Rose wrinkled her nose. "Well, I don't know about now. But when you and Fisher weren't together, he was ..." She shot Rory a quick look as if she'd offer some backup.

"He was a ... *virile* young man with an active dating life." Rory for the win.

I was getting tired of Angie's string of shocked expressions. Even at eighteen, I hadn't been *that* naive. Whether I liked it or not, I had to acknowledge Fisher liked sex, and he wasn't the godly man who worried about love or marriage before sticking his dick into someone. Or part of his dick, in my case.

Angie drained the rest of the wine in her glass. "You know ..." She twisted the stem of her glass in one direction and then the other. "We weren't exactly being careful about birth control before the accident. Which was crazy. I had a wedding to plan. A dress purchased. But part of me ..." She shook her head and laughed. "I wanted to get pregnant. I was even late with my period and thought ... this is it." Her grin vanished. "But it wasn't. I got my period the week before his accident. And I know it's stupid, but had I been pregnant, I think, even with the accident, we would have been married by now. That's just Fisher. Maybe he's not the exact same person he was before the accident. But at his core, he's still the same good man. He would have done the right thing. And I know ... I just know we would have eventually fallen in love again because it's us. It's always been us."

I had to hand it to Angie. She unknowingly brought her A-game. It wasn't the orphan standing in front of a full-length mirror, but it still packed a punch. My desire to keep my hands up, fisted in front of my face, dissipated. Maybe because it was easy to forget that Fisher didn't remember our love the way I did. His love for me spanned months, not years.

Was I getting too comfortable? Too confident? Could four days in Costa Rica derail us?

I finished my wine and pushed my chair back a few inches. "I'm going to finish cleaning my bathroom."

"Happy Thanksgiving if I don't see you before then." Angie smiled.

"You too. Do you have plans?"

"Fisher's parents' house, of course." She shrugged like, *duh*.

Duh indeed.

I should have known. I think I did know. But ignorance really was bliss when it came to my boyfriend and his fiancée.

"Tell them hi for me."

The woman they don't know they're supposed to love yet.

"Sure thing."

I sulked to the bathroom. Scrubbed the hell out of the shower and then the floor with Matt Maeson's "Hallucinogenics" blasting through my earbuds.

CHAPTER TWENTY-SIX

My grandparents were scheduled to arrive on Wednesday, a nice buffer between Rory and me. Things were better, but she wasn't completely giving up all her anger. I had let it slide, but if she didn't shake out of it by Thanksgiving, we were going to have a "You Went To Prison" talk. For the rest of my life, I reserved the right to play that card. She abandoned me during the most delicate and influential years of my life.

Basically, all my imperfections would be blamed on her temporary absence. Okay, not really. But I did have every intention of using that excuse when things got rough. And since the *incident*, things had been rough.

"Fisher's coming over," Rory announced Wednesday morning as I read a book on the sofa while Rose knitted something that resembled a scarf from the chair next to me.

"Okay," I said in a controlled tone, even if inside she'd lit a fire of anticipation with her news. "Why? Are you two back on speaking terms?"

"He's coming over to quickly install a rail by the toilet. My mom can't get on and off the toilet that well right now. Her knee is bad."

"Nothing like waiting until the last minute," I said.

"She wanted him to do it last week, but she stopped talking to him, so he had no way of knowing," Rose said, tossing my mom a wry grin.

"Anyway, I'm just letting you know. He's coming over to *work*."

With wide eyes, I nodded slowly. "Okay. Thanks for telling me. Otherwise, I might have thought he was coming over to have sex with me since you spoiled my last chance at it."

Rose snorted and quickly covered her mouth. Rory narrowed her eyes at me.

Biting my lips together, I kept a fairly straight face.

Seconds later, there was a knock at the door. My tummy flipped several times and my heart did its crazy thing where it liked to skip a few beats.

"Hey," Fisher said to Rory when she opened the door.

"Thanks for doing this," Rory said almost begrudgingly.

"Sure. I would have done it sooner had I known you needed it."

"Well, I've ... been busy." Rory led him to the bathroom.

But Fisher glanced back and saw me and Rose in the living room, and his face exploded into what I'd decided was his Reese Only smile.

I bit my lower lip, but it hid nothing.

"Fisher, are you coming?" Rory all but barked at him.

Rose sniggered as did I.

"Yes, ma'am," Fisher said.

While he installed the bar, Rory made stuffing to be cooked the next day and Rose worked on pies. I had no cooking jobs yet, so I meandered down the hallway to the bathroom.

"Leave him alone so he can finish up," Rory instructed.

"Yeah, yeah," I pretty much ignored her. I was twenty-four not four. "Need help?" I asked, standing in the doorway as Fisher finished drilling holes in the wall.

"I'm good." He stayed focused on his task.

I loved watching focused Fisher. It was foreplay for me. The stern focus on his face. The bend and stretch of his arms and large capable hands. The way his tongue would make a lazy swipe along his lower lip when he was measuring something and marking it with the pencil he kept behind his ear. The fact that his jeans rode low but only showed the side waistband of his briefs instead of plumber's crack. Poor plumbers ... it wasn't like they all had big guts, poorly fitting jeans, and seemingly no underwear.

"Whatcha thinking about?" He caught me off

guard when he shot me a quick glance over his shoulder.

I smirked. "You don't want to know."

Fisher's gaze made a quick, appreciative swipe along the full length of my body. "Don't be so sure."

"I was thinking about plumbers' cracks."

"I don't have a plumber's crack."

"I know."

"Because you're staring at my ass?"

"Yes."

He chuckled without turning toward me again. "How's it look?"

"No comment. Rory probably has the room bugged. I'd hate to be in timeout for Thanksgiving. Have you uh ... remembered anything new since I saw you on Sunday?"

"Yes."

"Oh? What's that?"

He screwed the plates onto the wall. "I remembered my senior prom."

"That's ... interesting. Did something prompt it?"

"Yes and no. I think there was a trigger, but the memory wasn't immediate. It came to me later while I was sleeping."

"What triggered it?"

"Angie stopped by and showed me something. And I think that did it." He attached the bar to the plates.

"That's vague. What did she show you?"

"The dress she bought for her cousin's wedding and the coordinating tie she bought for me to wear."

They were going to wear coordinating outfits to her cousin's wedding. How vomit-worthy. "And that triggered memories from prom?"

"Yes. The coordinating outfits."

"So you dreamed of what? Shopping for a bowtie, cummerbund, and pocket square to match her dress?"

"Not exactly." Fisher tested the rail, using it to help him stand, pushing down on it with his weight.

"Then what exactly?"

"You'll take it wrong."

"I doubt it," I said reflexively.

As he returned his tools to his tool bag, he blew out a slow breath. "We had a hotel room that night. A friend who graduated two years early, but also went to prom because his girlfriend was younger, got the room for us when he booked one for himself and his date. I remember staring at her light pink dress on the floor the next morning and yes ... my matching bowtie and cummerbund."

The next morning. I swallowed past the thick lump in my throat. He was two for two. Both of his memories thus far about Angie involved sex. It wasn't exactly how he presented them to me, but I could read between the lines.

They had sex ... she got pregnant.

They had sex ... the next morning he stared at their clothes on the hotel room floor.

He was remembering sex with Angie while remembering Happy Meals with me.

"See..." he derailed me from my train of thought "...

you're taking it wrong." He brushed a little drywall dust off his shirt and jeans.

"I'm not taking anything wrong. You're remembering sex with Angie." I lifted a shoulder and dropped it like a ten-pound weight. "Was it good sex?"

Resting one hand on his hip, he dropped his chin to his chest and pushed another long sigh out his nose. "I don't want to have this conversation with you. You asked me a question. I wanted to be honest with you. But I don't want the strange cherry-picking of memories my brain seems to be doing to drive us apart. Just ... don't let it go there."

Go there. I wasn't supposed to let my brain go there, but his brain could go wherever it wanted to go. "I don't feel like that's an answer to my question." Self-destruction was a lit fuse.

You saw it.

You sensed its impending urgency, it's impending doom.

You felt panicked.

But you also felt helpless to do anything to stop it.

Fisher glanced up at me with a frown on his face. "If I say no, you won't believe me. If I say yes ... well, I don't know how you'll react. So why can't I just plead the Fifth here?"

I may have been ten years younger than him, but that didn't mean I was born yesterday. If it hadn't been memories of good sex, he would have said as much, and he would have gone to great lengths to make me believe the truth. That wishy-washy explanation was a yes. He remembered having good sex with Angie.

Fantastic ...

So a week before he was set to go with her to Costa Rica (her and her new lingerie and a king bed), he was having good sex dreams about her.

Forgive me, but I *was* still human with a tendency to have irrational feelings and an instinct for jealousy.

I drew in a long breath of courage, weak courage at best. Then I exhaled it. "Well, it's wonderful that you're slowly getting your memory back. And at least you're getting a sense of why you fell in love with her and agreed to marry her. The sex was good. But I think I already knew that because I came to your house that morning after the two of you had good sex that was apparently my doing because I questioned your ability to get and sustain an erection." With a fake smile, I averted my gaze to the floor. "I'll get the vacuum."

"Reese ..."

I didn't pause. My heart had already shifted into defense mode. Fight or flight.

"Did he finish the job?" Rory asked as I retrieved the handheld vacuum from the entry closet.

Yes. He finished crushing my heart.

"He did. Just needs to clean up the drywall dust." I held my breath or at least most of it while taking only tiny inhales and exhales like a woman in labor while I shouldered past him blocking the doorway.

"Reese ..."

I turned on the little vacuum which silenced him,

and I took lots of time making sure I sucked up every speck of drywall dust. Before I got it shut off, he squatted behind me, his hand taking the vacuum from mine and shutting it off.

"I love you today," he whispered in my ear.

Nope. Wrong four words. I loved those words on any other day. They just fell flat when all I could think about was him having sex with Angie because it seemed like that was all *his* mind cared to remember about her. Rory's words replayed in my head.

A virile young man.

I highly doubted *virile* young men were immune to sex dreams, especially the lingering thoughts they provoked. Just because one didn't want to think about something didn't mean they had control over it. There was no way I wasn't going to be thinking about him and Angie having sex, and it *definitely* wasn't because I wanted to think about it.

"Thanks for putting up the bar. I'm sure my grandma will really appreciate it."

"Are you punishing me for my honesty?"

With pursed lips, I shook my head a half dozen times.

"You asked me."

My head shake quickly transitioned into a series of nods. "I did. Stupid me. I think I'm done asking you about anything."

"Reese." He took a step forward and reached for my waist.

"No." I shifted to the side, wedged between the

toilet and the vanity as I held my hands up to let him know I didn't want to be touched.

"It means nothing ... at least nothing that you're worried about."

I grunted a laugh. "You're going to Costa Rica with her. It might end up meaning something."

"Why don't you trust me?"

I rubbed my temples. "We've been over this. Even if I convinced myself it's safe to trust you, I don't trust your memories lurking at every turn. One trigger after another. I mean ... that's all it could take. One trigger to remember why you said yes to her. And what if that comes on the heels of a beautiful wedding where everyone is in the mood for love? Good friends. Food. *Alcohol.* Dancing. Coordinating outfits. A shared hotel room."

"You're being ridiculous."

"And you're being stupid!"

Fisher flinched. And the noise in the kitchen silenced. Everyone and everything was silent except the lingering echo of my outburst.

"If you're done, it might be time for you to leave." Rory appeared a few feet from the bathroom door. "What do I owe you, Fisher?"

Keeping his back to her, he stared at me, but I kept my attention focused on the floor between us.

"Nothing. You owe me nothing." He snagged his tool bag off the floor and headed straight to the front door.

Click.

It closed behind him.

"Want to talk about it?" Rory said.

"No." I still had lots of anger to unleash as my "no" came out a little harsher than intended. "I don't want to talk to you, not after more than a week of you not talking to me. I don't want your opinion, a lecture, a long string of I-told-you-so's. Just ..." I handed her the vacuum and made a sharp left into my bedroom, slamming and locking the door behind me.

CHAPTER TWENTY-SEVEN

Dᴇᴀʀ Lᴏsᴛ Fɪsʜᴇʀᴍᴀɴ,

I'm really mad at you right now. And I don't care if it's rational thinking on my part or not. Sometimes a person just needs to be irrational. This front that I've been holding up is exhausting. One can only show bravery for so long. Even the strongest people break sometimes. I wish I was immune to insecurities, but I'm not. I wish your I-love-you's made me feel more confident in us, but they don't.

I know Angie's still dazed with disbelief that you can't remember the first girl you ever loved. The girl you met when you were six. I get it. Because I'm struggling with us. It's equally as hard for me to imagine us falling in love twice without you remem-

bering the first time. And I can't even articulate how badly I wish you would remember us. Not deduce the fact that you must have liked me a lot to show me your nerdy cruciverbalist heart, but actually feel what that really meant. I can't tell you how many times the eager words have sat on the end of my tongue, desperate to jump out and just tell you. Tell you that we were in love. Tell you that you were my first and forever love. And in my gullible, fairy-tale head, you magically remember everything and we live happily ever after.

Fuck fairy tales.

Seven across. Hint: Disloyal. Ungodly.

Faithless.

I was angry. Angry that it was Thanksgiving and she was with him.

Angry that I had to endure the long stares from Rose and Rory while my grandparents yapped about their aches and pains.

Angry that Fisher hadn't tried calling me to apologize for … I didn't even know. But *something*. Really, he needed to apologize for something.

And if I were being completely honest, I was angry that he got on his motorcycle that day. Angry that he lost his memory. Maybe that meant I wouldn't have moved back to Colorado. That might have meant we wouldn't have had the possibility of a second chance.

But as I simmered like a pot of soup left on the stove too long, I started to think Michigan sounded pretty good.

"How's your job, Reese?" Grandma took a breather from her winded explanation of ailments and their corresponding medications to finally show a little interest in her granddaughter.

"It's the best job. I love the midwives I work with. I'm so excited to start my master's program next year."

"She does love it. We get to see her come home with no sleep after a long birth but boundless energy because she loves it so much." Rory, for what felt like the first time in nearly two weeks, shared a genuine smile.

"That's amazing, dear. We're so proud of you. Is everything else good? Do you have a boyfriend? Or a girlfriend?"

I loved the way they accepted my mom for who she was. The way they loved Rose. If only my dad's parents could have been so loving. Like God. I believed God loved everyone. It was just what felt right to me ... when I started thinking for myself.

Thanks to Fisher.

"I have a boyfriend."

Rory and Rose visibly stiffened.

"And where is he today?" Grandpa asked.

"Having Thanksgiving dinner with his family."

And his fiancée.

"Will we get to meet him before we go home?"

Grandma asked as she wiped her red painted lips with her napkin.

"I'm not sure." I used my fork to fiddle with the remaining food on my plate.

"What does he do?" Grandma kept coming with the questions.

"He works in construction."

"Oh," she replied quickly. "Rory, doesn't your old landlord do that too? What's his name?"

Rory grabbed another dinner roll and took a generous bite while nodding. "Fisher," she mumbled over the roll.

"Does your boyfriend happen to know Fisher?"

I grinned. "He does, actually. They're really close."

Rose cleared her throat and fisted her hand at her mouth to hide her unavoidable laughter. Rory didn't find it quite as funny.

"That's nice, dear. Is it serious? Will I be attending my granddaughter's wedding soon?"

"It's serious, but no wedding. I'd like to finish school first."

Rory ...

The epitome of a mother waiting for her daughter to get her heart broken. And she wasn't wrong. There had already been a lot of heartbreak with what felt like unavoidably more to come.

"Well, I do hope we get to meet him."

"Me too."

"Speaking of Fisher ..." Grandpa spoke up, and for a second I'd forgotten that Fisher's name was just mentioned. I thought my grandpa magically knew or figured out my secret. "How's he been since the accident?"

"Yes," Grandma jumped in. "Has he remembered his fiancée?"

"He's doing well." Rory plastered on a believable smile. "Getting back a few missing memories, but not enough to remember being engaged to Angie. So that's been a little rough. And I'm not sure if they'll stay together, to be honest."

"Why is that?" Grandma questioned.

"There might be someone else in the picture."

"What?" Grandma's hand pressed to her chest on a gasp.

"It's complicated at the moment, but we highly suspect he has found someone else."

"Well, someone needs to talk some sense into that young man. He can't just abandon his fiancée. And what kind of woman would even dream of swooping in and stealing another woman's man after a horrific accident?"

Rose eyed me like an older sister who just realized her younger sister was about to get in trouble.

"Well, Mom, in all fairness to Fisher and this other woman, *if* there is another woman, he doesn't remember Angie. She's basically been this stranger claiming to be his lifelong friend and the love of his life. We can't totally blame him for not feeling what he doesn't know he's supposed to feel and therefore finding it easy to … get distracted by someone else."

"I'll give Fisher a pass, maybe." Grandma frowned. "But not the slut moving in on him."

Rory's mom was outspoken like my dad's mom, just in a different way. However, they probably would have both agreed that I was a slut.

Rory flinched and so did Rose. Me? Nope. I didn't flinch. I could see it from both sides. And because I could see it from both sides, I thought we all needed a little coming to Jesus moment.

"It's me," I said.

"Sorry. What, dear?" Grandma said, smiling at me … the slut.

"I'm the slut."

"Reese," Rory whispered, closing her eyes and shaking her head.

"Excuse me?" Grandma squinted.

After taking a sip of my water, I calmly set it on the table and grinned. "*Fisher* is my boyfriend. And we fell in love over five years ago. And as wrong as that probably seems to everyone else, the only thing that was wrong was the timing. But we have an unexpected second chance. And we've fallen in love again. Well, I've never stopped loving him, but he … he's fallen in love with me again. And he doesn't remember what we were before now. And that's heartbreaking and frustrating. But it's also beautiful and maybe even perfect. And I realize this is a really hard pill for everyone else to swallow, but our love has nothing to do with Angie. I don't think her ties to the man who doesn't remember her makes what *we* have wrong. So let's all take a timeout here and not call people sluts when we haven't walked in their shoes. I realize it's often the Christian way, but I think I can love God *and* love every single one of his children without judging anyone. And the last I checked, you're also sitting at the same table as my lesbian mother and her partner, whom we love so very much. And it's hard to imagine anything about their love is *wrong*. Wouldn't we all agree?"

Rose wiped a tear from her face, and Rory's emotions shined in her eyes too.

My grandparents held an even mix of shock and embarrassment in their expressions.

I stood, tossing my napkin onto the table. "I'm going to take a few minutes to myself. Call me when pie is served."

Nobody said a word. And I was grateful. I didn't want apologies or awkward attempts to explain away the previous conversation where I was labeled a slut. Had I not been the slut, it could have been somebody else's daughter or granddaughter.

Everyone means the world to someone. Or at least they should.

When I collapsed onto my bed, I called Fisher. After multiple rings, it went to voicemail. So I called again ... and again.

On the fourth call, he answered. "Hi," he said in a neutral tone. "I'm eating dinner. What's up?" He was eating dinner with his family. His whole family and Angie.

"I love you today," I said.

Silence.

More silence.

"Say it. Say it back to me, Fisher. Like you mean it. Like it matters."

"Can we chat about this later?"

"I said it. In front of my grandparents ... after they unknowingly called me a slut. I said it. I'm tired of not saying it. I'm tired of feeling guilty. Just ... say it and let everyone else *fucking* deal with it."

He cleared his throat. "So you clogged the garbage disposal?"

I pressed *End*.

Throwing my arm over my face, I grumbled and growled, just like the old Fisher. I was angry with him and the rest of the world. And I know it wasn't fair for me to ambush him like that—after all, he stood up to Rory and unapologetically told her that he loved me.

But I wanted him to make the gesture without getting caught first. Was that too much to ask?

Maybe.

"Stupid ..." I whispered to myself. "Stupid. Stupid. Stupid." Just minutes earlier, I had given my family a long speech on being kind and not judging others. I just left the kitchen with the words *everybody means the world to somebody* in my head.

Was Angie someone's world since her parents died and Fisher lost his memories of her? It was such a kind thing of me to ask Fisher to destroy her in front of his entire family on Thanksgiving. I was ashamed of myself.

And tired.

Getting a call that a baby was ready to come into the world was exactly what I needed. But that call never came.

"Hey." Rory smiled at me when she opened my door a crack. "Pie is being served."

"Okay," I said, staring at the ceiling.

The door clicked shut, but it did so with Rory on my side of it. Then the bed dipped. She laid herself next to me, also staring at the ceiling, as she reached for my hand.

"I know he loves you," she said. "I just want you to have it easier than I had it. I don't want love to be this complicated and messy for you."

"Messy ..." I laughed a little. "That's how we know it's real."

"I adore Fisher ... or I did. And honestly, it's just all been *a lot.* I was hit pretty hard, completely out of the blue. It would have been a lot to handle five years ago, but add in the accident, his memory loss, and Angie ... well ... it's more than my heart and brain can reconcile at the moment. And I know ... I *know* I have no right to say this, but I'm going to say it anyway. Seeing you and Fisher that day in that situation was not what any mom wants to see."

I laughed and laughed some more. Rory started to giggle too. She definitely had *no* right to say anything to me. She saw Fisher enjoying my breasts. I saw Rose doing so much more to her.

Rolling toward her, I tucked my hands under my

cheek. "I know it's not the way you imagined ... it's not the way I imagined ... but your little girl is in love. And it's big. And all-consuming. It's scary. It's exhilarating. And real. So if you want to be the mom you didn't get to be when I was going through my teenaged years, then I'm going to need a hand to hold and a shoulder to cry on as I fight like hell to get my prince."

"Your prince ..." She gave me a sad smile and rested her hand on my cheek.

"I need you to want my happiness more than Angie's. And I know that's hard because Angie is a good person. And her love story with Fisher is pretty amazing. But it's not forever. I just ... I know it."

Rory nodded slowly. "I've got you."

CHAPTER TWENTY-EIGHT

A<small>FTER</small> <small>PIE</small>.

After an apology from my grandparents.

After playing six games of Hearts.

Fisher called me.

"I'm calling it a night." I excused myself from the game when I saw his number on my phone's screen. It was close to ten-thirty at night. "Hi," I answered in a meek voice just as I reached my bedroom.

"I'm in your driveway."

My heart sucked at staying in chill mode or staying mad at him very long.

"Want to go for a drive?"

"I suppose." That was my version of chill, even though I was already grabbing a hoodie to wear over my leggings and heading down the hallway.

"Take your time."

"Okay." I ended the call while I pulled on my wool-lined boots.

"Going somewhere?" Rory asked as they picked up the cards and glasses from the table.

"I am." I grinned.

"Okay. See you in the morning."

Was she assuming I was coming home after they went to bed or not until morning? I was twenty-four. It didn't matter. But what did matter was I knew she knew who I was leaving with and she didn't give me anything but an honest smile.

"Goodnight."

Everyone else told me goodnight as I went out the front door. A few snowflakes swirled in the cold air, and my lost fisherman was in his truck waiting for me.

When I climbed in, he gave me a reserved smile. I felt certain that was all he dared to give me after my unexpected call to him during Thanksgiving dinner with his family.

Fisher drove us to his house, and I wasn't surprised. We didn't speak on the short ride. When we arrived, he climbed out, but I didn't. Stopping at the front of the truck, he looked at me expectantly for a few seconds before he made his way to my door and grabbed the handle. But he didn't open it right away. He paused and that look spread across his face. The concentration. The wrinkled brow and narrowed eyes.

Then he lifted his gaze and kept it on me as he slowly opened my door.

"I opened your door for you, but I acted like I didn't want to do it. I told you to pull the lever to make it open. I think I was an asshole to you."

I couldn't help but wonder if all his memory loss was physical from the accident or if some of it was psychological. Did he have emotional reasons for not wanting to remember his love for me? His love for Angie?

"Sometimes." I nodded, but I grinned too. I had a love-hate relationship with Fisher's asshole side.

I turned to get out, but I wrapped my arms around his neck and my legs around his waist instead. "I'm sorry *I* was the asshole today when I called you. It was stupid. I don't know what got into me." I buried my face in his warm neck and kissed it.

Fisher shut the door and locked his truck before carrying me inside the house. "It's all going to be over, settled, done. Soon. It just ... has to be."

I released him, easing to my feet. We took off our boots and he slipped off his fleece jacket as I pulled off my sweatshirt.

"Drink?" He curled my hair behind my ears.

"No," I whispered, gazing up at him.

"Bed?" A hopeful grin stole his lips.

"No," I whispered.

"Then what can I do for my beautiful girl?"

"Dance with me."

Fisher's eyebrows lifted a bit. "Dance?"

I nodded.

"I'm not sure I'm a dancer."

I shrugged, retrieving my phone from my sweat-shirt pocket. Taking his hand, I pulled him to the kitchen. "Dim the lights. I know you love ambient lighting."

"How do you know that?" He turned on some accent lights and dimmed them while I tapped a song on my phone. Judah & The Lion's "Only To Be With You."

"Because I know you."

"What if I want to know you like you know me?" He pulled me into his arms, and we swayed in a slow circle.

"You do, my lost fisherman ... you do."

"Did we dance? Are you trying to bring back more memories?"

"No." I kissed his neck as his hands slid from my lower back to my butt. "Just making new ones."

We danced and we kissed.

One song led to another song. It didn't matter that he wasn't a dancer and neither was I. Our bodies molded and moved, perfectly together and in sync with each other's own rhythm.

Fisher's hands stayed on the outside of my clothes, yet touched me intimately.

The graze of his hand over my breast, my butt ... the slide of his fingers up my inner thigh.

Open-mouthed kisses.

Soft moans.

More dancing.

We weren't sneaking around. We weren't rushed. It was just us, and we had the whole night.

I was exhausted with no desire to sleep.

I was turned on, but not wanting to take it any further *yet*.

I was perfectly content, but insanely eager.

We were messy and alive and living in the moment. Our love only mattered for a day.

A kiss.

A breath.

Eventually the songs ended, leaving us in silence dotted with the soft sounds of our kisses. Yet we kept swaying like we made our own music, like we had our own rhythm. I couldn't help but imagine a life with Fisher. A real life where we'd enjoy dinner and talk about current events, work, or plan a trip.

After dinner we'd do the dishes and listen to music like tonight. It would lead to dancing and kissing, a seemingly unhurried passion, but we'd still leave our clothes in a trail down the hallway because we would forever be that couple. We'd make love in a frenzy before falling asleep in each other's arms, only to wake in the morning and do it all over again, only slower and with the soft glow of the morning sun on us. We'd look into each other's eyes the whole time, starting everyday perfectly connected.

Or ... and I liked this dream the best ... we'd eventually have to give up our morning sex because we'd wake to the pitter patter of tiny feet charging toward our bedroom to wake us up. And we'd steal long minutes every morning to tickle little bellies and kiss soft cheeks while a chorus of giggles and squeals filled the room.

And on mornings, if we were lucky, we'd distract

them with a thirty-minute show on a television or a tablet while we jumped into the shower ... together.

"What's going through that beautiful head of yours?" Fisher asked before kissing the top of said beautiful head. My cheek had been resting on his chest, feeling his heartbeat, as we swayed in silence.

"I want this," I murmured.

"Want what? More dancing?"

Lifting my head, I gazed up at him and smiled. "More ... everything."

Fisher blinked several times as his knuckles brushed my cheeks. He knew. He knew what *more* and *everything* meant. "Me too." He kissed me while walking me backward out of the kitchen. And I begged for it to be like my dream.

It was.

He broke our kiss to remove my shirt. And we sneaked another kiss before we removed his shirt. More kisses.

My bra.

His back against the hallway wall while I kissed his chest and unbuttoned his jeans.

More kisses and more steps ensued as he inched my leggings south, but just barely past my butt. Fisher's strong hands slid inside the back of my panties, gripping me, pulling me close, rubbing me against him.

The brush of his bare chest along my nipples while his tongue teased mine ... it was intoxicating. Everything about us felt all-consuming. We were memories in the making, ignited by a past he couldn't remember and fueled by a desire for a future that seemed painfully just out of reach.

"You're so..." he kissed down my body, kneeling in front of me "...fucking beautiful." His tongue teased my navel as his hands worked my leggings and panties the rest of the way down my legs. "And sexy ... god you're so sexy." His mouth moved lower.

My hands found their place in his hair, and they curled into fists, forcing him to look up at me. "I had the biggest crush on you." More heat found its way to my cheeks, taking me back to that eighteen-year-old girl, out of my mind infatuated with him.

A slow smile worked its way up Fisher's face as his hands slid along the back of my legs, coming to a rest just below my butt. "Yeah?"

Why was I embarrassed? Why did my heart go wild in my chest making my tummy feel nervous? I wasn't retelling our past to him. I wasn't telling him how he felt about me. I wasn't telling him anything he had to reach for to truly understand. They were *my* feelings.

They shaped me as a woman in ways he'd never know even if he did remember everything. And I wanted him to see me. All of me.

"Yeah." I bit my lower lip for a second. "I had no idea sexy wore jeans, a faded tee, and work boots. I had no idea sexy drove a truck and mowed the lawn without a shirt. Well ..." I giggled. "I should've known sexy mowed the lawn without a shirt. On mornings we rode to work together, I was so giddy. I practically sprinted to your truck, slowing at the last minute to act cool and controlled. Then I prayed you had music playing so you didn't hear my heart so out of control. And I'd stare at your hands on the steering wheel, those veins up your arms, your full lips as you'd lick them after taking a sip of your coffee." I slowly shook my head. "I was in deep, feeling things I'd never experienced before. And it felt so wrong, but I couldn't stop. And you didn't help ... you and your effortless sex appeal just ... *every single day*."

He stood slowly, kissing my chest and neck on his way to my lips. And before he kissed me on the mouth, he paused, letting his gaze ghost along my face. "I didn't think I could love you more." He swept my hair away from my face before weaving his fingers through it. "I was so fucking wrong."

We kissed.

Clothes vanished along with the rest of the world. And I knew we were an unstoppable storm. But ... how much damage would we do in our pursuit to be together?

I died a little when he sank into me. It felt different. We felt different.

Fisher's heavy breaths washed over my cheek as his lips found my ear. "*You* are my favorite place in the world."

I gripped his backside as my legs wrapped around him.

That spoke to my soul, that *place* that defined us because we were everywhere our souls took us. And maybe that was Heaven. And maybe that was Hell. But in that moment, it was in a bed of messy sheets and tangled limbs.

It was a pretty *fucking* amazing place.

A LITTLE BEFORE four in the morning, I wormed my way out of his enveloped arms. I kinda loved that he held me so close, like he didn't want to ever let me go. After peeing, I stole a hoodie from his closet and pulled it over my head. Closing his bedroom door behind me, I tiptoed to the kitchen and opened the fridge.

"Score." I grinned at the plate of holiday leftovers he must have brought home from his parents' house. Pulling off the plastic wrap, I swiped my finger through the cold mashed potatoes. "Oh my gosh, those are good." I skipped the fork and made a second swipe through the mashed potatoes with my finger. They had a buttermilk taste to them.

"Are you really eating my lunch?"

I jumped and turned toward Fisher, licking the potatoes from the corner of my mouth.

He sauntered toward me in nothing but his charcoal gray briefs that hugged him in *all* the right places. "Stop eyeing my cock while licking your lips."

My gaze snapped up to meet his as my tongue made a quick retreat back into my mouth. I grinned. "These are the best potatoes I've ever had. And if you tell Rory that, I'll kill you."

"Why are you eating cold potatoes?" He ducked and kissed me.

My hand pressed to his warm chest. "Because I love almost everything cold. After my dad died, I lived on leftovers. My grandma made huge batches of everything, and we'd essentially eat leftovers for a week. And I was either hanging out with friends or working, so I often grabbed cold leftovers and ate them on the go." My fingers made a return trip to the potatoes, and I held it up to him.

Fisher wrinkled his nose. "I'm not a fan of cold potatoes."

"No?" I tilted my head to the side before slowly sucking my finger.

An unhurried grin curled his lips. "Was I snoring?"

I shook my head. "I had to pee. Then I decided I was hungry."

"I like this on you." He tugged the strings to *his* hoodie. "Not as much as I like me on you, but it's nice."

Popping a piece of cold turkey into my mouth, I teased the waistband of his briefs with my other hand. "How was Thanksgiving with your family?"

Fisher watched my fingers at his waistband for a few seconds before lifting his chin along with one slightly raised eyebrow. "It was okay. Lots of kids. Lots of everything. My mom gave a sappy toast that was more like a speech about how grateful she was that my life had been spared. It started a cry fest. I'm glad to be alive, but can we stop talking about it?"

I giggled. "How dare your mom express such gratitude for her child on *Thanksgiving*."

"I'm just not a fan of being the center of attention. That's Arnie's thing. Not mine."

"Try being an only child. There's no escaping the center."

He nodded slowly. "So ... you told your grandparents about us?"

"I did." I smiled. "It felt amazing, like we were real." I covered the plate with the plastic wrap.

Fisher grabbed the plate and returned it to the fridge. "We are real."

I reached across the island to grab an apple from his big bowl of them. "You know what I mean. *Official*."

"I don't know what you mean."

"Oof ..." I sucked in a sharp breath when he pinned me to the counter, my chest stretched over it with a shiny green apple in one hand.

"I don't know what you mean, because I heard nothing after you bent over my counter." His fingers teased my outer thighs. "And I discovered you're not wearing *anything* under my sweatshirt."

"Fisher ..." I gulped. It was a compromising position I hadn't been in before. He restrained me using his body and the counter instead of zip ties, but the effect was the same.

"You can't be in this position..." he hiked the hoodie up, completely exposing my bare butt "...with callipygian tattooed on your very sexy and shapely ass..." his knee nudged my legs apart a little wider "... and not expect me to fuck you."

Before I could respond, the head of his hot, wet cock slid between my legs, teasing my clit. I liked the new Fisher too much to spend much time missing the old Fisher, but when he talked dirty to me, letting me know I was going to get *fucked*, pinned against the countertop, I welcomed the glimpse of old Fisher and every ounce of the forbidden he brought with him.

"WANT TO COME IN?" I asked Fisher when he drove me home a little before nine Friday morning.

"I actually have a few jobs to check on."

I frowned. "You're making your crew work the day after Thanksgiving?"

"Deadlines, baby."

"One cup of coffee."

"Dinner tonight."

On a sigh, I gave him a reluctant nod. "Here. With my grandparents."

It was his turn to frown. "Is Rory ready to have me over for dinner? It killed her to ask me to install that bar by the toilet."

"She adores you."

"She has coffee and wine with Angie. And she does Angie's hair."

"She does?" I narrowed my eyes.

With a tight smile, he nodded a half dozen times.

"Huh. I didn't know that."

Fisher's gaze shifted to the front door as Rory and Rose came out in their sweatshirts, jogging pants, and tennis shoes.

"They must be escaping my grandparents for a walk. I bet it's a long walk."

They eyed us as they made a big production of stretching on the porch.

"Call me when you get home." I reached for the door handle.

"No kiss?"

I shot him a sideways glance. "I figured you didn't want to kiss me in front of them."

"I'm not the one getting grounded. What do I have to lose?"

Rolling my eyes, I leaned over the console. "I'm twenty-four. I think my grounding days are over."

He slid one hand behind my neck and grinned just before kissing me with no urgency to stop, with lots of tongue, and a little moan on his part. "Bye, beautiful."

Fisher lit up my world in the most spectacular fashion.

"Have a good day." I climbed out of his truck and strutted my stuff to the front door as Rory and Rose gave Fisher a tiny wave.

"Good morning," Rose said.

"Mor ... ning ..." I singsonged, wearing a grin that was nearly too big for my face.

"Did you have a *fun* night?" Rory asked before smirking.

I reached for the door handle. "Fun night. Fun morning. Fun shower. Just so much fun."

Rose snorted a laugh.

"So help me ... if Fisher doesn't make this all okay in the end, he's not going to live to see his next birthday."

"Wow, babes. Prison really toughened you up," Rose said, grabbing my mom's hand and dragging her toward the sidewalk.

I didn't want Fisher to miss his next birthday, but I loved seeing my mom on my team. It meant everything to me.

CHAPTER TWENTY-NINE

FOR EVERY STEP we took forward, it felt like we took two backward.

Fisher had to cancel dinner with us because his family (including Angie) were getting together when some of his extended family paid a surprise visit. That visit lasted the rest of the weekend.

Work on Monday and a mom of twins going into labor on Tuesday spilled over into Wednesday. I crashed when I finally got home. And by Thursday morning, Fisher was on his way to the airport with Angie for four days and three *nights* in Costa Rica.

I kept my chin up and feigned any confidence that tried to slip away when I had time to think about something other than pregnant mamas. On Friday morning, Fisher called me.

"Hey!" I answered my phone on my way to work.

"Good morning. You working?"

"On my way now."

"Well, I fucking hate that I didn't get to say goodbye in person."

"It's life." I meant it, but it still didn't ease my own disappointment. I want to say what a mature adult would've or should've said in that situation.

"Not the life I want."

I smiled.

"Yeah, in-person goodbyes should be mandatory. How is Costa Rica?"

"Green."

I laughed.

"What's on the agenda for today?"

"Apparently massages and rehearsal dinner."

"Massages, huh?" I pretended it was news to me. "Sounds relaxing. I could use a massage."

"I'll massage you when I get home."

"Mmm ... that would be amazing. How's your room?"

With the king-sized bed.

"It's nice."

Nice. That was what he gave me. And I didn't have the nerve to ask about the specific sleeping situation. It would have led to the "why don't you trust me" speech.

"Where are you?"

"Just finished jogging on the beach. I'm in the lobby. I need to go back to the room and shower."

Was he going to lock the door to the bathroom?

Jealousy, irrational or not, whacked away at my chest, making me hurt everywhere.

"Angie doesn't jog?"

"She was still asleep."

"Oh ... are you sharing a room?"

Ugh! I hated playing dumb. Fishing. Waiting to catch him in a lie. But I couldn't make myself stop. It was a terrible feeling.

"Uh ... yeah. The place is booked."

"So you tried to get your own room?"

He sighed. "Reese, don't do this. Nothing good will come of it. I'll be home Sunday night. It's just two more nights. I'm not happy about this situation, but we've discussed this ad nauseam. One month. It ends in one month. We've got this, right?"

I nodded. Of course he couldn't see my nod or my pouty face.

"I love you today."

I kept nodding.

"Reese?"

"Yeah."

"I love you. You. *Youuu*. Okay? Don't doubt that for one second. Go to my house. Crawl in my bed. And think of all the *things* I'm going to do to you when I get home on Sunday."

"Yeah."

"Jesus ... stop. Give me more than a 'yeah.' Tell me you love me. Or be honest and tell me you're pissed off that I agreed to come here. Give me something more than one emotionless word."

I pulled into the clinic's parking lot. "I love you. And I'm pissed off that you agreed to go to Costa Rica with your fiancée."

"Stop calling her my fiancée," he said with a defeated tone.

"Is she still wearing the diamond ring you gave her? When she introduces you to everyone at the wedding as her fiancé, are you going to correct her? If not, then she's your fiancée. And I'm the slutty mistress."

"Reese Capshaw, knock that shit off."

I cringed, rubbing my hand over my face. Why couldn't I stop? Why was I in self-destruction mode? And why couldn't I get out of it?

The unfairest part for him was he had no way to make it right. Not while he was there with her. Fisher was helpless. And I was hell-bent on making him feel terrible. It wasn't one of my finer moments, but it was honest. It was human.

"I'm at work now. I have to go."

"This ends. When I get home this ends. I'm not doing this any longer. Fuck my memory. Fuck family loyalty. I can't do this another month. I want you. That's it. You. So go sulk. You have three days for your pity party. Then I'm going to tie you to ..."

Oh shit. SHIT.

I knew it happened the second it happened. And not only was I not with him, but I was not even in the same country. And it freaked me out. It scared me for a million reasons.

"Jesus ..." he whispered.

And me? I ended the call. The equivalent of turning and running away as fast as my feet could take me.

Running to hide from the truth.

Running to escape reality.

Running to slow down the inevitable catching me.

Fisher triggered a memory by himself. A big one. The one I wanted him to remember in McDonald's where I could do damage control. Help him make sense of it. Help him understand why ... why I did what I did.

"Oh god." I stared at my phone as Fisher tried calling me back. "No. God no. Shit. Shitshitshit! FUCK!" I tossed my vibrating phone into my bag and covered my face with my shaky hands.

I was late for work, and Fisher was in Costa Rica with the memory of him zip-tying me to the stool in his workshop.

"I'm so sorry I'm late," I said to Holly as I hustled to peel off my jacket and toss my bag into the cubby.

She laughed looking at her watch. "I'm not sure two minutes counts as late. Is everything okay?"

"Yes. No." I shook my head before taking a deep breath. "It's a crazy situation."

"Well..." Holly leaned back in her recliner and sipped her tea "...Isabella had to cancel her appointment this morning. So I have time."

I twisted my lips. "It's really messed-up. Promise not to judge me?"

She chuckled. "Oh, Reese, you have no idea how

sordid my life was before I became a midwife." She smirked. "Grab your coffee. I'm all ears."

It only took a few more seconds for me to nod and grin. "Okay."

My story took up the full two hours we had free that morning, and Holly scowled at me when I left her with the Costa Rica cliffhanger. But I didn't have any more to give her because the story was still being written.

When I took a break that afternoon to grab a snack and check my phone, there were a string of twenty-five missed calls and a string of messages from Fisher. Messages with all caps and exclamation points. And a few screen shots.

"Oh no ..." I cringed, scrolling up through the messages. It was the first time Fisher had messaged me since five years earlier which meant when he brought up my name in his messenger, he saw those five-year-old texts.

Innocent texts telling me to drive myself to work or informing me of what time we'd be leaving. Then there were texts of him apologizing for telling his family that I had tummy issues.

Fisher: *I'm sorry.*
Fisher: *Are you going to stay mad at me forever?*
Fisher: *I'll call my family and tell them it was a lie. That I just wanted to be alone with you.*

That was one of the screen shots. Along with the message:

Why did I want to be alone with you?

Another screen shot.

Reese: *Hi. Rose isn't going to tell Rory or anyone.*

Tell Rory what?

Where are you?
Answer your phone.
I'm sorry.
Please pick up your phone.
Don't make me call Rory.
Or the police.

WHAT THE HELL?!!!!

Fisher: *If you're not dead, text Rory and tell her you made it safely to Houston. Don't be a total asshole about it.*
Reese: *Go fuck yourself!*

PICK UP YOUR GODDAMN PHONE!!!!!
MESSAGE ME THE FUCK BACK!
I ZIP-TIED YOU TO THE STOOL IN MY SHOP! WE
WERE MORE THAN FRIENDS AND YOU GODDAMN
KNOW IT!

The last text I received was five minutes before I checked my messages.

Who are you? Why did you do this to me?

My eyes filled with tears. I shouldn't have hung up on him. Not only were we not together, I left him with crazy pieces to what must have felt like an unsolvable puzzle.

I panicked.

I panicked because I was angry at the Costa Rica situation.

I panicked because I didn't have time to talk.

I panicked because I couldn't see his face and he couldn't see mine. I thought he would remember pieces of our intimacy when I could give him a look, and he could maybe see at least what I felt for him even if his feelings for me at the time were still missing. He wasn't supposed to be so far away.

With her.

And her lingerie.

And her sexy dress.

And her sleeping in the same bed with him.

It wasn't supposed to happen that way. Life seldom did.

I didn't have time to call him, but I needed to do something.

Don't be mad. PLEASE don't be mad. PLEASE let's talk about it when you get home. I love you.

After I sent off the text, I grabbed a glass of water and stared at my phone, waiting for him to read the text or text me back.

Nothing.

Maybe he was getting a massage. With her. But that at least meant he wasn't so mad he no longer cared to reply to me.

My short break ended, and I had to get back to work without a response from Fisher. Just ... a bunch of angry all caps messages from him.

How did I never think about our texts? How did he not scour through all his messages right after his accident to piece together some missing memories?

I'd imagined so many scenarios. Memories lost forever. Retrieved memories. The possibility of him remembering something big about him and Angie. And that something taking him away from me. What if she would have been pregnant?

But never did I think *our* time together would be the pulled thread that threatened to unravel everything. And it ate at me the rest of the day. I couldn't think of a worse scenario than him being angry and confused because of me and Angie being the one there to comfort him.

On my way home, I called him, hoping he wasn't at rehearsal dinner yet.

"I can't talk now." That was how he answered his phone.

My heart clenched and a new round of tears stung my eyes. "I love you. I've loved you for *so* long."

"I can't talk now." His voice was so cold.

"When can we talk?"

"When I'm ready."

I swallowed my shaky emotions. "Are you with Angie?"

"She's still in the shower."

Still ... what did that mean? *They* were in the shower and she stayed after he got out? It made me feel nauseous.

"I couldn't talk earlier. I was late for work."

"Well, I can't talk now. I guess we'll talk if or when it works out."

"If? Don't do this. Don't cherry-pick pieces of your past and try to piece them together by yourself. Making assumptions. Nothing about us was simple."

"No shit."

"Fisher," I said as my voice cracked.

"Angie put it all on the table. What the fuck did you do? Was it a game?"

"No! It wasn't a game. I wanted ..." I sighed. It sounded so good, so *right* in my head for the longest time. It made sense. It felt romantic even. So why did it feel all wrong when it mattered the most?

"I have to go."

"Fisher ..." I grasped for every last second, but all I could do was say his name. "I love you."

"I have to go." Fisher ended the call.

I batted away my tears and drew in a shaky breath. He needed space, but he wasn't getting space. He was getting Angie, and there wasn't anything I could do.

CHAPTER THIRTY

THAT NIGHT, it felt like all the bad things I had done in my life were being served back to me in the cruelest revenge. Like God was mad or Karma was having a nasty case of menstrual cramps.

"Do you uh ... happen to follow Angie on Instagram?" Rose asked after dinner, glancing at her phone while on the floor.

Rory was just above her on the sofa, stroking Rose's hair with one hand while holding an open novel in her other hand, readers low on her nose. "Me?"

"No," Rose said. "You, Reese?"

I'd reread the same page in my book for nearly an hour, thinking only of Fisher. "No. Why?"

"She has pictures from the rehearsal dinner with Fisher. And it's captioned 'Time to cut him off.'" Rose held up her phone.

I scooted to the edge of the recliner and leaned forward, squinting. Fisher was sitting at a table, laughing while holding a beer in one hand. The table space in front of him was filled with empty beer bottles.

"Looks like he's having a good time." Rose cringed. "Of course, he's going to feel like shit for the wedding tomorrow."

"Good." I frowned.

That got Rose's and Rory's attention.

"Trouble in paradise?" Rory asked, eyeing me over her readers.

"Kinda," I frowned. I wasn't going to say anything, but I couldn't keep my mouth shut any longer. Not with Fisher drunk in Costa Rica with Angie.

"This morning I talked to Fisher on the phone right before I had to be at work. He said something that triggered a memory of us. An intimate detail. And I freaked. Major panic. Completely lost my head and hung up on him when he started to question me. And by the time I got a break, I had a million messages and missed calls from him. He *just* found our texts from five years ago. They are confusing, and they did nothing but fuel his anger. So he knows we were more than friends, but only from a few vague texts and another cherry-picked memory." I stared off to the side, chasing away the emotions that threatened to make me cry. I didn't want to fall apart. Not yet.

"And now he thinks you lied to him. Or the omission of the truth which feels like a lie," Rory said.

Biting the inside of my cheek, I nodded.

"He'll be home Sunday. That's not that far away. You can talk it over then."

Another nervous nod.

"Reese?" Rory said my name slowly.

I forced my teary-eyed gaze to her.

"He won't do anything stupid." She read my mind.

But I wasn't so sure.

Did he like me more than a friend when he had sex with Teagan the orthodontist? Did he even think twice before having sex with Angie after his accident? I mean ... it wasn't that long after that he decided he liked me. What if sex wasn't a big deal to men like it was to women? Not that I could talk ... I gave away my virginity to Brendon when deep down I knew I was never going to marry him.

"What if he does?" I whispered.

"He won—" Rory started to reassure me.

But Rose cut her off. "What if he does?" she asked.

"Rose. Stop," Rory said, tossing her book aside and sitting up straight. "You're not helping."

"What if I am helping? What if preparing your heart for the worst is the best idea? So let's do it ... let's imagine the worst. Fisher has sex with Angie in Costa Rica. And maybe they fall back in love. Or maybe it brings back more memories and he remembers really loving her. Then what?"

I captured my tears with the arm of my sleeve before they fully escaped. "I don't know," I whispered.

"You do," Rose said. "You know. You know you'll be heartbroken. You know it will take time to get over him, and maybe you'll never get completely over him. But you'll go on to pursue your career. You'll go on to find new love. You'll survive. You'll live. So there you have it. That's your worst-case scenario. Once you accept it, then every other scenario won't seem as bad."

"Rose ..." Rory frowned. "It's not that easy and you know it. And honestly, that's not necessarily the worst-case scenario. If Fisher has sex with Angie, but then comes home and tries to say it meant nothing, *that's* a pretty bad scenario. Because Reese won't be able to trust him. It would be easier to know that it's just over. Done. But trying to move on and rebuild trust would feel torturous. I don't know how anyone truly gets past that. I mean ... Fisher fell in love with Reese and they ...well..." she grimaced "... had an affair or cheated or whatever you want to call it, but he didn't know or feel his love for Angie. I'm not sure that makes it right, but it at least makes it *different*. And even taking his memory into consideration, I don't know how Angie will ever be able to forgive and forget, even if he does decide he wants to be with her."

My tears were gone. All I could do was sit idle in the chair and slowly blink at them. "You two are the worst. I want to go on record saying you are *the worst*."

They shot me shocked expressions.

"I feel zero percent better and one hundred percent worse. I ... I ... I can't believe you just said all those terrible things. How am I supposed to sleep? How am I supposed to function or even breathe for the next two days with images of Fisher and Angie having sex?"

"Sweetie, we were just trying to ..." Rory shook her head frantically as if she could take it all back, as if there was a rewind button.

"Yeah, Reese, I wanted you to prepare yourself just in case. I'm not saying I think that's what's going to happen," Rose said with a lot more concern in her words.

"I told you he would never do anything. And I mostly meant it. Is that what you want? Do you need us to sugarcoat it, to possibly lie to you? Do you want us to tell you that Fisher is above every other man and that no amount of anger, alcohol, or temptation would ever lead him to do something he shouldn't do?"

"Yes! That's exactly what I want you to tell me."

Their eyebrows shot up their foreheads, lips parted.

I sighed, dropping my head into my hands. "I should have told him everything. Me and my stupid fantasy about him falling in love with me a second time without remembering or *knowing* anything about the first time. I did this ... this one is on me." My head lifted to look at them. "He might have sex with her." A new round of tears burned my eyes, but I kept them at bay. "I'm not stupid. He's human. Even the best humans make mistakes. Maybe by not telling Angie, sneaking around, pretending that time would make things less painful for her and his family, we were really just setting ourselves up to implode."

After a few silent moments, Rory murmured, "Maybe he thinks about it, tells Angie everything, and comes home to the woman he loves."

That made me cry.

I WASN'T friends with Angie on Instagram, but her account wasn't private, so I had the opportunity to drive myself *fucking* insane for the next two days.

Rory and Reese attended some family fun event at the school. So on Saturday, I spent the day stalking Angie hard on Instagram. Looking at every picture she'd ever posted and reading every caption. Had I known about it or looked for her account earlier, I'm not sure things would have progressed as far between Fisher and me.

I mean ... I knew social media rarely portrayed the real stories of people's lives, but it was easy to get caught in the trap of believing it. A picture was worth a thousand words, right? Take that times another thousand because I swear Angie had nearly a thousand pictures on her page.

A lot before the accident.

Some since his accident.

All of them said she and Fisher were in love.

My Saturday would have been less destructive and less tragic had I spent it overdosing on pills or slitting my wrists. Seriously, Angie's Instagram page was a dark hole of death for me.

Kissing.

Laughing.

Big smiles.

Photos in the mountains.

A ton of photos of Fisher with his shirt off. *MY naked fisherman.*

His family.

Some outing on a boat.

Kiss. Kiss. Smile. Smile.

She even posted photos of them in bed! Not porn, but definitely a little racy. Him sleeping with the sheets low, obviously naked beneath the sheets. A weird-angled photo of his arms around her waist and his legs scissored with hers. The sheets covered the right areas, and she captioned it: soul mates.

What was that acronym everyone used? Oh yeah, FML. Really ... *fuck my life.*

Recent photos included the shot that Rose showed me of Fisher getting his fill of alcohol, but also of their room in Costa Rica confirming that they only had one bed. An hour earlier, she'd posted a shot of her reflection in the mirror of the hotel room. She was in the bathroom with a towel wrapped around her body and another one wrapped around her head, and Fisher was already dressed in his suit for the wedding, looking out the window with his hands casually slid into the front pockets of his pants.

My heart cracked again and again, barely hanging on.

Her caption was: My Future Husband. With a heart emoji.

My level of obsession hit the most destructive low when I heard Rory and Rose pull into the garage. I grabbed a bottle of wine and an opener and ran to my room and closed the door. When one of them knocked and opened the door a crack, I remained perfectly still on my bed, with my back to the door, so they thought I was taking a nap. When the door softly clicked shut again, I sat up, pulled the hidden bottle of wine out from under the blanket, and opened it.

Over the next hour, Angie documented the wedding in her Instagram story with a nice mix of still photos and short videos.

The venue on the beach.

Clips from the ceremony.

Her and Fisher holding hands, posing next to the bride and groom.

"We're going to dinner. Pizza? You coming?" Rory knocked on my door. I quickly set the bottle of wine on the floor where she couldn't see it, nearly falling out of bed onto my butt. Then I grabbed a book from my nightstand and buried my nose into it just as she opened my door.

"I'm uh ... good." I couldn't tell if my words were slurred, so I yawned to hide anything that might make her suspicious. It was incredibly hard to pretend you weren't drunk when you were.

"Sure you don't need a break? Or you can bring your book."

"Good." Another yawn. "Totally good."

"You sound exhausted. Might want to go to bed early and get more sleep, in case you get called for a delivery."

Oh my gosh ...

She was right. I was on call and drunk. Only Rory didn't know I was drunk.

"Okay," I managed.

Once I heard the back door to the garage close, I stumbled out of bed and drank a hundred gallons of water to flush out the alcohol ... give or take ninety-nine gallons. Then I spent the next hour on the toilet peeing out all the water, eating chips from the bag, and monitoring Angie's Instagram page.

Kill me now.

I'd always felt like saying "yes" to Brendon, and then losing my virginity with him when I knew I wasn't going to marry him, was my lowest of lows.

Wrong.

My self-destructive drunk ass on the toilet, stalking Fisher and Angie in Costa Rica was my new low. I should have deleted the app and gone to dinner with Rory and Rose. When my bladder gave me a break, I took my pathetic self to my bedroom, and I deleted the Instagram app. Then I prayed, on-my-knees-hands-folded prayed, for God to make it stop. I left it up to Him to determine what that meant. I just wanted something ... anything ... everything to stop.

While I waited for his answer, I grabbed my Bible from my bookshelf and plopped onto the bed.

Suddenly I was inspired to read some 1 Corinthians about love and marriage inspiration.

It doesn't envy. Well ... too late.

It doesn't boast. It is not proud. Clearly Angie needed to spend a little more time in God's Word.

So many things love was not supposed to be.

Rude.

Self-seeking.

Easily angered.

Keeping no record of wrongs.

Never delighting in evil.

Demanding its own way.

Had I believed all that, then the only conclusion I would have come to was ... I couldn't love Fisher.

But for the record ... neither could Angie with her mega boasting and larger-than-life pride.

Thou shalt not judge.

It wasn't all restrictive. There were a few things love *was* supposed to be.

Patient.

Kind.

Rejoicing in truth.

Hopeful.

Enduring in every circumstance.

Wow! Was I incapable of loving Fisher the way God intended for humans to love one another?

Feeling a little nauseous and mentally broken, I slid my Bible onto my nightstand, pulled my blankets over me, and fell asleep.

CHAPTER THIRTY-ONE

Sunday morning was rough. My head felt like it had been shaken with a 6.0 magnitude earthquake.

"Muffin?" Rory asked.

She and Rose eyed me from the kitchen table. They wore matching white robes and big smirks.

Squinting against the light from *all* the window shades drawn open, I shook my aching head.

"I knew something was up when I asked you about dinner last night. But the un-flushed toilet, empty bag of chips on the bathroom floor, and empty wine bottle next to your bed this morning confirmed it. Not to mention your Bible next to your bed. Wanna talk about it?" Rory slowly sipped her coffee.

I poured myself a cup of coffee and filled a tall glass with water before taking two pills for my head. "So you knew I wasn't right, but you went to dinner anyway?" I shuffled my feet to the table and plunked my butt onto the chair.

Rory shrugged. "What's that saying ... something about the only way to get past something is to go through it? I noticed you were going through it. And I didn't want to stop your progress."

With a grunt, I sipped my coffee. "Yup. I'm making amazing progress. Here's what I now know. Angie posts *everything* on Instagram. Fisher loved her. Maybe does again. And I have no clue how to love. I'm an expert in anti-love. I should move back to Michigan. Finish my master's. And forget I ever met Fisher Mann."

"Ouch." Rose wrinkled her nose. "So much for clarity after a rough night."

Resting my elbows on the table, I rubbed my tired eyes. "Isn't life just a rocky road of mistakes? A journey to enlightenment or Heaven or wherever? I mean ... what do we really know when we die? What did we really learn?"

"What's the point?" Rory said.

"Exactly." I gave her a tight-lipped smile. "And what is wrong with the world? Why do we have to spend so much time recording our lives and sharing them with the world? Granted, I didn't get a cell phone until I was nearly a legal adult, and I do have social media accounts, but why does something that's so time-consuming make us feel so terrible most of the time? And why do we do it? Why do we voluntarily subject ourselves to it? What a waste of life."

Rory chuckled. "I spent five years in prison, so I agree with you. But let's talk about the real issue. How much time did you spend on Angie's Instagram account yesterday?"

I sighed, hanging my head. "All of it. Every single picture she's ever posted and every single caption she posted with them is burned into my brain. It was the most suicidal thing I have ever done." I took another sip of my coffee. "I'm not proud of it. And I deleted the app." I retrieved my phone from my hoodie pocket and brought up the screen. "But then I downloaded the app again this morning. And I officially hate Fisher Mann and his *fiancée* Angie." I showed them the post from late last night, after I'd already gone to bed. It was a photo of him sleeping on his stomach, arms next to his head, sheets *so* low on his back that it seemed unlikely if not impossible that he was wearing anything at all. Angie captioned it: My Whole World.

Rose and Rory blinked slowly at the phone screen, but Rose's gaze drifted away from it first. She had already seen it. They had nothing to say. And I had no tears left to cry. I told Fisher I was in it for as long as I felt like I was actually *in* it.

Well, I was no longer in it.

"Reese ..." Rory said softly as I pushed back in my chair and stood.

I shook my head. "It's fine. I actually feel sorry for her. The only way she can feel like he loves her is if he hates me. And I think this weekend ... he's hated me."

I think Elliott Trenton Davies decided to announce his impending arrival Sunday afternoon just so I could avoid dealing with my so-called life. Around four in the afternoon, I received the call from Holly with permission to "not rush" because she knew Elliott's mom's contractions were years apart. But she was a first-time mom who required some guidance in being patient. And Holly excelled at patience. Even though she knew the new mom would not be holding her baby anytime soon, Holly shared in her excitement and vowed to be with her every step of the way. That was code for Holly would sit in the corner of the room, reading a romance novel, while the mom and scared but eager dad worked through tiny contractions together. As long as the mom was still smiling, Holly knew no baby would be arriving soon.

So I took my time, taking a shower, eating dinner, and packing my bag with my own books, snacks, and lots of water.

"Hope it all goes well." Rory smiled as she unloaded groceries.

I hiked my bag onto my shoulder and tucked my feet into my shoes. "Me too. I don't know when I'll see you. This could be a *long* labor."

"Wouldn't that be a blessing."

I knew what she meant. And I felt it too. Fisher and Angie would be home later, and I needed to *not* be home. Not be available to him and his anger or pathetic excuses. Not put myself in the position to explode and say things that would make everything exponentially worse.

"Yes." I scrounged a smile for her. "It really would be." I shut the door behind me.

Elliott's mom did, in fact, labor for almost twenty-four hours, during which time, I received one text from Fisher.

I'm home if you want to talk.

If I *wanted* to talk. Not "I'm home, we need to talk."

I replied as soon as I had a quick chance.

I'm at a birth.

He didn't reply.

It was almost seven o'clock Monday night before I made it home.

Rose and Rory were decorating the house for Christmas.

"Hey, sweetie. How'd it go?"

On a sigh, I smiled—a tiny one. "Good. A boy. Seven pounds, nine ounces. Mom cried. Dad cried."

"Did you?" Rose asked.

I shrugged. "I might have got a little teary eyed because I just ..." On another sigh, I frowned.

"You're tired. Emotionally drained." Rory said.

I nodded. "*So* drained. I'm going to crash. I'll see you in a hundred years."

"Love you."

"You too," I mumbled, dragging my feet and slumped body to bed.

THE NEXT MORNING, I woke a little before five and couldn't get back to sleep. It also didn't help that it sounded like someone was mowing our lawn. I peeked out the window. It had snowed overnight. A lot. And Fisher was snow blowing our drive and sidewalk.

Of course he was ...

Rory and Rose's room was tucked in the back corner of the house, so they likely didn't hear him. Lucky them.

Ten hours of sleep was enough for me, so I showered and dried my hair. By then it was five-thirty, and I no longer heard the snowblower. When I peeked out the front window, Fisher was loading the snowblower and his shovel into the back of his truck.

Without a real goal in mind, I slipped on my jacket, hat, and boots and went out the back door, opening the garage door which turned on a light. Fisher glanced in my direction for a second before closing his tailgate. He made his way up the driveway as I stood in the garage between the two cars with my hands in the pockets of my jacket.

"Thanks for doing that," I said with reserved emotion. My heart hurt too much. There was so much to say. And I didn't know where to begin or if it was even the right time to have the conversation. Did he have other driveways to clear? Work to do?

"It's no big deal." He dusted snow off his jacket and coveralls. His scruffy face was wet from the snow.

"Do you have time to grab coffee?" He pulled up his coat sleeve to look at his watch. "Starbucks opens in fifteen minutes."

Starbucks. He could have invited me to his house for coffee so we'd have total privacy, but he invited me to Starbucks. I didn't know how to interpret it. But I also knew I needed something from him. And maybe that was his goal too. Maybe he needed something from me. Were we going to Starbucks to break up? Were we even still together? Were we *ever* really together?

I nodded once. "Okay. Let me grab my purse."

"Okay."

After I grabbed my purse, we headed down the driveway, Fisher's gloved hand held mine, but it wasn't an intimate gesture. It was a friendly gesture, just making sure I didn't slip and fall.

After we got in the truck, it only took a few minutes to get to Starbucks. Not a word was murmured on the way, and it only intensified the pain in my chest.

Again, Fisher held my hand as we made it through the parking lot that hadn't been plowed and into the empty Starbucks, save for two employees behind the counter.

"My treat. You plowed the driveway," I said like I would have said to a kind stranger. "Coffee. Black?"

He nodded and headed in the direction of a table

while I ordered our drinks. And instead of taking a seat and waiting for my name to be called, I milled around the registers reading all the advertisements for their holiday drinks. Anything to put off the inevitable.

"Here you go." The guy at the register set the two drinks on the counter.

I took a deep breath and made my way to the table. Fisher had his gloves on the table and jacket off, but his beanie still on, and a sad look on his face. Once I got seated and unzipped my jacket, it took a few awkward seconds for our gazes to lock. But once they did, I knew there wasn't any more small talk to be said.

"We were more than friends," he said like it physically pained him to say it.

I thought it was a statement, but maybe it was a question. Maybe he needed confirmation that what he remembered was real.

"We were more than friends," I echoed, giving him confirmation.

"And you didn't tell me this why?"

With a tiny head shake, I rubbed my lips together. "For several reasons. At first, I didn't think it was beneficial information to share given the fact that you were engaged and we hadn't seen each other in five years anyway. And I didn't want to give you something you couldn't remember and make you feel like you owed me something in return. Some sort of emotional acknowledgment. And honestly, I didn't need it. I liked where we were going. I liked our present. And the closer we got, the less I cared if we shared the past."

I stopped. I had a truckload of other things to say, but I had to pace myself and get a feel for where his head was after recent revelations.

"So we ... what? We were just fucking around?"

"There was a physical attraction. And we messed around, yes."

"Messed around. But we weren't sleeping together because you already told me you gave that other guy your virginity. Correct?"

I nodded.

"Did I try to have sex with you?"

I took a sip of my coffee and then another sip, buying *all* the time before clearing my throat. "No."

He blinked several times, an unreadable expression pinned to his face. "Why not?"

"Because I was upfront with you that I wasn't going to have sex with you."

"But oral didn't count?"

My cheeks filled with embarrassment as I glanced toward the counter to see if anyone seemed to be listening to us. "Do we have to go into such detail? Does it matter?"

"I'm just trying to understand."

"Well..." I kept my gaze pointed to the counter "... you have amnesia, so you might not ever really understand."

"Maybe if you give me all the facts, all the details, then I can understand."

"Like Angie? She gave you everything. Do you understand your love for her? Or should I say, before you left for Costa Rica, did you understand your love for her?"

"What's that supposed to mean? Before I left for Costa Rica ..." He narrowed his eyes.

"Did you have a nice time? Was the couples' massage in the same room? And how does that work? If they do, in fact, think you're a couple, does that mean you undress for the massage in the same room? Did you take off all your clothes for her? Did she take hers off for you? What about the room where you stayed? Were there two beds? Because in the photo on Instagram, it looked like there was only one bed. And before you answer that, fair warning ... Angie told me, Rose, and Rory all about her plans for you two on the trip. She requested a room with one bed instead of two. The couples' massage. Oh, and we must not forget the sexy lingerie she bought to wear for you. How did you like that? Did you try to have sex with *her*? Or did you settle for oral like you did with me? Was it all-night oral? Because the photo of you on Instagram sleeping in bed made you look thoroughly exhausted. Oh ... and it definitely looked like you were naked under the sheet resting so low on your torso."

I was so angry my hand shook as I gripped my coffee. My heart raced. And my jaw worked overtime grinding my teeth.

"Are you done?" he asked, looking completely unaffected by my long spiel.

I stood. "I think *we're* done."

Fisher's gaze fell from me to his coffee cup, and

after a few seconds, he nodded, pulling on his jacket and sliding his gloves onto his fingers.

I didn't mean it. I was just *so* mad and so hurt. And tired. Rory was right. I was emotionally spent for the next hundred years. Why didn't he have a defense? One single comeback or explanation for his actions? Why couldn't he at least lie to me, show a little desperation like the idea of us ending affected him? Was it because everything I said was true? Did he not have a defense? Did he want things to end between us?

"I'll take you home." He took my hand to lead me to the door, and I yanked it away. Falling in the snowy parking lot would have been less painful than enduring another second of him touching me after touching her.

Fisher had the nerve to give me a little flinch, like he was scarred by my gesture. I brushed past him to the door and trekked through the snow to his truck.

When he pulled into my driveway and put the truck in *Park*, he turned toward me. "Am I him?"

I grabbed the door handle and gave him a slow glance. "Who?"

"Your first love? You told me he wasn't ready to be found. And you call me your lost fisherman. Am I him? Did you fall in love with me? Am *I* the schmuck who wouldn't take your virginity even after you offered it?"

That moment was the very reason I never told him about us. It was a terrible feeling to be so emotionally exposed without an ounce of recognition. I didn't want the "did you love me?" I wanted the "I loved you, and I remember it. Every feeling. Every moment. Every single emotion."

I opened the door and spoke the only truth I knew for certain at the moment. "I will never regret not giving you my virginity." I jumped down and shut the door, not looking back for a single second.

As soon as I opened the door, Rory and Rose were right there. They'd been watching out the window. And while they had no idea what had been said between us, the look on my face must have said everything.

"I'm sorry," Rory's brow wrinkled as she took a step forward with open arms.

I couldn't take any steps. All I could do was fall into hundreds of pieces and hope my mom could catch all of them.

I thought we were strong enough to make it through.

I thought it was finally our time.

I thought wrong.

CHAPTER THIRTY-TWO

Babies made everything better.

On the one hand, they reminded me of the life I wanted for myself, the life I'd imagined with Fisher. But they were also symbolic of transition, transformation, moving forward. A reminder that we are such tiny parts of something so much bigger.

How many babies were created from a love that died? Yet they moved forward. Love can live in small ways even after it dies. Fisher nudged me, he shifted my journey in life. And while we didn't have a tiny human to show for our love, I was a nurse and a midwife in training because I met Fisher Mann, and he was the reason I went with Brendon. Had *he* been the one to take my virginity, I wouldn't have had the strength to leave.

Fisher's love led me to a job I loved. A purpose that meant something to me. A feeling of accomplishment and unfathomable personal satisfaction. And I could hate him for a lot of things, but I couldn't regret us or all the reckless moments that sent us spinning in a whirlwind of passion and love.

Love. It *was* love.

I knew it always would be love. A tragic love, but nonetheless *love*.

"Are you married?" Abbie asked me as I weighed her four-week-old daughter in the clinic.

I smiled. "Not yet. I've been a little unlucky in that department." I handed Abbie her little peanut.

Abbie sat in the rocking chair with her and breastfed her while we waited for Holly to join us for the well-baby check.

"I feel ya." Abbie chuckled while gazing adoringly at her little girl. "Drew and I have actually been married twice."

I looked up from my table after recording the weight. "Seriously?"

She nodded. "We got married right out of high school against our parents' wishes. But we were in love. Neither one of us had any idea what we wanted out of life. We just knew we wanted to be together. But being together didn't pay well, neither did our minimum wage jobs. It got increasingly hard to squeeze happiness out of a love that nobody supported. And it led to fights and resentment. Then it led to divorce in less than a year. And we didn't see each other again for ten years. Crazy, right?

"He went to college. I went to college. Drew ended up in Maine, and I came back here for a job. We both had been in several serious relationships. And when Drew came home one Christmas, we ran into each other at an Avalanche game. And it was instant sparks. He was in a relationship at the time and so was I. But it didn't matter. I swear we both knew it too. I actually remember thinking, this is going to get messy."

Messy.

Of course she said messy.

"So hearts were broken and lives were disrupted again so you could have your second chance?"

Twisting her lips for a second, she nodded. "Pretty much. But look at this little princess. I have no regrets."

Before I could say any more, ask a single one of my twenty questions, Holly came into the room.

But Abbie's story haunted me for days.

Saturday morning, I woke to voices in the other room. After throwing on my robe, I opened the door a crack.

Angie.

WWJD?

WWJD?

Really, what would he do?

I wasn't okay. It had been two weeks since the Costa Rica trip. And I hadn't talked to Fisher since our morning at Starbucks, and neither had Rory or Rose to my knowledge.

Was Angie there to gloat? Should it have mattered?

Jesus needed to tell me what to do because I wanted to tell her everything. Woman to woman. If she was going to marry the man I loved, she needed to go into it with her eyes wide open. Jesus would've told her the truth, right?

As I opened the door a little farther, I could hear their conversation.

"Did he say who?" Rory asked.

"Nope."

"Did he say how long it's been going on?" Rose probed.

"He said it didn't matter. I asked him a ton of questions, but he said the answers didn't matter." She sounded so defeated, her voice weak and even a little shaky.

"Does his family know?"

"No. I asked him not to tell them until I leave." She sniffled. Yeah, she was crying.

"Leave?" Rory sounded surprised.

"I'm going back to California. And after I have time to make sense of this, to figure out what I did wrong, I'll either come back and face his family or I'll at least call them. They are my family too, but they're his real family. And I don't want there to be sides to take. That's not fair."

"It was unexpected. A tragedy in so many ways. He could have died. He could have been crippled for life," Rose said. "But he lived. And sometimes when we love people, we have to give them what they need even if it's not us. Life takes so many unexpected paths. Forever is rarely realistic."

"I miss him already," Angie said.

And dang it anyway, I teared up. I teared up because she had no idea that anything she had done was hurting me. I teared up because she was just a woman who fell in love with Fisher Mann. And it was nearly impossible to not fall in love with him.

"H-he lived ... but I still l-lost him."

I wiped my eyes as I leaned against the doorframe and listened to the *mess* I helped create.

"I'm so sorry for your pain," Rory said, and I imagined her hugging Angie. Someone needed to hug her.

I gently closed my door and sat on the edge of my bed. When did he break things off with her? Did that change things between us? Did he sleep with her in Costa Rica? A goodbye of sorts? How did I feel about him?

So many confusing and unanswered questions.

Did I feel her words? Did they ring true for me too? Did I lose Fisher, but he didn't die? Did I lose Fisher, but he didn't end up with Angie?

Was that the right choice all along? Did he need to start fresh? Walk away from the past he couldn't remember and find someone completely new?

I didn't know. And by that point the pain was rather numbing.

A while later, there was a knock at my door.

"Yeah?"

Rory opened the door. "Morning."

I smiled. "Morning."

"Were you listening?" She gave me a sad smile while taking a seat next to me on the bed.

"For a little while."

"He ended it."

I nodded. "When?"

"The night they got home from Costa Rica. Angie had to go out of town for work the following week, probably for the best, and so this has been her first chance to tell us. She'll be okay."

I glanced over at Rory, eyes narrowed. "I heard enough of the conversation to know that she's not going to be okay anytime soon. Why would you say that?"

Her nose wrinkled. "I'm Team Reese and I don't want you to feel responsible because you really are not responsible. Had he not fallen in love with you, I don't think he was going to fall back in love with her."

"So two weeks ..." He'd broken up with her when we went to Starbucks, but he said nothing.

"Give him time, sweetie. I think he's dealing with his own loss. He's lost hope of getting his memory back, and that has to be hard to accept."

He lost faith too. Faith in me. Faith in us.

I knew from experience that losing faith sucked. And it was lonely. And you did reckless things. You made poor decisions.

Maybe we needed another five years apart like Abbie and Drew. Or maybe it was really *never* going to be our time.

"It sucks that she's losing her new job over a guy."

"She's not. She put in for a transfer, that's all."

I nodded. "That's good, I guess."

"So ... Christmas is next week. I think we should make cookies today. Pop popcorn to string on the tree. And maybe drive around and look at lights tonight. I think we could all use a little Christmas cheer."

"Yeah," I said, lacking all cheer.

"Rose and I are going to run errands. We have some shopping to finish up. And then we'll grab groceries on the way home so we can make cookies."

I nodded. "Give me twenty minutes to shower and I'll go with you."

Her nose wrinkled. "We can't buy things for you when you're with us."

"Fine. I'll stay here and watch movies."

"Now, that's a great idea. You've been working a ton of hours. It's about time you just relax."

I handed her a fake smile and even faker enthusiasm. She rolled her eyes. "See you in a few hours."

After she left, I grabbed a shower, dried my hair, and dressed in my comfiest sweats and fitted long-sleeved tee.

Fuzzy socks.

Hot chocolate.

Netflix.

Halfway through the first movie, a sappy love story, and drunk on chocolate and spray whipped topping, I brought up my messages, specifically my texts with Fisher. And I typed a message.

It was you, my lost Fisher Mann. I loved you. And you loved me. Just wanted you to know that in case you never remember. It was messy, but we were real.

I stared at the message and thought of all the reasons to send it. Then I thought of all the reasons not to send it. Then I pressed send because my heart needed more closure than leaving his truck and telling him I would never regret not giving him my virginity.

After all, he most likely took Angie's years ago, and where did that get her? Them?

I felt like the note he wrote in his graduation card to me was his way of getting closure. Five years after the fact, but clearly it was something he needed to say to move on and marry Angie.

But I didn't want to be engaged to another man and suddenly feeling unsettled emotions for Fisher. I wanted closure before I moved on.

Fisher: I know.

I know? Really? That was his reply? It seemed ... well, a little arrogant. Like ... of course I loved him?

I started to send another message but I had no idea what it needed to say. What was the comeback to "I know?" If I was looking for closure, then I got it. I said what I needed to say, and it shouldn't have mattered whether he responded or not. Yet there I was with a frown on my face, feeling like it *did* matter.

Taking a deep breath, I let it go. That was all I

could do. Just let it go. Accept the closure. After all, I clearly wanted him to know since I sent him the message. So what was the big deal with him replying with "I know?"

Maybe I should have replied with an "Okay. Great. Just making sure. So ... nice knowing ya. Have a good life."

I continued playing the movie for all of two, maybe three minutes, before I shot to my feet. Grabbed my keys, jacket, boots, and marched to my car. It took me less than two minutes to get to Fisher's house.

Knocking on his front door several times, I hugged my arms to my chest. The door opened. "What exactly does—" I bit my tongue and my face morphed into a constipated feeling smile. "Hi," I said to the stranger opening Fisher's door.

"Hey. Can I help you?"

"I ... um ... was looking for Fisher. But I'll come back later."

"He's downstairs. We're playing pool. I just happened to be up here grabbing more beer, so I answered the door. Come in."

I shook my head. "No. I'm fine. I'll come back." I started to back away from the blond dude with dimples and an overly friendly grin.

"Did someone knock at the door?" Fisher popped his head around the corner from the top of the stairs.

"You have company, I think. The more the merrier. But she's a little skittish." Blond dude chuckled, patting

Fisher on the shoulder and disappearing to the kitchen and probably the basement.

"Speaking of company, I didn't know *you* had company. I'm leaving." I turned.

"Reese, you can come in."

"Nope. I'm good."

"Did you need something?"

"Nope." I got to my car but the door was locked. I didn't remember locking the door. And I also didn't remove my keys from the ignition.

It beeped. How did I not hear it beeping? Oh, that's right, I was on a mission until Dimples ruined it.

"Reese ..."

"Nope." I needed another word, but suddenly it hurt to be so close to him. Suddenly I wasn't okay with us being over no matter how much closure I tried to get from him.

I started down the sidewalk, heading home to get the spare set of keys to my car.

"Reese ..." Fisher was closing in on me, so I took off running. "Jesus ... what ... why are you always running from me?" He chased me down the sidewalk, but I wasn't that fast in my snow boots.

Before I could turn the corner, his hand grabbed the back of my jacket. I stopped and wriggled out of his hold, turning toward him, breathless and a little rabid.

"I'm always running from you because you are the worst, Fisher Mann. The. Worst. You make it impossible to love you and just as impossible to *not* love you. But the worst part is you make it impossible to be with you. And you just ... let me go. All the freaking time. And you go off to Costa Rica and screw around with Angie and sleep in the same bed and do god knows what else with her. Then you *again* let me get out of your truck that morning after coffee and you. Let. Me. Go.

"AND I had to find out from Angie that you broke things off with her. Why? Why did I hear it from her and not you? So you don't want to be with me. Fine. But have the decency to say *something*. Don't be an arrogant jerk who says 'I know' when I get the nerve to message you about how I loved you. So yeah ... I'm running from you because you are bad for me. And I should have known it years ago. But more than any of that..." I turned and tucked my cold hands into my pockets as I continued trekking toward my house "...I'm running away from you because I locked my *fucking* keys in the car."

"You kept the truth from me when it could have been the thing that gave me my memory back."

"Angie gave you the truth. It didn't give you your memory back."

"Why keep the truth from me? Why do it after you already knew I was in love with you?" Fisher stayed a few feet behind me.

"You wouldn't understand, and it doesn't matter now."

"Well you drove to my house because *something* must still matter now."

"It was a mistake. I shouldn't have texted you. I

shouldn't have driven to your house." I picked up my pace again, but not to a run. "I thought I needed some sort of closure, but I was wrong. Being away from you is all the closure I need." I batted away the tears and made sure he didn't catch up to me, didn't see my tears.

"Say it. If you don't say it, you know you'll regret it."

Screw my tears.

I whipped around. "I didn't tell you because I wanted you to remember us and how you felt about me all on your own. And I wanted to be there when it happened. I wanted to see the look on your face. And I wanted it to convey the feelings I had when I realized you were falling in love with me for the second time without ever remembering the first time. I wanted to know if you felt this sense of awe and fate like it was impossible for us to not fall in love at every possible opportunity."

Fisher deflated. He couldn't even look at me.

So I turned and continued my journey home.

"We messed around on the pool table. In your bedroom. My closet. My bed. The downstairs kitchen. My workshop."

I halted at his words, but I couldn't turn around because I wasn't sure if I was really hearing what I thought I was hearing.

"And we slept on the screened-in porch one night after I went out with Rory and Rose. You tripped at one of my job sites and ended up with a nail in your hand. I carried you to the truck. And the whole way I smelled your hair. And I thought ... if I could spend the rest of my life smelling her hair, I'd die a happy man. Did *you* know that? Did you know how much I liked the smell of your hair and the floral scent of your skin, and whatever you put behind your ears and down your neck? Yeah, that shit drove me crazy insane."

I couldn't turn around. Or blink. I could barely breathe. But I could cry. And I did. So, so much.

He thought. If he thought. He knew. If he knew. He remembered ... everything.

"Five years ago, I loved you and you loved me. It was really fucking messy ... but we were real. It just wasn't the right time. Our timing seems to always suck. And I'm sorry about that. But you're here. And I'm here. And my best friend from high school is in town for the next two weeks, and you should come play pool with us."

I turned a degree every second, like a ticking clock, until I faced him—that gleam in his eyes.

"I love you today." He shrugged a shoulder. "And I'm going to wake up and do the same thing tomorrow."

I had so many questions. *Did* he have sex with Angie in Costa Rica? That was my biggest question, or so I thought. But as I inched my feet in his direction, I realized it didn't matter. If I wanted to cross that threshold back into his life, it couldn't matter. If I accepted his love and gave it freely back in return, there were Biblical rules about love I'd have to follow.

It was never jealous or demanded its own way.

It wasn't irritable.

It didn't keep record of being wronged.

Love never gave up.

Never lost faith.

Love was always hopeful.

And it endured through every circumstance.

However, before I could take that final step back to him, there was a question he had to answer.

"Were you ever going to come for me?"

Fisher smiled that glorious, unmatchable grin, and it instantly sent a new round of burning tears to my eyes. It blew my heart up like a balloon, and it rattled my stomach, sending those familiar, tiny wings aflutter. "I was thinking about it."

"I found my lost fisherman," I whispered as I took that final step and wrapped my arms around him, our lips reuniting after too long apart.

When we pulled back an inch and gazed at each other, he grinned again. "I told you, all you needed to do was go knock on his door." He wiped his thumbs along my cheeks. "Don't cry. I don't want Shane to think I made my girl sad."

"You remember."

He grinned. "I remember. I just had no idea the memories of us would be so ... NSFW. And when it happened, when I remembered the *feeling*, it felt indescribable, in some way like the universe was laughing at me. How could I have not known? Not like my brain forming the memory, more like my soul tapping on my heart and saying, 'Yo, dumb ass, remember her? We love her. 'We will always love her.'"

I rested my forehead against his chest and laughed. "Not safe for work ..."

"No joke." He took my hand and led me back toward his house. "You know, I can't play pool anymore without getting an erection. Do you have any idea how awkward that is when you're playing against a dude?"

I giggled.

When we reached the basement, Fisher released my hand and grabbed a beer. "Shane, this is Reese. Sorry we disappeared. She's a little skittish."

I narrowed my eyes at Fisher.

"Nice to finally meet you. This guy hasn't shut up about you in days. After two beers, everything turns into Reese-this and Reese-that." Shane sipped his beer in one hand while resting his other hand on the pool stick.

"That's not true." Fisher rolled his eyes while opening his beer bottle.

My scowl turned into a smirk. I felt ten feet tall, even if he was doing all this *thinking* and *talking* about me while I was miserable assuming he no longer wanted to be with me.

When I turned back toward Shane, Fisher stood behind me, snaking his hand possessively across the top of my chest as he ducked his head and whispered in my ear. "It only takes one beer for me to talk about you. But I think about you all the time. And sometimes..." his whisper got even softer "...I touch myself." He playfully teased my ear with his teeth eliciting another giggle from me.

"Who's playing?" Shane asked.

"Reese. She's freakishly good at whatever she does. She kicked Arnie's ass in ping-pong."

I glanced back at Fisher, and he winked at me.

Over the next two hours, we played pool. Shane told me all about Fisher's shenanigans in high school. And Fisher called Shane out on a few of his own. I had to resort to college stories, which were much more recent because I went to a Christian academy and therefore had no exciting stories during that time in my life. The most taboo thing I had ever done was pull Fisher's towel from his waist and give him head in his closet, but Fisher already knew that, and Shane *didn't* need to know it.

"I have to get home." I glanced at my phone screen. "Rory and Rose were shopping, but now they're home and looking for me. We're making cookies." I returned my pool stick to the rack. "Nice meeting you, Shane. I hope we get to hang out again before you leave."

"Yeah, that would be great." He plopped down onto the sectional and turned on the TV.

"I'll walk you upstairs." Fisher took my hand and led me to the front door. Always ... *always* me following Fisher off a cliff or to the ends of the earth.

"I have a million questions." I trapped my lower lip between my teeth and wrinkled my nose.

"And I'll give you a million answers. Just not until Shane leaves town."

Nodding slowly, I whispered, "In two weeks ..."

"But I'll answer one now. So pick the one that matters the most."

I rolled my eyes. "That's not fair."

"Ask me."

Did you have sex with Angie?

"When did you remember ... everything? And *do* you remember everything? Do you remember all your memories of Angie?"

"That's three questions."

"Fisher ..."

He kissed me once. "I remembered after I got drunk off my ass at the wedding ... because I was so pissed off at you."

I frowned.

Fisher didn't. He kept grinning and kissed me again. "And I remember all my memories of Angie."

Another kiss.

"I remember everything."

Another kiss, but slower.

When he released my face, I stood motionless for several seconds. "You *knew* that morning we had Starbucks? And you didn't tell me? Not only did you not tell me, you completely played dumb about it. You asked me questions you already knew the answers to."

He shrugged. It was an arrogant shrug, like he had every right to not tell me the truth that morning at Starbucks. As I started to protest his arrogance, my conscience got the best of me, halting my words. I slid into my jacket and pulled on my boots.

"Shane doesn't know I lost my memory."

I narrowed my eyes before returning a small nod. I wasn't sure why he didn't tell him, but I figured it didn't matter.

As I opened the door, he grabbed my wrist, and I turned back toward him. A slightly pained expression stole his beautiful smile. "You. I've told you about my memory. That's it. No one else."

"What do you mean?"

"I mean, I didn't tell Angie. And I didn't tell my family. Not Rory or Rose. Not anyone at work. Just you."

Still a little confused, I added another nod. He wanted to tell them, so he didn't want me saying anything.

"I'm not going to tell them. You know. And you're the only one who ever needs to know. Except my doctor. I'll tell my doctor."

"W-why?" I shook my head.

"I know I hurt Angie. And when I told my family, they were hurt too."

That answered another one of my questions. He told his family.

But did he tell them about me?

"But it would have been worse for everyone had they known I made the decision knowing how I felt about her before the accident. I think it's easier for them to believe that I can't marry her or that I've fallen in love with someone else because I simply can't recall my feelings. They are *all* so sure that I would marry Angie tomorrow if I only remembered. So that's the deal. I don't want them to know. I'm not going to tell them. And I don't want you telling anyone either. Not even Rory and Rose. Can you do that?"

I didn't know. That was a big ask on his part.

Fisher pressed his lips together and canted his head. "Need I remind you that you kept a big secret from me ... because you thought it was for the best?"

"And look how that turned out."

He grabbed the collar to my jacket and brought his lips to mine without touching them. "I *am* looking at how that turned out."

He won. Fisher always won.

"When will I see you again?" I changed the subject, realizing that I'd lost.

"Shane's on East Coast time, so he goes to bed by ten. What kind of cookies are you going to bring me? You know I have a thing for your cookies ... your muffins ... your whole damn bakery."

I matched his grin. He remembered that conversation.

"Now you're just flexing."

He barked a laugh and released my jacket. "Not yet. I'll do that for you later ... after I eat your cookie. Maybe bring extra frosting. I have an idea."

"So you have time to eat my cookie, but I can't ask you any more questions for two weeks?"

"Exactly."

Grumbling in the naked fisherman style, I headed out the door to walk home.

CHAPTER THIRTY-THREE

"Spill," Rory said the second I walked into the house.

"Spill what?" I unzipped my jacket.

"You were over at Fisher's. We drove by there."

"Oh that..." I hung my coat in the closet and padded my way into the kitchen to wash my hands and start helping with the cookies "...yeah, we're back together." I could not have been more coy.

"What? How? Who? WHAT?" Rory tossed me a hand towel as she and Rose cornered me.

My coyness quickly vanished. "Yes!" I fisted my hands at my chest and squealed. "I texted him, basically for closure. And he texted me back this weird, vague response that just ... ugh ... *ate* at me. So I drove over there. Some stranger answered his door. Turns out, it's his best friend from high school who's staying with him for the next two weeks. That was awkward, so I went to leave and Fisher ..." Then it hit me.

His speech. Our big moment. I couldn't share it

with them because it was all about him remembering us—remembering everything. And how he felt about me. Carrying me to the truck and smelling my hair. Sure it might have sounded weird to anyone else, but it was so romantic.

AND I COULDN'T TELL ANYONE!

"And Fisher what?" Rose asked. She and Rory had wide eyes and hung on my every word.

"Uh ... well ... Fisher felt really bad for not having called. But after breaking up with Angie and telling his family, he needed some time. And out of respect for both Angie and his family, he thought it was best to keep his distance from me. And he knew I was angry with him, so he thought we both needed to take some time and space. But..." my enthusiasm rebounded after that rambling version of the half-truth "...he was so excited to see me. And it was like nothing else mattered."

They seemed disappointed in my story. And it wasn't the most dramatic ending to a love story, but it was all I could give them.

"So you talked? Worked everything out? He told you everything that did or didn't happen in Costa Rica?" Rory eyed me suspiciously.

I nodded.

"And did he have sex with Angie? Because I can't see you being okay with that." Rose gave me the same untrusting look that Rory gave me.

I made my decision before I stepped into his house. I chose us, even if he had sex with Angie in Costa Rica.

If I believed the giving of my body to another in that way was the most sacred part of a relationship, the defining characteristic of love, then I would not have given my virginity to Brendon without marrying him. I would not have been interested in Fisher, the furthest thing ever from a virgin, and I would not have been able to love him after he and Angie had sex the night before our Target trip.

"He didn't have sex with her." That was my answer. And maybe that was a lie. Another lie I would never confess to Rory and Rose. And maybe it was the truth. I didn't know. And it wasn't going to change my love for Fisher. The second I hung up on him and didn't return his calls or texts, that was the moment I could no longer call him mine.

I abandoned him when he needed me the most.

That worked. They smiled and hugged me. "So happy for you, sweetie. Both of you."

"Thanks. So ... let's make some cookies."

MARIAH CAREY BELTED out the lyrics to "All I Want For Christmas Is You" while we made cutout sugar cookies, chocolate crinkles, and peanut butter blossoms because Rory thought Fisher might like them. I didn't break her heart by telling her that Fisher wasn't the peanut butter fanatic he used to be.

Then we strung popcorn for the tree and used the rest of the popcorn to make a batch of caramel corn.

After that, we nearly passed out from too much sugar while watching *Last Christmas* and *Elf*.

And finally, I grabbed my spare keys, packed up some cookies (and frosting), and headed to Fisher's house after Rory and Rose went to bed. Tapping lightly on his door, I shivered from the gusty cold wind that night that promised to bring more snow by morning.

"Hey." Fisher answered the door with a very pleased expression.

"Cookie delivery."

He chuckled. "We've been waiting for them."

We?

I stepped inside to a kitchen filled with guys. "You have ... more company," I said with a tight, fake grin.

"Yeah, Shane rounded up the whole crew for dinner and ... they're still here." Fisher took the container of cookies.

"Yo, Reese!" Shane said with a drunk man's boisterous enthusiasm. "Fisher said you were coming with cookies."

"Yo," I replied with a very bummed girlfriend's dismay as I removed my jacket and boots.

Fisher opened the container and set it on the counter for the pack of wolves to devour, but not before snagging one of each for himself and putting them on a paper towel. "Guys, this is Reese. These are the guys."

They laughed and I rolled my eyes. It was all too reminiscent of his pathetic introductions when I met his family.

"The game's on downstairs. Let's go." One of the guys said, and the rest of the pack followed with their beers and cookies.

"This isn't what I saw happening tonight," I murmured to Fisher as we brought up the rear.

"Me neither. But they're here, and I can't just abandon them."

I bit my tongue. Abandoning groups and sneaking off to be alone was our thing. Did he not remember that?

A few of the guys sat at the barstools, two other guys played pool, and the rest of the group sat on the sofa or floor in front of the sofa to watch the game.

I snagged a blanket from the back of the sofa and plopped down next to Fisher.

"I don't need a blanket, baby. It's plenty warm," Fisher said.

"It's not that warm yet." I covered him with the blanket, eliciting a frown from him. It lasted a full five seconds before his body went rigid and his lips parted with an audible inhale.

"Reese ..." he whispered.

"Huh?" I turned my attention to the television, wetting my lips while he grabbed my arm—the arm attached to the hand down the front of his jeans and briefs.

I wasn't sure what got into me, but I suspected it had something to do with repression. Fisher was finally mine, and I didn't have to hide it from the world anymore. We were no longer forbidden lovers. And while his friends knew nothing about our forbidden love, and therefore I had nothing to prove to them, I still felt the need to claim Fisher in a public way.

My guy.

My hand on his cock. (Now MY cock)

All the kisses belong to me.

All the nights out belong to me.

Me in his tub.

Me in his bed.

Me. Me. ME!

My unsettled possessiveness seemed to spur on my hand, and Fisher whispered, "Fuck," under his breath while yanking my hand from the inside of his jeans and then yanking me off the sofa.

"Be right back," he said to whoever was in earshot as he dragged me up the stairs. I didn't miss the few looks in our direction. They knew what we were going to do, and while that made my face flush a bit, I didn't care. In fact, it was really out of our way to go upstairs when there was a perfectly good pool table right there.

When we reached his bedroom, we heard someone in his bathroom.

Fisher growled and pulled me toward one of the spare bedrooms, but one of his friends was sitting on the bed, talking on his phone. He held up a finger like he would be just a minute.

Fisher growled and pulled me to the guest bathroom. The door was locked.

Another growl.

His grip on my hand tightened. Frantic Fisher was

my new high. Anticipation zipped through my veins. I liked him out of control with his need for *me*.

"The pantry?" I laughed, a little in disbelief as he pulled me into the walk-in pantry.

"Really?" He turned me to face the wall with a few hooks on it and random things like bags, a broom, and some grilling tools hanging from them. "A hand job in front of my friends? Who are you?" Fisher pressed my hands to the wall and yanked my sweatpants down to my ankles followed by my panties.

"I hope ... I'm yours," I said in a shaky breath, rattled by what he was doing to me and how much it thrilled me.

He chuckled. "You're mine alright." I liked his fast hands. He was impatient boot-shopping Fisher with his cock out as he thrust into me in a matter of seconds.

"Fishe—" I wasn't prepared for that quick of an invasion.

He silenced me with his hand over my mouth and a harsh "shh" in my ear. Fisher moved with intention with one hand giving attention to my clit while his other hand snaked up my shirt and used my breast like a handle.

It was quick and dirty ... and I liked it.

And we finished, just minutes later, he fetched a new roll of paper towels and handed me several squares.

My hero. I laughed at the thought.

My hero also leaned against the corner of a shelf and opened a bag of popcorn, eating it while watching me pull up my panties and sweats. Then he grinned while I looked around for a place to put the wad of paper towels that had *his* mess in it.

I slipped it into my pocket.

He smirked. "Don't forget to take that out before you wash those. It's like Kleenex. It'll make a mess in the washer and dryer."

"You look a little too pleased with yourself." I snatched the bag from him and grabbed a handful with my non-cleaning hand.

"You started it."

"You invite me over for bakery fun. I brought extra frosting! Then I get here only to discover it's a sausage fest."

"I want you to come to Christmas dinner with me. Rory and Rose too, of course."

"How did we go from sausage fest to Christmas dinner?"

"I want my family to know it's you." His hand dove into the bag of popcorn. Fisher discussed our relationship and the sheer gravity of telling his family like it was nothing more than an invitation to grill out with neighbors.

It was Christmas with his family! The family who just learned about the end of his engagement to the woman they loved like their own.

"Yeaaahhh ..." I grimaced. "But do *they* want to know quite so soon?"

"Yes. My mom's words were, 'Well, dear, if you're in love with another woman, she must be really special. So you need to bring her to Christmas dinner.'"

I fed my anxiety with another huge handful of popcorn, then I mumbled over it, "I think you should tell them ahead of time." I chewed a bit and swallowed. "There is no reason for a surprise. Unless you're a celebrity, nobody likes to be the mystery guest at a party."

He shook his head, stealing the bag back and closing it with a chip clip. "It will be fine."

"Let me rephrase it for you. If you don't tell them ahead of time, I won't go with you. And I'm on call this week. When you dumped me after coffee at Starbucks, I volunteered to be on call over Christmas with one of the other midwives. So I can't make any guarantees, even if you do tell them ahead of time."

His head jerked backward. "I didn't dump you. I dropped you off at your house, but I didn't dump you. *You* were the one who left me with the parting words of 'I will never regret not giving you my virginity.'" Fisher used a feminine voice while mocking me.

"Well I don't." I tipped my chin up. Even with a pocketful of his cum, I had no regrets.

"You had me. Before I got my memory back, you had me. I thought this first love of yours was a total schmuck for not taking it if you offered it. But now I remember why I wasn't camping out all night to be first in line for the virgin lottery."

I bit my lips to keep from laughing. *Virgin lottery?*

"You carried that V-card like a bomb. I wanted

nothing to do with it. The responsibility? Given the fact that you were eighteen and clueless as to where you were going in life? No thank you. You can 'not regret' not giving it to me all you want. But I 'not regret' not taking it from you even more."

I like riled-up Fisher. I'd always liked that version of him. It was hot. There was no other way to describe it.

Virgin lottery.

V-card bomb.

Double-downing on not regretting his decision.

The intensity in his jaw when he clenched his teeth, showing a little animalistic anger. That was a "yes, please" from me.

"Wanna do it again?" I said, reaching for the button to his jeans.

"Fuck yeah, I wanna do it again." He grabbed my face and smashed his mouth to mine.

CHAPTER THIRTY-FOUR

I MAY HAVE JINXED Christmas that day in Fisher's pantry. While Rory, Rose, and I were enjoying potato leek soup and lots of cookies on Christmas Eve, I got called to a birth.

Twins!

Magnus Andrew Howard and Minnie Ann Howard.

Two little five-pound bundles of holiday joy born on Christmas, just after three in the afternoon.

Fisher's family had Christmas dinner scheduled for noon to accommodate his sisters' schedules with their in-laws. I texted him and told him to eat without me.

I finally arrived just before seven that night. Lights and wreaths adorned their house. I barely got a second knock on the door before Fisher opened it.

"Merry Christmas." I gave him a sad smile. It was

an amazing day, but I was disappointed I missed Christmas dinner with his family.

As soon as I stepped inside, before I could get out of my coat or remove my boots, he framed my face gently and kissed me. And I melted. It was exactly what I needed after a long twenty hours at a birth. "Merry Christmas." He looked up and nodded to the mistletoe.

I grinned, and that was when I noticed the onlookers in the living room. Just his parents, Arnie, Rose, and Rory. And that was the moment. Yes, Fisher had told them ahead of time that I was the other woman. But it did very little to ease my nerves in that moment. "Hi," I said a little sheepishly because I didn't see them there before Fisher kissed me. "So sorry I missed dinner."

Fisher took the bags of gifts in my hands and my coat while I toed off my boots and glanced down at myself. I did a quick change in the car before heading to his parents' house in the dark. It was possible I had my sweater on backward or some rogue sock from the laundry stuck to my jeans.

"You had more important things to do. Merry Christmas, honey." Laurie met me halfway and hugged me. It felt genuine. Not for one second did I feel like the less desirable replacement to Angie.

"Merry Christmas."

Pat stood and hugged me too with an equally generous embrace and sincere "Merry Christmas."

"Bro stole my girl. Not cool." Arnie winked before getting in on the hugfest.

"Hi, Arnie." I had to bite my tongue because I almost said, "He stole me before I was *your girl*."

I headed straight to Rose and Rory for hugs too since I hadn't seen them yet that day.

"How was the birth?" Rory asked.

"Pretty special. I don't know if anyone could be having a better Christmas than them. Two perfect little peanuts."

"That *is* hard to beat." Rose nodded and smiled.

"Hungry?" Fisher asked when I turned around to look for a place to sit.

"Yeah, I'm kind of starving."

"Let's get you fed. Come on." Laurie took my hand, very Fisher-like of her, and led me to the kitchen.

Fisher stayed in the great room, leaving me with just his mother.

Laurie set out tray after tray of leftovers. "There's a plate in that cabinet to the left of the sink. I can heat it up in the oven or the microwave. Do you have a preference?"

"Cold," I said, eagerly dishing food onto my plate.

"No, honey. It's really no problem. You can't have cold Christmas dinner."

"She can." Fisher appeared in the kitchen after all. "She's an odd duck. Likes everything cold."

That wasn't totally true. I liked my fisherman hot.

And impatient.

And a little dirty.

He swiped his finger through my potatoes as I had done with his Thanksgiving leftovers. I grabbed his wrist before he got his hand to his mouth and I sucked it off his finger.

His eyebrows lifted a fraction as he made a quick glance at his mom. I think I may have made him blush. Typical guy ... a little finger sucking sent his mind reeling into inappropriate territory.

"She's been working, Fisher. I wouldn't blame her for biting your finger off for attempting to steal her food." Laurie returned everything to a nice PG rating.

"Mmm ... yes. My girl is ferocious." He playfully kissed me, licking the side of my mouth.

My girl.

I liked being his girl, even if I was a woman. The truth of time still remained unchangeable—I would always be ten years younger than him.

Laurie rolled her eyes at Fisher's obnoxiousness. "Make sure she gets anything she wants or needs, Fisher. I'm going to sit down," Laurie said before leaving the kitchen.

"Hear that?" I leaned against the counter and held my plate with one hand while shoveling food down with my other hand. "Anything I want or need. Wanna know what I need?"

Fisher smirked, chest puffed out, chin up. "What?" He waggled his eyebrows suggestively.

"A bed," I said with my mouth full. "I'm so tired it hurts."

"Oh, baby …" He took my plate from me and pulled me into his body.

I could have fallen asleep right then and there. We stayed another hour, everyone drinking wine, and some crazy cocktail Arnie put together, and opened gifts.

Me?

I didn't drink a drop, and my gifts from his family sat piled on the floor in front of me. The second I sat on the sofa next to Fisher, I was out, nestled into his side. The next thing I knew, he was gently waking me while everyone stood by the door saying their goodbyes.

His parents gave me hugs goodbye while Fisher put on my coat and guided my feet into my boots like someone would do to a child. I was *so* tired.

"Keys?" Fisher felt around in my pockets and found my keys. "Who's driving her car?" he asked Rory and Rose.

"I can drive," I mumbled.

A chorus of nearly everyone chimed, "No you can't."

Rose grabbed my keys and Fisher wrapped his arm around me and helped me to his truck as Arnie followed with the gifts.

"You bringing her home?" Rory asked.

"What do you think?" Fisher replied while I climbed into his truck.

"I think you're stealing my daughter from me," she said.

"Then you think right," Fisher replied after helping me fasten my seat belt.

I didn't remember the ride home. I sort of remembered Fisher carrying me into his house, but that was a little fuzzy at the time. The next thing I remembered with any clarity was waking in his arms, naked save for my panties and his T-shirt. A warm ray of sun squeezed through a tiny gap in his blinds as I sat up slowly.

"Stay in bed," he mumbled.

I chuckled, hopping out of bed. "I have to pee."

"Fine," he said with a little grumble. "Then come back."

While I washed my hands, I noticed something different about his closet, but it was too dark to say for sure what it was, so I tiptoed to the entry and turned on the light.

One entire wall was exposed, open to the closet of the guest room.

"Thought you were coming back to bed?" Fisher slid his arm around my waist from behind me while kissing my shoulder.

"What are you doing to your closet?"

"I'm making an access door to the other room."

"Why?"

He kissed his way to my neck. "Because it's going to be a nursery."

I turned slowly, eyes narrowed.

"I'm pregnant," he said.

"Stop." I giggled.

"I think it's yours, but I'm not going to lie ... Shane and I had a few drunk nights."

More giggles as he bent down and picked me up, tossing me over his shoulder and swatting my butt.

"Fisher!"

"Bed. We are not getting out of this bed today. I took the day off just to be naked with you."

I laughed when he deposited me onto the bed. "Tell me. What are you really doing in your closet?"

He settled between my legs, kissing my neck again while inching my shirt (his shirt) up my torso. "I'm going to ask Nurse Capshaw to move in with me, and I know she has a lot of scrubs, so I'm giving her more space by stealing a few feet from the other closet."

I wriggled to the side to get out from under him, scooting to the back of the bed like home base. "You're going to ask me to move in with you?"

Still on his stomach, he lifted onto his elbows. "I'm going to ask you a lot of things, but that's coming up soon on the list. Spoiler alert ... you say yes."

My lips did that twitching thing where I tried to hide my amusement or maybe it was just unfathomable happiness. "Wow. The man who couldn't remember the best hand job of his life is now predicting the future?"

"Absolutely." He army crawled toward me.

"Fisher ..." I opened my bent legs. He filled the space with his broad shoulders, and instead of doing what I thought he was going to do ... what I was offering him ... he rested his forehead against my stomach and slid his hands along my outer thighs. "Can I do it now?"

"Do what?" I asked with a soft voice, running my fingers through his messy hair.

"Can I love you *forever*?"

I swallowed a little emotion that had been building since I saw the closet. "Yes."

EPILOGUE

FISHER

SHE SAID YES ... and she never stopped saying yes.

Yes to moving in with me.

Yes to weekend trips to ski.

Yes to movie nights or Arnie's concerts.

Yes to helping me in my shop.

Yes to waffles for dinner and cold pizza for breakfast.

Yes to long baths and quickies in the shower.

Then I made her a crossword puzzle that was a treasure hunt.

"I'll see you soon, if you're as smart as you say you are." I kissed her head and handed her the puzzle and a pencil.

"Where are you going?" she asked when I got to the back door.

"You'll see." I left.

It took her just over an hour to solve the puzzle and follow the clues they spelled out which led her to me.

"Really?" She rolled her eyes as she walked toward my table at McDonald's. "All that for a Happy Meal?" She eyed the sack opposite me.

"It's probably cold since you took so long." I sipped my chocolate milk.

"The average person wouldn't have known half of those words. You're such a geek." She pulled out her hamburger and apples. "No fries?" She nodded to my empty burger wrapper.

I shook my empty sack. "I've had two orders waiting for you."

Another eye roll just before she took a bite of her sandwich. "I'm going to make you a puzzle that takes you to the grocery store. A list of the things we need."

"Sounds fun." I rested my face in my hands.

"Why are you acting so weird?"

I shrugged. "Am I?"

"Yes." She chuckled, setting her hamburger down after three bites. That was her ritual whether she realized it or not.

Three bites of her sandwich.

Half of her apple slices.

One big sip of her juice.

And then a fishing expedition for the toy in the bottom of the sack.

She pulled out the toy and frowned. "This is an old one. How on earth did they have this to offer?" She inspected the Sponge Bob treasure chest, cracking it open to reveal a diamond ring. After several blinks she glanced up at me.

I nodded to the small group of kids who volunteered literally fifteen minutes earlier to help me. They yelled at the same time. "Will you marry the fisherman?"

Reese jumped and shot her gaze to them. Most of them fell into goofy fits of giggles with their hands covering their mouths. And the small gathering of parents at nearby tables all looked on with big grins, maybe even a few nervous grins. I mean ... what if she said no?

Reese turned back to me, and I was waiting on one knee because that's what you did when you wanted your girl to say yes more than anything.

"Are you going to say yes?" I asked after she blinked a thousand times.

Lifting one shoulder, she relinquished a grin. "I'm thinking about it."

"Thinking is overrated." I took the ring and placed it on her finger just before kissing her. "Say yes," I mumbled over her lips.

She kissed me while nodding, and when the kiss ended ... it was another glorious *yes*.

As I waited for my bride to make her way down the aisle in the church that would have made her dad proud and *did* please her dad's parents, I got a little emotional for reasons that had nothing to do with the stunning woman in white.

She never asked. Not once.

I promised a million answers after that Christmas, but Reese never asked. It was like Angie no longer existed in her mind.

She never asked if I had sex with Angie in Costa Rica. I didn't.

She never asked about my memories of Angie—our engagement, how I felt about her, or why I said yes when she proposed. And unless Angie told someone, the truth remained buried in the past.

I said yes because she was my friend. I said yes because my family adored her. I said yes because she had just lost her mother. I said yes because we were *good enough* together. And I said yes because I had already let *the one* go.

But the most revealing part of my memory returning involved the morning of the day of my accident. While the accident itself still remained a black hole in my mind, and for good reasons probably always would, I recalled the heated argument I had with Angie.

Irritation.

Pressure.

Regret.

She had been moving a hundred miles per hour with wedding plans, and it made it hard to breathe. What should have been a happy time in my life felt like impending doom. So after she showed me tux swatch number eight hundred and fifty and asked my opinion on ten different shades of fucking white for the linens at the reception, I cracked. I said some things I instantly regretted. As tears rolled down her cheeks, she muttered the words, "Do you even want to marry me?"

And I spoke my truth with a whispered, "No."

I wasn't engaged when the truck knocked me off my motorcycle. And Angie shared everything about our past that suited her narrative, her desperation to keep me. And given the short amount of time between breaking off our engagement and the accident that afternoon, nobody else knew the truth.

The funny part? I wasn't mad. People did desperate things for love. Angie didn't know about my relationship with Reese. She didn't think her slight omission was hurting anyone. Her actions, although dishonest, were also out of love. She did love me. She did take care of me after my accident as I had taken care of her after her mom died. And maybe she thought I would fall in love with her again. My accident serving as a reset on our relationship.

So what?

It didn't stop me from falling in love with Reese for a second time.

It didn't stop her from giving me all the yeses.

And since I never told anyone but Reese and my doctor about my memory returning, it really didn't matter.

So as Rory and Rose walked Reese down the aisle,

I fought the ache in my chest, the feeling that I was undeserving of such perfection. She was about to marry me without the answers to her million questions. Reese loved me like I had always imagined God (if He existed) loved us.

My heart pounded so violently; it was hard to hear past the whooshing sound in my ears. But the second Rory and Rose took their seats, and Reese placed her hand in mine, my heart found its normal rhythm again, and I could hear the final notes of the harp and her whispered, "Hey, handsome," as she grinned.

I swallowed so hard and fought to keep my shit together. There was no way I was going to cry when my girl showed such control, like marrying me was just the next simple step in her journey.

I made it to the end with dry eyes, but just barely. Reese gave away a tear or two when I said the words "I do." And my thumbs quickly caught them as the minister gave me permission to kiss my bride.

For a guy who was in no hurry to get married, I walked my wife out of that church with a puffed-out chest and the cheesiest grin.

"It's likely I won't be able to answer my phone, but I'll call you as soon as possible. If things get really sticky, you know my mom and Rose will happily come help. If it's an actual emergency—"

"Call 9-1-1. Got it," I said.

Reese frowned. "Of course, but I was going to say, call Holly. She's not on call, but she lives across the street from the birth center."

"You know ... this isn't my first rodeo." I rocked our little girl like the fucking pro I was while our three-year-old son played in his room. It was Reese's first full day back to work (her first birth) since maternity leave.

I knew how to warm milk and thaw more if needed.

Diapers? No problem.

Crying? I had the best football hold and most soothing gait in the whole damn state, and my wife knew it.

It was the weekend, so there was a one hundred percent chance her family and mine would be popping in nonstop to get their baby fix or take Aiden to the park and to get ice cream.

"Fisher ..." She frowned before leaning over to kiss Claire's tiny cheek as she rested on my chest in the recliner.

"You've been spoiled. Most working moms don't get to wear their babies to work. You can't wear her to a birth. So just go before the baby arrives without you."

Reese had been so spoiled that way. She looked like a woman from Ghana wearing Aiden and now Claire to work ... magically tied to her with some long piece of material. And that worked for clinic days when no one was in labor.

After she kissed Claire, she hovered over my face,

surrendering enough of her pouty demeanor to offer me a tiny grin because she knew I was right.

"She won't take a pacifier, so don't even try."

"I know." I smiled. "She's like her dad ... only the real deal will satisfy her."

I managed to squeeze a bigger smile from her as she rolled her eyes.

"Are you going to kiss me?"

She slowly rubbed her lips together, teasing me as usual. "I'm thinking about it."

The End

ACKNOWLEDGMENTS

I have to thank my amazing readers first and foremost. As I experimented with different ways to publish this story, you stood by me, eagerly awaiting my words in whatever form I decided to share them.

Thank you, Jenn, for dealing with the chaotic summer version of me—juggling a million projects and constantly changing publishing schedules.

Thank you, Nina and the hardworking team with Valentine PR for all the Zoom calls and sheer love of this story. It's an honor to work with people who believe in me.

My editing team! These souls have a very special place in the afterlife for making sense of my gibberish and polishing it into something worth sharing with the world. Max, I can't wait to take this new journey with you as not only my editor, but also my agent. Leslie, Kambra, Sian, Monique, and Amy, thank you for sacrificing your enjoyment of my stories to make me look like a competent author. I feel like my success belongs to you as well.

As always, a big thank you to my family for supporting me during moody times, frantic schedules, a million frustrations, and everything in between. You inspire me.

ALSO BY JEWEL E. ANN

Standalone Novels

Idle Bloom

Undeniably You

Naked Love

Only Trick

Perfectly Adequate

Look The Part

When Life Happened

A Place Without You

Jersey Six

Scarlet Stone

Not What I Expected

For Lucy

The Fisherman Series

The Naked Fisherman

The Lost Fisherman

Jack & Jill Series

End of Day

Middle of Knight

Dawn of Forever

One (*standalone*)

Out of Love (*standalone*)

Holding You Series

Holding You

Releasing Me

Transcend Series

Transcend

Epoch

Fortuity (*standalone*)

The Life Series

The Life That Mattered

The Life You Stole

Receive a FREE book and stay informed of new releases, sales, and exclusive stories:

Mailing List

https://www.jeweleann.com/free-booksubscribe

ABOUT THE AUTHOR

Jewel is a free-spirited romance junkie with a quirky sense of humor.

With 10 years of flossing lectures under her belt, she took early retirement from her dental hygiene career to stay home with her three awesome boys and manage the family business.

After her best friend of nearly 30 years suggested a few books from the Contemporary Romance genre, Jewel was hooked. Devouring two and three books a week but still craving more, she decided to practice sustainable reading, AKA writing.

When she's not donning her cape and saving the planet one tree at a time, she enjoys yoga with friends, good food with family, rock climbing with her kids, watching How I Met Your Mother reruns, and of course...heart-wrenching, tear-jerking, panty-scorching novels.

www.jeweleann.com